The Brittany Files

Hostile

By Melissa Logan

Smashwords Edition

Copyright © 2014 Melissa Logan

Published by Melissa Logan at Smashwords

Chapter 1

"Seriously, why do they pick the *hottest* day of the year to make us run out in the country where there is absolutely no shade?" I whined as I struggled to keep up with Haley Lincoln, a junior on my cross country team. Our coach had ordered us to run five miles and pointed us in the direction of the country roads. Asphalt with only cornfields for shade was not my idea of a good time and we were all struggling to keep running.

"To torture us?" Haley joked, wiping the sweat from her face with her shirt. "I'm about to start running in my sports bra. I don't care if I get suspended, this is ridiculous."

"I just want to slap that damn bottle of water out of Coach K's hand when they drive by too."

"Right? It's so bad they don't want to run out here, but they make us?"

"Jerks." I giggled. "On a positive note, I'll probably shed fifteen pounds in water weight today."

"There's always a positive side." Haley laughed.

"There's the turnaround spot up ahead." She gestured with a jerk of her head.

"At least we're not the boys." I smiled. "Running even further would bite." She nodded her head, slowing her pace so we could turn around at the bare tree standing in the middle of nowhere.

"Truth." The two of us stopped as we made a wide turn and started going back the direction we came. We were way ahead of the rest of our team, so we were safe to walk for a bit. It was just a little after eight in the morning and already a hundred degrees, not to mention the humidity made you feel as if you were walking around with a wet towel on your body.

"Why don't we ever run with a bottle of water?" Haley asked with a chuckle.

"Because it would be boiling over by now." She just nodded her head and stretched her long arms over her head.

"Could you imagine how nasty the football players must feel now in all that gear?"

"Ugh, I can't even imagine. What is worse is they have to do it three times a day! That's pure dedication, or insanity."

3

"Insanity." She laughed as we heard footsteps pounding the asphalt. We started at a slow jog, knowing one of our teammates wouldn't rat us out for walking, but we still didn't want to get caught.

"Great job Trin." Haley grinned as she cheered on Trinity Liscom, another freshman on our cross country team. She just nodded; she also looked like she was ready to pass out.

"Thanks...I sure didn't think I was this close to y'all." She mumbled with a forced chuckle.

"You're doing great." I said cheerfully. She nodded again, put her head down and ran right past us. The next two miles consisted of us cheering on our teammates as they passed by. Sadly, just as we were finishing two of the senior boys were close on our heels. They had run seven miles, which meant they were bionic or something.

Haley and I stretched out and waited for the rest of the team to return, sucking down the water we had left on the benches in front of the school. Coach dismissed us quickly and I said my goodbyes before I trudged to the parking lot where my brother's beater car sat. He had packed a cooler in the trunk filled with ice and Gatorades so

4

he and the guys had something to drink if they needed it during their breaks. I got to the old Pontiac, opened the driver side door and popped the trunk. I grabbed out a red drink, slammed the trunk shut and made my way to the football field to wait for my older brother, Drake, to finish with practice.

The football team starts practice at six in the morning, so they finish their three hour practice right around when mine is ending, but it was just the beginning for them. For the next few days, they were doing three a days until school started.

"Damn, I love me a hot and sweaty girl." One of my good friends, Justin Harper, flirted as he came up and grabbed me in a bear hug.

"Well, I *don't* love a smelly guy!" I teased as I tried to dart away from him. Justin was drenched in sweat and covered in mud, but he didn't seem to notice.

"I'm hurt." He laughed as he gave me another hug for good measure.

"Nice practice today, Harper." Drake said, giving him a high five as he came up behind us. "I heard the coaches talking and they're looking at you for varsity. You hit harder than guys three times your size."

"Thanks." Justin said blushing. "McHalley was tearing it up out there...I've never seen a guy run so fast in my life."

"I know, he'll be on varsity too this year. I thought losing Mason and the others was going to be a bad thing, but I think you two will fill the void nicely." Drake replied looking back at where Bret McHalley was walking up behind us.

"You need a ride Justin?" I asked, praying he would so he could save me from Bret and my soon to be stepbrother, Marc Curren.

"No, mom will be here in a few minutes." He answered. "She is still working on trusting me again." Not very long ago, my best friend, Aaron Dalkman passed away from cancer and soon after, Justin was hanging out with his cousin when a drug bust took place. It was a case of being in the wrong place at the wrong time, but his mother didn't care and sent him off to a scared straight boot camp. He came home earlier than expected because his cousin came clean about Justin not having anything to do with the situation. However, she is still convinced the whole incident was her son acting out from the grief of losing his friend.

6

"She'll come around." I murmured as I gave him a half hug and rested my head on his shoulder.

"Hopefully soon, or high school is going to suck." He chuckled as he walked to the front of the building. I nodded with a laugh before I turned around to where Drake was waiting with Marc, his best friend Bret and two boys from the football team that I didn't know.

"I am *so* jumping in the pool when we get home." I said, pulling my ponytail away from my sweaty neck as I climbed into the front seat of Drake's car.

"I think we'll join you." Marc replied, glancing at Bret. "I don't care how early we practice; the temperature still feels the same as if we were practicing at noon." Drake dropped the other two kids off, then steered us to our new house. We'd only been living there for a few weeks, so it was still weird to drive here rather than to the house we'd lived in since I was born.

As soon as we pulled into the long driveway that led to our massive house, I sprinted upstairs to change into my bathing suit and jumped in the pool before the boys even got downstairs. Diving into the cold water was like Heaven to my skin.

"Thanks for waiting." Drake cracked as he did a cannonball into the water. Bret and Marc climbed in a little slower, but didn't waste time sinking all the way under to cool off. We all swam and played around in the pool until lunchtime. It was the first time in the last month that Bret wasn't extremely quiet around me.

I had only been officially broken up from my boyfriend for a week's time. Michael Rhodes had been someone I'd known all of my life, but our relationship became more serious a little over two years ago. However, when I found out about Aaron's illness I became his girlfriend, as well. Because of the situation, Michael hung back and didn't protest because he knew how close Aaron and I were. Isn't that weird?

Anyway, Michael and his three older brothers; Mitchell, Mason and Matt, are in a band together called Rhode House, they moved to Nashville, Tennessee to pursue their dreams of becoming country music superstars. It won't be long before they make it big, I know that for certain.

"So the date with Jeremy wasn't all that great, I take it?" Marc asked as he climbed out of the pool and sat on one of the lounge chairs. I shot him a funny look as I shrugged my shoulders. I had gone on a date with another freshman, Jeremy Font, a few days ago. Bret, Marc and I had gotten into a huge argument when they found out; apparently, they don't really care for Jeremy. When I first met my stepbrother, the three boys were together a lot, I didn't know what happened to change that, but they were not thrilled I had accepted a date with him. Actually, now that I think about it, when the boys found out about my date was when Bret had started acting distant around me.

"I guess not." I said as I rolled my eyes. I had only gone on one date with Jeremy and he never asked me on another one, so I don't understand what the big deal is all about. I knew going in that Jeremy was a jerk, but I'm stupid sometimes and think there is something else under the crude exterior or that I can change the guy. I'd seen Jeremy out at a party since our date, he hung all over me until he found another girl who would actually make out with him. Marc just nodded smugly.

"I'm beat, I think I'm going to go veg out in the basement." I said with a shake of my head as I climbed out of the pool by the ladder. Too much time out in the sun was making me really drowsy and I needed to get out before I fried like a chicken.

"Way to run her off Marc." I heard Drake chuckle as I grabbed a towel, wrapped it around myself and padded into the house. I ignored them. I wasn't in the mood to fight with the boys over my choices of dates. After all, I was pretty new to the dating scene, considering I'd really only dated in my group of friends throughout grade school and that really didn't count.

I went straight to the kitchen to grab something to eat; I was starving. I made myself a sandwich, grabbed a bottle of water and hurried up the stairs to change out of my wet bathing suit. Twenty minutes later, I was downstairs in our basement mindlessly watching reruns on the television. It only took about five minutes before the boys joined me.

"So, Brittany Hoffman has a date tonight, I hear." My older sister, Lindsay, said just after the boys had retreated back to the basement after their second football practice of the day.

"Where'd you hear that?"

"Oh, I know everything sweetie." She teased. "Chris

Kaplan, huh? You sure do like the older guys."

"He's been asking me out daily since the first time I met him, I figured I'd be nice and give it a shot." I replied shrugging my shoulders.

"Why didn't *I* hear about this?" Drake questioned.

"Do you not listen in the locker room?" Marc asked disgustedly.

"Not to Kaplan, he makes so much stuff up I never know when to believe him." Drake answered.

"He's been bragging about it ever since she said yes." Marc stated, rolling his eyes.

"And you haven't warned me about him yet?" I asked in shock.

"You didn't listen about Jeremy, I figured I'd be wasting my breath." Marc declared.

"Well, at least you're learning."

"He's a jerk and a little weird, Brittany. But *you* do whatever you want to do." Bret said shrugging his shoulders. "I heard he was in a mental hospital for a little while. I've also been told he likes to smack girls around."

"Do you like anyone *but* yourself?" I shot, ignoring the rest of his comments. I figured he was just saying whatever he thought would get me away from Chris. Bret obviously didn't want me, he's had plenty of opportunities to ask me out and never has. So why didn't he want anyone else to date me either?

"I'm just telling you now, so you can't blame us later for not warning you about him."

"I don't say anything about the airhead cheerleaders you flirt with constantly, so keep your mouth shut about the guys I date." I instructed coldly.

"Ouch." Drake said. "Lay off dude, he's just trying to look out for you. And don't hate the cheerleaders, they're people too."

"You do know he's not in high school, right? I'm not sure how mom and dad will feel about that." Lindsay interjected.

"Not in high school? What do you mean? He's at every football practice."

"He got hurt last year and is trying to build his strength back up so he can walk on at U T next season." Drake answered with a shrug of his shoulders. "Coach is listing him as an assistant coach

12

because he owes his dad a favor."

"So, if anything were to happen between you two, he could go to jail." Lindsay teased.

"Whatever." I rolled my eyes and went into the kitchenette to grab a snack. I was a little floored by the information, I hadn't seen that coming and I really was not keen on the idea of going on a date with an older guy. Bret's comments were also bothering me, not what he actually said, but that he continued to feel the need to badmouth everyone I chose. Aaron had told me on more than one occasion that adding another brother into my family would be a good thing, so far, I wasn't seeing it.

My parents had been divorced for almost three years and I held on to the hope they would reconcile. Since the divorce, my father hadn't really been around but he was also an emergency room doctor at the local hospital and he had really crazy hours. At the beginning of the summer, Marc and his widowed father moved into the house next door to mine. At the same time, my mother made friends with Bret's parents on the base where she works. They invited her to church with them and then introduced her to Captain

Jerk, AKA Marc's dad. It all went downhill after that, mostly

because Marc comes attached to Bret McHalley. I had enough

overprotective guys in my life, I really didn't want anymore. I didn't

think my sanity could handle it.

Chapter 2

"Chris is here." Lindsay announced as she poked her head in my room. I nodded slowly as I pushed myself off the bed. "Don't let the boys get to you sweetie, they just worry about you."

"I know." I sighed. "It's just frustrating and annoying. I thought when Mason moved, I'd be through with that."

"Drake and Marc do it out of genuine concern, I think Bret is jealous. I'm pretty sure he has a thing for you."

"Whatever." I chuckled as I rolled my eyes. "I am definitely not his type." She shrugged her shoulders and looked down the steps.

"I've heard the same rumors Bret has heard about Chris though, so just be careful okay?" I nodded my head.

"Now that I know how old he is, I really don't even want to go. I'm not…he's going to want more than I'm willing to…give."

"You'll be fine. Keep your phone close, okay? I'll call you in about an hour and if you feel uncomfortable, fake puking and call me to come get you." I laughed and nodded my head.

"Thanks sissy." Lindsay gave me a hug and then followed me out of my bedroom. I took the steps slow, dreading the fact that Chris and the boys were downstairs in the living room together. I could hear them talking about football, Chris giving Bret tips on how he can get better. From what I've seen and heard, Bret McHalley is one of the best players to ever come through Stitlin High School, pretty sure he didn't need Chris's advice.

When I walked into the living room, all conversation stopped and all eyes turned towards me awkwardly. I instinctively looked over at Bret; he smiled at me and stood up. I was lost in those deep blue eyes, forgetting Chris Kaplan was sitting five feet away expecting to take me on a date. Someone cleared their throat, I closed my eyes and shook my head.

"You ready?" Chris asked as he took a step towards me. I took a step back and nodded my head, hurrying out before he could touch me. Actually, I was trying hard not to run away. It would be extremely rude to tell him I didn't want to go on a date because he was creepy old.

"We'll probably see you guys later, I'm sure we'll end up at the same party." Drake called after us, his way of telling Chris

16

to behave. I walked out of the house before I could hear Chris's answer and waited on the porch. There was a red Iroc sitting in the driveway, something straight out of an eighties movie, but not in a good way.

"I hope you're up for a party." He said with a grin as he led me to his car. He climbed into the driver's side as I crossed over to the passenger door. I nodded my head, thinking to myself that being in a group setting would be the best idea. I didn't want to be alone with him. I had originally accepted the date just so he'd leave me alone and because I had nothing better to do, but the more I was around Chris, the more creeped out I got. Of course, maybe it had everything to do with the fact that he was three years older than me and that made me nervous.

Chris rambled in the front seat and I stared out the window, wishing I were elsewhere. I bet I sound like a real witch, right? You have to remember, this is technically the second date I've ever been on that hasn't been with someone I've known all my life. I'm so used to being in the safety of my close friends that I don't know how to act around outsiders.

"I hope you like beer." Chris said as he looked over at me hopefully. "Brittany?" He asked again when I was still staring out the window.

"Sorry, what?"

"Do you like beer? That's all that will be there."

"Yeah, that's fine." I murmured with a small smile. I crossed my arms in front of me self-consciously and leaned back in the seat.

"Don't be nervous, Brittany." He said with a big grin as he leaned over and patted my knee. "I won't bite." I moved a little too quickly away from his touch and his smile dropped. "I don't want to hurt you." He said in a soft, pleading voice.

"I know I'm just…I've never really been…" I inhaled and then looked out the window again. "I've only really ever been on one date and it was the other night with Jeremy Font. I'm new to this and I thought I was ready, but I'm really not."

"According to Font, you didn't seem to have any issues then." He said in a flat tone, his hands gripping the steering wheel tighter.

"Jeremy is also the same age as me." I snapped. "I

thought you were too."

"You're nervous because I'm nineteen?" He laughed as he shook his head.

"I thought you were eighteen." I said quietly. He laughed harder now.

"Age doesn't mean anything, Brittany. It's all just numbers." He reached over and squeezed my knee, but he didn't take his hand away this time. I tried to scoot away from his touch and he locked down on my knee so I couldn't. My heart started beating a little faster and it wasn't because I was crushing, it was straight fear.

I was grateful to see the party up ahead because it meant I could get away from Chris in just a matter of minutes. My heart slowed down a bit as we pulled into the driveway of someone's house and Chris put the car in park. I couldn't get out fast enough and almost fell flat on my face as I tripped out the door. He was out of the car and caught me before I could though. I stiffened, got my bearings and pulled away.

"Thanks." I mumbled.

"No problem." He leered as he tried to put his arm around me. I darted away, saw Haley and made a beeline for her.

"I'll get us something to drink."

"Why didn't you tell me he was nineteen?" I asked in a loud whisper as I grabbed her arm and pulled her as close to the house as we could get.

"I thought you knew." She laughed, her face went solemn when she looked at the fear in my eyes. "Did he try something?"

"No. I just...I do not feel comfortable dating someone who is nineteen." I said as I looked around nervously. "I've never...I'm not ready for anything and he..."

"Did he try something?" She repeated. I shook my head.

"I'm just scared he will." I mumbled. "I'm being ridiculous I know. You probably think I'm a big baby. It's just that...Justin Harper, Michael Rhodes and Aaron Dalkman are really the only guys I've ever dated. Michael and I didn't break up that long ago and I'm just not ready, I guess."

"There's nothing wrong with that. Did you tell Chris?"

"Not the part about the guys but...I told him I didn't

think I was ready to date anyone, especially not a nineteen year old, and he pretty much ignored me."

"Well, just fake you're not feeling well in a bit or we'll just leave without telling him and I'll take you home." She shrugged as she slung her arm around my shoulders. "I'm an ace at avoiding people so you came to the right girl." I giggled and nodded my head. She led me to where the alcohol was, but grabbed two bottles of water for us. "We need a clear head to avoid."

"Good point." I said as I looked around. Chris was nowhere in sight, thankfully, but I immediately locked eyes with Bret. He was walking next to Marc and they were headed for us, Marc was talking but Bret was staring at me instead of paying attention to my soon to be step brother.

"Why haven't you asked him on a date yet?" Haley asked with a shake of her head.

"What?" I gasped with a shocked and nervous giggle.

"You'd have to be blind not to see the way you two look at each other. I just don't know why you haven't jumped on him yet."

"I am not his type."

"Does he have a type?" She asked with a raised eyebrow.

"Cheerleaders and the like." I answered with a roll of my eyes.

"I've never seen him date anyone, cheerleaders and everyone else flock to him but I've never seen him interested really. Of course, I've only known him a month or so." She said with a thoughtful shrug. "I guess I've only really seen him check you out."

"You're senile." I said, rolling my eyes again.

"Where's your date?" Marc asked sarcastically as he and Bret sidled up next to us.

"Around." I answered as I rolled my shoulders and looked around as if I were bored.

"Not going well?" He asked with a raised eyebrow and a quick glance at Bret.

"Y'all would love for me to answer yes to that, wouldn't you?" I snapped.

"Is that bad?" Bret asked flatly. "You can seriously do better than that creep."

"You're the only creep I see." I said flippantly.

"Aren't you missing your gaggle of cheerleaders?"

"What are you talking about?" Bret asked as he moved closer to me.

"You know, you're entourage of dimwits." I bit. Bret shook his head.

"I can't help that those girls follow me, I certainly don't encourage it."

"Yeah, that's hilarious."

"Someday, you should really try to get to know Bret." Marc said drily, shooting me a dirty look. "He's not the ass you believe him to be and you would know that if you'd stop being a bitch to him."

"What is your problem?" I snapped. "Why can he bad mouth the guys I choose and I can't say anything about the girls he dates?"

"If you weren't so self-absorbed you'd see that he's not going on dates with anyone." Marc hissed.

"Marc." Bret interjected as he put a hand on his friend's shoulder.

"And that he's telling you the truth about the idiots

you're choosing because he cares about you."

"I don't need any more people to look out for me."

"You ever think I'm not doing it out of brotherly concern?" Bret mumbled. I took a step back, shook my head and walked off. I could hear Marc apologizing to Bret behind me, but Chris interrupted anything good I could hear.

"Here's a beer babe."

"I am not your babe." I snapped quickly as I shot him a dirty look. "And I have a drink, but thanks."

"Water?" He asked with a laugh. "That's not a drink."

"Pretty sure it is." I said rudely. "I have a headache and beer will only make it worse."

"I have some Tylenol in the car, do you want some of that?" He asked quickly, genuinely concerned.

"Yes, thank you." Chris reached down and squeezed my hand before he headed back to the car. I looked over at Haley and raised an eyebrow.

"Why do you fight Bret so much?" She asked quickly, her eyes widened as if she were surprised by what had just fallen out of her mouth.

"He's too good." I mumbled, I shrugged my shoulders and turned around to see Justin and Alex headed towards us.

"Too good? What does that mean?" Haley asked quickly.

"He's like a...choir boy and I'm far from being a good girl. I'm not even a virgin and..."

"You *are* a good girl." Haley gasped in shock. "You shouldn't be so hard on yourself; you could miss out on something really amazing by doing so." I nodded my head, knowing she was right.

"Hey baby girl." Justin grinned as he enveloped me in a giant bear hug. I giggled and hugged him back. "What are you two up to?"

"She's supposed to be on a date and we're trying to avoid him." Haley giggled as she looked around for Chris.

"Good, I'm glad you realize how creepy he is, without me having to warn you away from him." Justin smiled innocently.

"Why is he creepy? He's kind of cute." Alex asked innocently.

"He's nineteen. I totally didn't know that."

"And he only hangs around high school kids?" Alex asked with a weird look on her face. "I guess if all his friends are in college right now, but still, you'd think he'd make new friends by now."

"Yeah, it's a little weird that he's still going to high school parties."

"He's just weird." Justin said with a shake of his head. "Some of the stuff he says to me doesn't add up. I'm all for people to be different, but he's different in a bad way. His stories never make sense either."

"Marc said he's a pathological liar." Alex said quickly. "I overheard him and Bret talking when they found out you accepted a date."

I just nodded my head and soaked it all in. Why don't my friends point out the people I should steer clear of, before I accept dates from them? Seriously, I have no doubt that if Mason Rhodes were still in town this crap would not be happening. Actually, if Mason were still in town, I'd probably never get a date because he'd scare everyone away.

We got off the subject of Chris, just in time for him to

reappear, out of nowhere and hand me two white pills. I took them

with a gulp of water and thanked him quickly.

"I saw some of my friends; I'm going to go say hi."

Chris said with a smile. "I'll catch up with you in a bit." I just

nodded my head. Maybe he finally got the hint I was trying to blow

him off? Regardless, I was grateful for him to give me an easy out.

Chapter 3

Alex

"Where did Chris go?" Brittany asked in a loud whisper an hour after her date had disappeared.

"Who knows?" Justin mumbled with a raised eyebrow. "Why are you whispering?"

"I'm not." She pouted. Justin looked at her hard, one eyebrow cocked. "I want Bret to take me home, not Chris."

"What?" Justin and I asked simultaneously.

"Has she drank anything tonight?" Justin asked Haley. The tall, willowy blonde shook her head. Brittany shrugged her shoulders and plopped down on a nearby bench.

"I need to sleep." She slurred sprawling out across the wood.

"B, why don't we just take you home?" Justin asked softly.

"No." She slurred adamantly. She sat back up, wobbling as though she were dizzy. "I need pee."

"We'll go with you." I said quickly as I flocked to her side.

"No!" She exclaimed, pushing me away as she stumbled towards the house.

"Are you sure she hasn't drank anything but water?" Justin asked Haley again.

"Positive. I've been with her all night and she's had water and Tylenol that Chris brought to her."

"That is not a reaction to Tylenol." Justin growled. "Go with her. I'm going to get Drake." I looked at Haley quickly as I turned in the direction my friend had just gone.

"Is he thinking Chris drugged her?" I asked.

"Surely he's overreacting."

"Not Justin." I mumbled with shake of my head as I went in the direction Brittany had gone.

She wasn't in any of the bathrooms, nor any bedrooms. I was starting to worry.

"I'll bet she's wherever Bret and Marc are." Haley said lightly, I nodded hoping she was right.

"Where's Brittany?" Justin asked a few minutes later

as he and Drake came up beside us.

"I don't know." I said quietly. "She's nowhere in the house."

"Where could she have gone?" Drake asked.

"Where is Chris?" Justin growled, his face hardening. I shook my head and started out into the crowd.

"Hey Jeremy." I greeted the tall, conceited freshman. "Have you seen Brittany?"

"She went towards the cars about ten minutes ago. She looked like she had a little too much to drink. I tried to help but…"

"I bet you did." I interjected drily with a fake smile as I headed in the direction he'd pointed. Jeremy Font is hot and, unfortunately, he knows it. I was relieved his date with Brittany wasn't repeated. She always thinks she can fix people. It's in her nature. Some people are just born assholes though and Jeremy Font was definitely one of those people.

I saw Bret and Marc surrounded by a few football players and a lot of girls. Two of which were attempting to hang on Bret. I thought about getting their attention but knew it would just draw attention that Brittany wouldn't appreciate.

I wove in and out of the vehicles until I saw Chris's head across the top of two cars. He was headed away from me and didn't see me. Seconds later, Justin hollered. I jogged over to him. Brittany was passed out, leaning against the tire of someone's Chevy truck, snoring softly.

"Where's your car?" Justin asked Drake as he shook Brittany awake.

"Why are you in my bed Justin?" Brittany giggled.

"You're not in bed babe."

"Really?" She asked as she looked around, she shrugged her shoulders and then closed her eyes. "I don't feel good." She mumbled before her face dropped and she turned to the side and retched in the grass.

"Are you positive she didn't drink any alcohol tonight?" Drake questioned. "She's acting like she's drunk."

"We were with her all night, she only had bottled water. And Chris gave her some Tylenol."

"I don't think it was just Tylenol." Justin hissed with a shake of his head.

"We should get her home." I mumbled quietly. "That way we're close to adults if he did drug her." Drake nodded his head and scooped his little sister up easily. Luckily he was parked nearby and we had her loaded quickly.

"Mom's not even home." Drake said with a shake of his head when we pulled into the driveway.

"Should we call your dad?" Haley asked innocently. She was answered with three simultaneous no's. Her eyes widened and Drake shook his head. Brittany fumbled to open the passenger side door and puked in the rocks just as her door swung open. Justin ran inside, got a bucket and followed with it as Drake carried her inside to the bathroom where she leaned against the toilet and purged everything inside her.

"I have to go." Justin murmured as he looked sadly back at our friend who was still puking, her body dry heaving every few minutes.

"What time is it?"

"Almost eleven." He shrugged. "Mom won't let me

stay, she thinks I'm trying to hide something if I don't plan it ahead."
He watched Brittany worriedly.

"I've got until midnight. I'll take care of her." I
mumbled. Justin nodded, squeezed my shoulder and pulled himself
off the tile floor. He hollered for Drake, looking for a ride home.
"Call me if anything changes." Justin said as he poked his head back
into the bathroom. I chuckled and nodded.

I could hear Justin and Drake walk out the front door. A few
minutes later, I heard the door open again, followed by footsteps
pounding up the stairs.

"Jeez Justin, go home! I said I'd take care of her." I
laughed as I shook my head in disbelief.

"What?" Bret asked as he walked by the bathroom and
poked his head in nervously.

"Oh, sorry. I thought you were Justin." I blushed.

"He just left with Drake." He nodded at Brittany, just
as she groaned and drug herself to the toilet. Bret moved quickly as
he rushed to help pull her hair out of the line of fire. "She drink too
much?" I shook my head, he looked up at me questioningly, his eyes
telling me to explain.

"She drank water all night. Justin thinks Chris drugged her."

"What?" Bret all but growled. I shrugged and watched my friend heave up nothing in the toilet.

"We have no proof, she could just have the flu or food poisoning, but she was acting as if she were drunk."

"Was Chris with her all night?"

"No. He tried to get her to drink but she wouldn't. She said she had a headache, so he brought her Tylenol and then disappeared. She went missing, about an hour later we found her passed out by a car and then she started puking and hasn't stopped." Bret looked at me long and hard before he did the same to Brittany. She finished puking and slumped against the toilet, not even coherent. He grabbed a wash cloth out of the linen cabinet, turned on the faucet and placed the cloth under the stream. He shut off the water, rang out the cloth and then crossed back over to Brittany. He got in the floor beside her, picked up her head and wiped her face with the cool cloth before he dabbed at her mouth. She barely stirred.

My heart clenched and I felt completely out of place watching how Bret was taking care of her. I longed for someone to give me even a third of the attention Bret gave Brittany.

My best friend always had the interest of most guys around us. She was so good, she just attracted it, but she never understood why boys were drawn to her. Most of the time she was clueless to their attention. I'd never hated her for that because she never tried to get all the guys, never made it a competition, not like Ashley Dalkman did. Ashley never wanted anything to do with Justin Harper, unless I did. Any guy she ever went for was because I mentioned having a crush. I was relieved when she left, because all the drama was gone.

"You know she won't remember this in the morning, right?" I asked.

"I know." Bret mumbled as he cleaned puke out of her hair.

"Then why are you doing it?"

"I'm not going to just leave her." He hissed, shooting me a dirty look. "I don't care if she knows I'm here or not, it's not why I'm doing it."

"Good to know." I said. "I'm also pretty certain you're smart enough to be scared of Mason and Drake, because both of them will kill you if you take advantage of this situation."

"Do you really think I'm that kind of guy?"

"No, I don't." I sighed. "I believe you really care about her, but I'm also not a very good judge."

"I wish *she* could see that I really care about her."

"Surprisingly, her self-esteem is pretty nonexistent. Almost every guy she's ever loved has left her behind…her dad, the Rhodes boys, Aaron, Justin even did for a bit. But even before that, she was always clueless of a guy's interest."

"So you're saying I should just come out and tell her?" He asked. I shook my head and then shrugged.

"I don't know really. She probably won't believe you, she thinks she's not your type." Bret snorted.

"She's exactly my type. Just because cheerleaders and whoever else ask me out, doesn't mean I'm interested in them."

"I know." I murmured softly. "Hopefully someday you'll prove that to her." Bret nodded.

"I'm going to move her to her room." He mumbled as he pulled himself off the tile. "She's out cold, so she'll probably sleep the rest of this off."

"I'll help and then I need to go." I said as I looked

down at my phone. "My parents will flip if I'm late." Bret nodded.

"You think you can get her into pajamas or something?" I nodded watching as he bent down, scooped up my friend and effortlessly carried her into her room.

I got her changed into a tank and shorts and Bret took her from me, put her in bed and tucked her in. She barely moved. He put a trash can and a glass of water by her bed.

"Night." I murmured. Bret mumbled a response, too worried about my friend to really acknowledge me leaving. I walked out of the room and found Drake heading up the stairs.

"I was just coming to see if you needed a ride home."

"Yup, thanks Drake." He nodded, turned on his heel and padded back down the stairs.

"Is Bret with her?"

"How'd you know?"

"Brittany is the only person oblivious to how he feels about her." I chuckled and nodded.

"Truth." I could tell her about my conversation with him until I was blue in the face and she would never believe me. Bret McHalley definitely had his work cut out for him.

Chapter 4

Bret

I'd been sitting at Brittany's desk all night watching her rhythmic breathing, praying she'd wake up fine. I could only hope Justin was wrong with his accusations. Chris Kaplan was definitely capable of doing such a thing but I hated the fact that he could've hurt her. I was livid hadn't listened to my gut and watch her like a hawk. I'd promised to protect her and I let this happen. It could've been so much worse.

She awoke definitely unhappy to see me watching her sleep. She was groggy, extremely dizzy. She sat up in bed and immediately puked from the movement.

"What the Hell?" She grumbled. "I don't remember drinking last night."

"You didn't." I replied, handing her a cold, wet cloth and a bottle of water.

"Food poisoning? Flu?" She asked as she slowly started to bring the bottle to her lips.

"Kaplan." She stopped drinking and looked at me. "Justin thinks he gave you something other than Tylenol."

"Justin is ridiculous." She mumbled as she rolled her eyes and took a swig of water.

"Maybe, but it makes sense."

"Was I alone with him?"

"Not that I know of."

"Was I alone with you? Is that why you are in here?" I nodded slowly, seeing immediately where this was going.

"You were with Alex, Haley and Justin most of the night. Alex had to go home and I took over. By then, you were already passed out."

"Did you change my clothes?"

"Alex did."

"Why are you in here?"

"I was worried you'd drown in your own vomit."

"I didn't, so you can leave now." She said harshly as she pushed her soft pink comforter into the floor. Her face paled and I fought the instinct to rush to her side. I gripped the chair and waited as she clamored for the bucket to retch in again.

"Do you need anything?"

"No." She hissed.

"It doesn't hurt to ask for help Brit." I said softly. "I don't have an ulterior motive."

"No, you just want to be a condescending asshole."

"I'm sorry if that's how I come off. I don't…I worry about you."

"I have enough people to worry about me." I nodded my head. Why did I always come off as an idiot around her? She thinks I'm smooth, that I have a different date every day but she's wrong. I'm not interested in any of those girls, so I don't waste their time. When it comes to the girl before me though I'm a blundering, bumbling idiot. I never say the right thing and I always come out looking like a jerk.

Truth is, I've had a crush on Brittany since the first time I saw her covered in mud, playing football with her friends and Drake. We had just moved here and I was hanging out with Font. He said then that she was off limits and told me her name, but it was another six months before I saw her when Marc moved in next door to her. It had been a nightmare of stupid stuff falling out of my mouth ever since.

40

"You can leave now." She grumbled.

"Ok." I said with a quick nod. "I'm sorry."

"Whatever." She said flippantly. I stood up and walked out of her room. I heard her groan behind me, but I kept walking, even though everything in me was shouting to help her whether she wanted it or not.

Chapter 5

Jeremy Font had been running his mouth about hooking up with Brittany since his date with her. It didn't matter if it happened or not, he didn't need to be blasting it through the locker room ruining her reputation before high school even started. He wasn't too stupid though, he knew to keep his mouth shut when Drake, Justin, Marc or I were near. Blake Allerton, another freshman football player had told me Jeremy had told Chris that Brittany was so easy even he could hit it. It made perfect sense as to why he was so adamant about getting a date with her.

Jeremy and Chris were talking about Brittany as we changed after practice. I usually ignore Chris because most of the stuff he says is lies. Blake came by and gestured for me to follow him.

"She was all over me." Chris said with a chuckle.

"Then why was she hanging on me halfway through the night." Jeremy asked.

"She got too drunk and stupid so I…" Chris mumbled.

"You didn't hit it?" Jeremy roared with laughter, other players started heckling Chris as well. "The girl will spread her legs at the drop of a hat and you couldn't hit it? Did you at least get a blow job?"

"Hell yeah I did." Chris said loudly. "She can at least do that right."

"Now we know why the Rhodes boys were all over her constantly, she was doing a little lap action for them. That bitch can definitely…" Jeremy's words died off as the roaring in my ears became deafening. I turned the corner and my former friend's face dropped, paled as he made gestures that he wanted me to stop. I heard nothing but the horrific things he was saying about Brittany, none of them were true but no one else would believe that.

I growled as I charged and speared Jeremy into the nearest locker, my fists flying without hesitation. Font took a couple swings to defend himself but he never stood a chance. I was bound and determined to shut his mouth for good.

"McHalley!" Jeremy was screaming. I felt bodies trying to get in between us, felt arms tugging at me before Justin was in front of me, both hands holding me against a locker.

"McHalley look at me!" Justin yelled. "What in the Hell are you doing?"

"Shutting his mouth." I hissed, feeling something warm and salty on my tongue. I turned my head and spit the blood out of my mouth, glaring at Jeremy. He was pushing everyone away from him.

"Chill out McHalley, I was just kidding. I was giving Kaplan a hard time, it's what we do."

"You were spreading lies about Brittany. If I hear you speak her name again, I won't hold back." I hissed, lunging for Jeremy again. Justin cried out as he pushed himself into me to keep me from hitting Font again. It didn't take long for the coaching staff to rush into the locker room looking for explanations. All eyes were on me.

Chapter 6

Brittany

"What happened to you?" I asked Bret as the boys filed out of the locker room and into the parking lot after practice. Bret's lip was busted open, a few seconds later Jeremy Font walked out trying to hide his messed up face.

"Nothing."

"Did you get into a fight with Jeremy?" I questioned. Bret shrugged his shoulders and got into the car. Before Jeremy could leave, my brother was banging on his car window.

"You're lucky McHalley got a hold of you before I did. Run your mouth again and *I* will put you out for the season." Drake warned.

"What's that about?" I asked Marc.

"Jeremy was talking shit about you. I told you he was a jerk."

"What?!?!" I exclaimed. "What was he saying?"

Marc shot me a look like 'c'mon, do you really need to ask that. Isn't it obvious?' My mouth dropped open as I glared in his direction.

"That's the kind of classy guy he is." Drake said. "You better not go near him again, Brittany."

"So why does Bret have a busted lip?" Again, Marc shot me another look.

"How can you not follow?" Marc asked shaking his head in disbelief.

"Why is he spreading shit now, our date was last week?"

"He ran his mouth then, just not in our presence. I guess he didn't realize Bret was on the other side of the lockers when he was giving Kaplan a hard time. He was asking him if he had hit it yet and when Kaplan said no, Jeremy said you were easy and that anyone could score with you."

"And Chris didn't do anything?"

"He's a wuss. Besides he didn't have a chance, Bret called him out and then just attacked him. They both got warned and they're suspended from varsity for two games." Marc explained. I looked over at Bret, but he stared at the ground.

"Hey." I called out to Bret a few hours later, as he walked past my bedroom. Bret stopped and poked his head in.

"You can come in, I won't bite." I laughed. He hesitantly walked the rest of the way into my room. "Um, thanks for…thanks for today. I'm sorry you got suspended."

"I still get to start freshman, it's not a big deal." He answered coolly.

"Well it is to me." I said. "Thanks."

"No problem." He replied as he started to leave.

"Wait!" Bret turned back around and looked at me questioningly. "I'm…I'm sorry about the way I've been treating you too. I've been a real jerk."

"It's not a big deal; I know I come off as a butt sometimes."

"Stop being so nice about it…I was a royal witch to you." I said.

"I'm over it." He replied with a shrug and walked out to Marc's room. I was really put off by his nonchalance of the whole situation.

I was thoroughly confused, why would someone who beat a guy up for spreading rumors about me, not care that I was a jerk to him? Wouldn't you think he had to care a little bit to be suspended for it?

Chapter 7

I hadn't been able to sleep for two days. My stomach was in knots, because high school was about to begin and it was already nothing like I had imagined it being. I'd always thought on my first day of high school I would walk in surrounded by Justin, Michael, Aaron, his twin sister Ashley and Alex. Justin and Alex were there with me, but it was honestly, extremely hard for me to not crawl into the fetal position and cry. I missed Aaron so bad that my stomach was hurting; I missed all of my friends and the normal our life used to be. As we stood in front of the building, waiting to go in, Justin slung his arm around my shoulders and gave me a squeeze. He was feeling the same emotions I was.

"He's here Britty," He whispered in a broken voice. "Don't ever doubt that." I nodded my head and wiped at my eyes.

I was completely nervous as well, worried I wouldn't know anyone in my classes and that none of my friends would be near me all day. Bret walked by me in the hallway and threw me a wink; he was on top of the world because everyone already knew his name from the buzz about his football skills. I wanted to hate him for that, things seemed to come pretty easily to him, but just that little gesture had my stomach calming down immensely.

"I get to see *your* beautiful face between every class?" Justin asked, realizing our lockers were side by side. "How did I get so lucky?"

"I don't know, but I'm happy I know *someone* by me." I answered with a genuine grin. "Alex is all the way down in no man's land. At least we have a class together. I have a few classes with Bret and one with Marc too, so that's helpful. I have lunch with both of them though."

"You have a class with me too and lunch." Justin reminded me, we'd been on the phone most of the night before, comparing our schedules and giving each other pep talks about today.

"Thank God. I guess we all have study hall together though."

"Yeah, freshman have their own in the cafeteria because there's so many of us."

"I'll be in there too." Chris interjected as he snuck up behind us. "They needed an assistant, because of the class size."

"Cool." I said with a blank face. "How are you

allowed at school, when you're not a student?"

"Can I walk you to French?" Chris asked.

"How do you…"

"I heard you talking to one of the cross country girls after practice yesterday." He shrugged. I looked back at Justin nervously, he rolled his shoulders and shook his head.

"Brittany, need a ride to French class?" Tucker Long, the boys Senior Cross Country Captain teased as he strolled by me.

"Sure, it'll be the one time today I don't walk into the wrong class first!" I laughed. Chris made a noise, almost a growl at Tucker.

"I offered first." Chris said in a whine.

"Should you even be here?" Tucker asked with a raised eyebrow. Chris glared back at him and I quickly grabbed my books and scurried away.

"Is he a teacher's assistant or something?" I asked Tucker when we walked into our French class. Tucker shook his head.

"No. He shouldn't be here, unless he said he was going over stuff with the football coach." He shrugged his shoulders and looked around the room for desks. He gestured for me to follow

him to the back of the room where he found two desks next to each

other. He sat down in one aisle and nodded for me to take the desk

next to him. "He got away with a lot of crap while he was here

though. Of course, with his dad being County Sheriff they pretty

much think he's an angel, which he's not."

"He creeps me out."

"Go with your gut on that guy." Tucker said with a

shake of his head. I shot him a weird look but Madame Clark

introduced herself and the classroom went silent.

Chapter 8

"Do you remember which way the cafeteria is?" I asked my cousin, Kristy Thomas, as we stood in front of my locker. She shook her head and then shrugged her shoulders.

"It's that way, maybe." She said as she pointed down the hallway. "Those are upperclassmen though, so they could be going to the parking lot because they can leave campus." I bit the inside of my cheek and nodded, I looked back at Kristy just as Justin, Marc and Bret came up behind her. Justin squeezed in, dropped his books in his locker.

"You going to lunch with us?" Bret asked. I grinned gratefully back at him.

"Sure." Kristy answered with a smile as she elbowed me quickly.

"Thank goodness." Justin said with a sigh as he pushed in between us and slid his arms around our shoulders. "It definitely looks bad if it's the first day of high school and we've got no girls with us. It sends a bad message."

"Justin, you realize you've known most of the girls in

this high school all of your life. They already know your message."
Kristy teased with a roll of her eyes as we started down the hallway,
in the direction Kristy had originally pointed.

"Ah, but there are some who don't know Brittany is
my best friend and not my girlfriend. Or that you still think I have
cooties."

"You do have cooties." Kristy laughed.

"What if I don't want people to think I'm your
girlfriend? It might attract the wrong guys."

"Can't attract any worse than the two you've already
gone on dates with this week." Justin said with a wink. I made a face
and nodded.

"What if you pretended to be my girlfriend?" Bret
asked quietly. "What message would that send?" My face blanked
and I quickly looked at Kristy waiting for her to answer.

"He's not talking to me." She laughed as she gave me
a playful shove.

"Um, that would put a target on my back. Every girl
would hate me without even knowing me."

"But it would keep all the jerks away from you." Marc

said thoughtfully.

"Don't you watch teen romance movies? Or have you not been around B enough?" Kristy asked. "If the star football player chooses a girl, it makes her insta popular, so the second they realize you're not together, she'll be the most sought after girl in high school."

"What?" Justin chortled. "That's Hollywood Kristy, not real life."

"Care to test it?" She asked with a smile.

"No." I said quickly, looking down at the ground as we came up to the cafeteria doors.

"That was a quick response." Justin lit.

"Don't use me, or Bret, as a lab rat." I said, rolling my eyes as Justin opened the cafeteria doors and motioned for Kristy and I to go in before him. "Or force me on Bret."

"Force?" Marc roared with laughter. Anything that was said next was drowned out by the noise and overwhelming size of the cafeteria. It was gigantic, with lines formed in four different spots. It reminded me of the hospital's cafeteria and I was completely thrown off by the different choices. Justin headed towards one line, the shortest, and the rest of us followed.

It didn't take long to be served burgers and fries, I was the last in line and the boys were already turned around looking for an open spot for our group to sit. I was grateful they were waiting for me. I didn't do well being left alone in new situations. I had no idea that high school lunch would be so overwhelming.

"McHalley!" A very large, muscular and short, upperclassman hollered, motioning Bret over to sit with them. He didn't hesitate to shake his head, looking back at the rest of us with a shrug.

"There's room enough for all of you." The guy mouthed. Bret looked back at us again, Justin was already headed over though and so the rest of us followed without hesitation.

"Hoffman, you're a freshie already?" Jonas Abbott, asked with raised eyebrows, as he gestured for me to sit next to him, Kristy followed behind me while the boys took seats directly across.

"Scary, isn't it?" I lit, the squat guy grinned back at me and nodded. Even though he's older, he and Lindsay had dated on and off all throughout grade school. He still had a thing for her but for whatever reason, Lindsay wanted nothing to do with him.

"How are you surviving without Papa Bear around?"

"I'm finally learning what freedom is all about." I smiled and giggled at the nickname he'd always called Mason around me, it was pretty accurate after all. "Although, I do miss him."

"Locker room is definitely not the same without those three around."

"Drake's little sister?" A gorgeous guy with short dark hair asked with a raised eyebrow as he leaned forward and looked around Jonas, directly at me. "The one Mason said to stay away from or he'd castrate us all." I nearly choked.

"He did what?" The guy laughed.

"Hawkins left out that Mason told everyone you were his little sister and did it out of love, not to be an asshole." Jonas interjected.

"I could see why he was worried." Hawkins said as he looked me over. His eyes darted between the three boys across from me. "Apparently, you all don't know Mason's reputation for following through on threats."

"She's my sister, sort of." Marc mumbled as he went back to eating his lunch.

"And Harper has amnesty." Jonas added with a chuckle. "I'm pretty sure McHalley isn't scared of Mason though, did you see Font when he finished with him?" The discussion erupted about Bret's beat down on Font and I went back to paying more attention to my food than anything else. I prayed the reason for the fight wasn't broadcast in my presence, I would be humiliated. I looked up at Bret and saw he was uncomfortable with the attention too, I gave him a small smile and he returned it, his face looking incredibly relieved.

"What class do you have next?" Jonas murmured as he leaned down close to me.

"Umm," I said, reaching for my pocket to pull out my class schedule. He chuckled as I dug for it. "Life Science."

"With Coach K?" He laughed. "Good luck with that."

"Great, thanks." I smiled. Jonas pushed away from the table and stood up. It was already time to head back to our next class. Lunch was incredibly too short. I let out a sigh as I finished my water and stood up as well. I stuck close to my friends as we disposed of our trays and then headed back out to the hallway. One by one somebody would veer off to their locker, leaving Justin and I walking

58

alone.

"Are you kidding me?" I muttered, stopping abruptly. Justin stopped too and looked back at me worriedly. His eyes followed mine, before they narrowed at Chris, who was standing in front of both of our lockers. "Why is he here?" Justin shrugged his shoulders and grabbed my arm supportively.

"Shouldn't you be...elsewhere?" Justin asked rudely as he gestured for Chris to move out of the way. The tall blonde shot my friend a dirty look, causing him to laugh. Justin Harper wasn't intimidated by much. I could feel the tension rolling off Chris and I squeezed Justin's hand before I let go and got into my locker. Apparently, Justin saw the issue as well because he hung out in his locker, pretending to look for something so he could eavesdrop.

"Hey, shouldn't you be out the door for lunch by now or something?" I asked, trying to get into my locker, but Chris continued to stand in front of it.

"I just wanted to say hi before I left. I feel like I haven't seen you all day." He said, leaning in to kiss me. I moved out of the way quickly, shooting him a dirty look.

59

"You just saw me two hours ago." I laughed. Justin looked at me questioningly and I nodded at him, to let him know I was okay. Therefore, he walked off towards his next class, leaving me alone with Chris Kaplan.

"I don't want you going to lunch with him anymore." Chris informed me as he nodded after my friend.

"With who?"

"Harper or McHalley for that matter. They're both trying to move in on you and I don't like it." Chris said.

"Justin Harper is one of my best friends and Bret is at my house so much he's practically family. They're just friends."

"You're wrong." He answered angrily, then his tone changed and he looked at me seriously. "I just don't want to lose you that's all. I'm sorry."

"You're not my boyfriend, Chris. We're not even dating." I said awkwardly. "I better go; I don't want to get a tardy in the first week. I'll see you in study hall I guess."

Chris leaned in to kiss me again, but I pretended not to notice as I rushed off to class. I turned around halfway down the hall, I could see he was fuming. A senior came up to him and pushed him into a locker playfully, Chris started to attack until he realized who it was. Well, this was awkward.

Chapter 9

"How was your first day of school?" Michael Rhodes asked on the other end of the phone.

"Decent. How was yours?" I teased, knowing their mother had started homeschooling them a few days ago so they could concentrate on their music.

"Different." He chuckled. "I think my mom is going to start hitting the liquor hard if she has to put up with us constantly."

"I don't blame her." I giggled. "Maybe I should get someone to buy her Christmas present from me then…I'll keep her stocked on Vodka."

"No need to suck up Britty, she already loves you." He laughed.

"Britty?" I heard Mason question in the background. "Give me the phone." There was a struggle as Michael yelled at his older brother.

"You're on speakerphone." I heard Michael growl.

"Hey B, how was your first day of high school?" I heard Michael's other older brother, Matt ask. I giggled.

"Not as bad as I imagined. Justin and I are locker neighbors, so that helps."

"I told you it wouldn't be so bad." Matt chuckled.

"Any guys bother you today sis?" Mason asked with a tight voice. I couldn't help but laugh. Mason and my brother had been best friends since kindergarten and since there were no girls in the Rhodes family, Mason had absolutely adopted me as his little sister. They all had really, but Mason referred to me as sis all the time and if anyone messed with me, they would have to go through him. I don't know how many times Mason had scared guys away from me just for the heck of it. When Michael and I broke up, Mason beat the Hell out of his own brother for breaking my heart.

"No Mason, no one bothered me." I said forcing a giggle as Chris Kaplan's face popped into my head.

"You and McHalley a thing yet?"

"Uh no." I said awkwardly.

"Don't say it like that…you will be." Mason laughed, as he no doubt gave his youngest brother a funny look. "And Michael will be kicking himself then."

"I'm taking it off speaker now." Michael said drily as I

heard a click. "Sorry about them."

"No worries. I miss you guys. Not being with you all today, sucked."

"I know. I thought about you all day. I'm just lucky I beat Mason to the phone because he's only mentioned calling you to see how your day was, oh about ten times."

"Awww, he's so sweet."

"That's supposed to be my job."

"Not anymore." I said sadly, as I took a deep breath. "Any news on the music business?"

"We're in the studio, starting tomorrow for the rest of the week."

"That's awesome."

"Hopefully something happens soon…a two bedroom apartment with the six of us is waaaaay too intimate for me."

"OhmiGod." I gasped. "Two bedrooms?"

"Yeah, it's all mom and dad could find on short notice."

"Yikes. Well, you're welcome to stay here anytime you need to." I offered with a laugh. "Or maybe Mason will be the better choice."

"I am always the better choice Britty." Michael said sadly. "You always used to think so anyway."

"I still do Michael." I sighed, talking to my friend for another hour before I was interrupted by my mother.

"You have a call on the house phone." My mom said in a loud whisper. "It's Mrs. Hawkins." She said in response to my funny look.

"I have to go Michael." I said quietly. "I'll text you later."

"K." He murmured I love you and hung up. My mom smiled back at me as she handed the cordless phone to me. Mrs. Hawkins and her husband were both ob-gyns that ran their own practice, they also had four year old twins that needed a babysitter most weekends. I'd been babysitting Bret's younger brother, Brian, sometimes too but the Hawkins were more consistent and paid incredibly well. Mrs. Hawkins was very efficient as well, she was scheduling her month and asked if I was available for the next three Friday nights.

Chapter 10

For the next month, I was either in for curfew after football games because of cross country or I was babysitting. When I was free, I was with my friends constantly. I had already told Chris I wasn't interested, repeatedly, I had told him over and over again that I was not ready for a boyfriend or anything serious at this point. He was not getting it, at all.

"So there's a big party Saturday night, we going?" Chris said closing my locker before I headed to change out for practice.

"Uh, we? No. I'm babysitting."

"Can't you blow that off?" He asked, clearly upset.

"No." I laughed. "I have priorities."

"It would be nice to be your number one priority sometimes." He pouted.

"We are not a couple Chris. I have told you repeatedly that I am not ready for a boyfriend." His eyes narrowed as he looked at the wall across from us, then back at me.

"You're constantly hanging out with your loser friends. They see you more than I do."

"Loser friends, huh?" I asked angrily. "If you don't like my friends, then you should definitely take a hike."

"And I'm your boyfriend, doesn't that count for something?"

"Boyfriend? Have you *not* been listening? I *do not want* a boyfriend right now!" I snapped. Chris took a step back from me and looked down at the floor as if I'd hit him.

"I'm just….nothing. I'm sorry I just wish I could have more alone time with you, that's all. What if I came over to the Hawkins after the kids go to sleep?" Was he serious? Was I saying this stuff out loud like I think, or is it all in my head?

"Uh, no. How do you know where I'm babysitting?" I asked quickly, knowing I never mentioned that to him, or anyone.

"Joey and his friends are over there all the time when you're babysitting." He said, referring to the Hawkins' son, who is a junior. "But not because I invited them…half the time I don't even know they're there."

"Hoffman…you coming?" Haley asked, shooting me a

strange look.

"I've gotta go, I'm gonna be late…and so are you." I said dismissively and ran off before he could say or do anything else.

"He cannot take a hint, no matter how obvious." I answered Haley's questioning eyes as we headed for the locker rooms.

"Yeah, I've heard that about him."

"And you're just now telling me?"

"You never asked, besides you can't always believe what you hear."

"Have you heard how to cut him loose?" I asked sarcastically. "Because he apparently does not understand the words that are coming out of my mouth."

"There are way too many hot guys around for you to be attached your freshman year anyway." She giggled.

"Thank you, oh wise one." I laughed. "I'm definitely not interested in being attached to anyone."

Haley and I entered the locker room and got changed out for practice, while gossiping with the other girls. I was quiet, my dilemma with Chris running through my head. I had to come up with some way to get rid of him, since being blatantly honest and rude was not working at all. It really bothered me that he was allowed free reign of the school, when he had graduated last year. Most schools were very strict with allowing people in the building when school is in session for obvious reasons, but apparently Stitlin High School didn't care. Everyone I had asked about it just told me Chris was able to do whatever he wanted and no one understood why. Justin thought I should go to a teacher or something and tell them he was harassing me but I worried it would get him kicked off as assistant on the football team. I wasn't desperate yet, but I would definitely keep that option in my back pocket. Every scenario I ran through my head was underhanded and I didn't like the idea of lying to get rid of him, or risk someone getting into a fight because of it. Chris had already, in a roundabout way, threatened to hurt Justin and Bret if I didn't distance myself from them. He never said that to them of course, because both boys probably would've just laughed in his face.

"You okay?" Haley asked as I grabbed my stuff out of the locker room. I nodded my head and walked over to the water fountain. I bent down, took a long drink before I stood up and looked back at her.

"Yeah, just trying to figure out a way to get rid of Chris."

"I'm sure Mr. McHalley would be very willing to take you off the market so Kaplan gets the hint."

"Pretty sure he's dating Charity Klein." I said with a shrug.

"And I'm pretty sure he's not." She giggled. "You are definitely not destined for the life of an investigative reporter, paparazzi definitely." I shot her a funny look, shrugged my shoulders and walked out to the parking lot with her. We headed towards her car and I climbed inside. The football team still had well over an hour left to their practice and Haley was nice enough to take me home every day and if she couldn't, I would wait for Lindsay to finish with volleyball practice.

"Are you sure you're okay?" Haley asked as we pulled into my driveway. "I've really never seen you this quiet before." I nodded again.

"I don't like being mean to people and I hate that I got myself into this situation with Chris."

"What situation? You accepted a date with him and

then told him you were not interested. This isn't your fault, just ignore him and forget about it. Have you talked to Drake about it? I'm sure he can scare him off."

"Drake alone isn't as intimidating as he and Mason were together."

"True, the entire school was pretty scared of them together." She laughed. "Talk to Drake though, I'm sure he can help you out of the problem. If nothing else, if what I hear is true, if you call Mason Rhodes and tell him about it, then he'll be here in two hours to get it taken care of."

"They're preoccupied with being in the studio." I shrugged. "I have no doubt Mason would be here in a heartbeat, but I don't want him to screw everything up because of me." She nodded her head in understanding. "Thanks Haley." I smiled as I opened the door to her silver Ford Taurus. She nodded her head, I said goodbye and headed into the house. Why did high school have to be so difficult? It was times like this that I missed Aaron the most, he would get me out of this situation in a heartbeat. However, if Aaron were still alive Chris Kaplan would've never been in my line of sight, ever.

Chapter 11

The next day they announced the homecoming court and I was one of the freshmen attendants. I was really shocked and certain the only reason I had been voted in was because of my last name. No one knew who I was except for my cross country teammates, the people I graduated with and my close friends. Everyone knew Drake and Lindsay though, so they probably just voted for me because they recognized my last name.

They had just made the announcements over the intercom and when I walked out of my last class for the day, I felt like everyone was staring at me. So I'm a little self-conscious if you can't tell.

*"Congratulations." Bret grinned as he sidled up next to me on our way to our lockers.

"Thanks." I said, smiling up at him. "Pretty sure I won by default, but I guess I'll take it."

"Pretty sure it wasn't by default." He chuckled as he shook his head. I shrugged my shoulders. "You headed to the locker room to change out?"

"Yup." I said with a sigh as I looked ahead and saw

Chris was standing by my locker waiting for me.

"I thought you told him you weren't interested."

"I thought I did too." I mumbled with a shake of my head. I closed my eyes and took a deep breath, until I felt Bret's hand on my wrist.

"Are you being nice or beating around the bush?"

"I've been blatantly honest, it's almost like he stops listening when I say it." I shrugged. "I'm going to be late for practice." I looked down at my locker where Chris was fuming, then back at Bret. There was no point in allowing Bret to get into another fight because of me, I was pretty certain Chris would attack and Bret would get the blame. "I'll see you later."

"Wait till I tell my brother that *I* am dating the freshmen homecoming attendant." Chris breathed as I walked up to my locker.

"We're not dating." I snapped, as I pushed past him to get into my locker.

"He was planning on coming home from school for homecoming, so you'll get to meet him."

"I didn't know you had a brother." I said, "Anyway,

can we talk later?"

"We can talk now." He said with a shrug and a smile. He looked up as if he were looking to see if anyone was around. His face grew tight when he saw Bret walking towards us. "McHalley needs to back off. He's trying to get in your pants. You need to stay away from him."

"Please don't tell me who to stay away from." I sighed. "You and I are not together."

"Are you going to wait for me after practice?" Chris asked as Bret got closer. He leaned in and tried to kiss me. I bent down, got my duffel out of the bottom of my locker and ignored the ticked off look on Chris's face.

"Actually, yes. I was hoping we could talk." Chris grinned, trying to kiss me again. I backed away quickly and fell into stride with Justin and Bret.

"What's that about?" Justin asked. I shrugged my shoulders and hurried towards the locker rooms.

"I don't know…I have tried being nice when I tell him I'm not interested and he's not listening. Apparently, I have to employ a little harshness."

"Good, I don't like him."

"I'm well aware Justin, I'm pretty sure you tell me that *at least* five times a day."

"So you do hear me then? I thought I was just thinking it." He teased. I shook my head and laughed.

"Funny, I think that when I'm talking to Chris a lot. I also still do not understand why he is allowed to be on campus all the time."

"They've tried getting rid of him, rumor has it his dad says he's here as an undercover agent to cut down on the drugs being passed around the school." Bret replied.

"And they believe that?" Justin shrugged his shoulders. I started towards the girl's locker room while Bret and Justin started towards the boy's locker room. Bret started to say something when Justin interjected;

"Let me know if your harshness doesn't work, I'll be happy to tell Kaplan that you and Bret are an item." Justin teased with a grin as he winked. My mouth dropped open and the two boys disappeared before I could protest.

After practices, I waited for Chris by the entrance to the football field. Of course, my brother and everyone made it out before him. I was tempted to just jump in the vehicle with them and avoid the drama that would surely be unfolding soon, but I fought the urge.

"Chris said he's taking you home?" Drake questioned.

"No, would you wait for me?" I asked hesitantly.

"Sure." Drake shrugged his shoulders and walked over to flirt with Haley.

"There's my favorite girl." Justin said picking me up in a sweaty bear hug.

"Put me down, you know I think your sweatiness is disgusting."

"Whatever…I know you just say that to play hard to get." He teased; I rolled my eyes at him. "Hey, mom wanted to say hi." He said with a toothy grin as he nodded to where his mom was parked. He took my hand and led me to his mom's Kia. Mrs. Harper got out of the car and gave me a big hug; it obviously runs in the family.

"Brittany was just voted onto the homecoming court, mom." Justin bragged.

"That's great." She exclaimed. "How exciting, congratulations. Stop by the house and see me sometime, I miss you kids so much. The house is so empty without having all of you guys running through the house all hours of the day, especially that Michael."

"Yeah, we all miss him." I said sadly. Out of the corner of my eye, I saw Chris staring at me angrily.

"Well, it looks like you have someone waiting on you." Mrs. Harper stated, before giving me another hug. "You've grown into such a beautiful girl, Brittany. And I'm so glad you and Justin are still such good friends. You're such a good influence on him."

"Moooommmm" Justin whined as he blushed. I laughed, hugging Justin quickly. I said my goodbyes and then headed towards Chris.

"He's introducing you to his mom?" Chris questioned angrily as soon as I was in front of his supped up car.

"Uh no, I met his mom when I was born. She was just saying hi."

"That's not what it looked like."

"Okay." I said shooting him a weird look. He grabbed my arm and roughly led me to the other side of his car, he opened the passenger side door and tried to shove me inside.

"No Chris, I'm riding home with my brother."

"I told him I'd take you since you wanted to *talk*." He answered putting an emphasis on the word talk, as if it held a different meaning.

"Chris...I....this is really hard for me, and I've tried to be really nice about it. I'm not interested in you at all. I lost my best friend to cancer over the summer, he was my everything and I'm just not...I can't. I can't do it. I don't want to date you or be your girlfriend or anything, okay?" I stuttered. Chris's face looked as though he had just heard his parents were killed.

"You don't mean that...." He started.

"Yes I do, I just think I jumped in too soon after Michael and I broke up..."

"No, did I do something wrong? I'm sorry, I'll try to change."

"Chris, there's no changing. I just...I'm just not ready to have a boyfriend again that's all. I am nervous about our age difference. Besides, I have way too much going on with school, cross country and babysitting it's just so overwhelming. It's not fair to *you*." I babbled nervously, not taking my eyes off the ground the entire time.

"Cross country will be over in a month, you said that yourself. It won't be as bad then and I'll try to help you out." He argued.

"No, I'm not interested. I'm sorry. I'm really sorry." I lied, praying he would finally listen.

"Yeah and you're a tease." He stated angrily.

"I'm going to go now before you say something you don't mean."

"No, I mean it. You're a tease and a cunt." He whispered angrily as he tightened his grip on my arm.

"Chris you're hurting me."

"It's okay for *you* to hurt me, but I can't…"

"Chris, stop, please?" I begged, fighting back my terrified tears.

"So just admit it Brittany, you really want to be single so you can *fuck* whoever you want, is that it?" He asked angrily. I shook my head, thinking I was imagining this whole conversation. When I looked up at him, his eyes had turned to a frightening black and his facial features showed nothing but hate. "You can sleep with Font and all of Hawkins's friends, but you can't so much as let me kiss you? Am I not good enough for you, am I not popular enough?" His grip tightened on my arm, fear filled me quickly.

"What are you talking about?" I asked as tears streamed down my face.

"Don't pretend to be so innocent. You're not fooling anyone. I know you're a slut, that's the only reason why I asked you out." Chris's grip was so tight on my arm that I couldn't pull away and it felt as though my bones were going to crack under the pressure.

"Chris, please, just let me go. I don't..."

"Brittany, let's go! We've got to meet dad for dinner in thirty minutes." Drake yelled, oblivious to what was happening.

"I need to go."

"No, you're going to stay right here." Chris answered angrily. "This isn't over."

"Is there a problem?" Coach Liebermann asked as she walked by. Chris's expression and tone changed in an instant, as though a completely different person had suddenly taken over his body.

"No problem at all, Coach. Brittany's just upset because I can't be her escort at homecoming." He lied with a smile.

"Are you sure that's all?" She asked, before moving on. I looked away but nodded my head so she would walk to her vehicle and not cause a scene. Chris let loose of my arm and tried to kiss me on the cheek. I dodged him and started away.

"I'll call you later babe." He hollered after me. This guy was freaking delusional.

I wiped my eyes quickly and scurried away to Drake's car, before Chris could grab me again. That went well.

Chapter 12

"*Hu-looh*, earth to Brittany." Drake said looking at me in the rearview mirror as we pulled out of the school parking lot. "What's your deal?"

"Sorry...I...I was just thinking about Michael, that's all. I saw something on his Facebook and it's bothering me. It's stupid, I know."

"Okay." Drake mumbled, shooting me a worried look. "What did Chris want?"

"Nothing."

"Why did he think he was taking you home? Haven't you told him you're not interested?"

"Yes Drake, I've told him repeatedly that I'm not interested. In fact, I was telling him for the five hundredth time and I still don't think he gets it."

"Want me to talk to him?"

"I can fight my own battles." I hissed. I leaned back in the seat and looked out the window. I was holding my arm, fighting the tears from the pain and fear that had enveloped me. Drake nodded his head and started talking to Bret and Marc, knowing he wasn't getting anything else out of me.

As soon as we pulled up to the house, I jumped out of the car and hurried inside. I didn't know how much longer I could reign in my emotions. I was not about to randomly cry in front of the boys, they would think I was crazy.

"What's wrong with your arm?" Bret asked, as he followed me into my room, I hadn't even noticed he was right behind me.

"Graceful as I am, I tripped in a pothole and landed on it during practice." I lied.

"The bruising looks like fingerprints, not from a fall."

"Chill out, it's just from me holding it, that's all. Now, I need to jump in the shower before I'm late for dinner with my dad." I answered rudely. He put his hands up in the air as if he was surrendering and started out of the room.

"I saw you and Chris arguing, he looked pissed." I nodded my head and looked away. "If he hurt you Brit, keeping it to yourself isn't helping anyone but him." I nodded my head slowly. I could feel Bret's eyes boring into my back, but I pretended not to notice. He let out a sigh, then walked out of my bedroom.

I grabbed a change of clothes out of my closet, rushed into the bathroom and closed the door quickly. As soon as I locked it, the tears flowed freely.

Chapter 13

My father did not show up for dinner. I should not have been surprised, it wasn't the first time he had stood the three of us up. Unfortunately, it won't be the last either. I get that he's an emergency room doctor and his schedule is unpredictable, but it would be nice if he would dedicate as much time to his kids as he does to that hospital and those patients.

Lindsay, Drake and I walked into the house where my mother and Mr. Curren were watching television in the living room. Both were working from laptops, half paying attention to the world around them. As soon as we walked in, they both shut the electronics off.

"How was dinner?" Mom asked with a smile.

"Wonderful, dad didn't show, of course." My mom's face dropped as she let out a sad sigh.

"I'm so sorry kids." She said as she stood up to hug each of us. "He swore he wouldn't let anything pull him away this time."

"Isn't that what he always promises?" Drake lit as he shook his head in disgust. My brother disappeared up the stairs quickly, going into his room to work out his anger at my father. Lindsay started up the stairs as well.

"Brittany, honey, you had something delivered about an hour ago. It's in your room."

"Delivered?" I asked as I looked back at my mother questioningly. She smiled and shrugged her shoulders.

"Go see."

"I need to get my homework done, anyway. Night." My mom gave me a quick hug.

"I'm really sorry about your father." She murmured. "Night honey." I nodded in response. I went into the kitchen, grabbed a bottle of water out of the refrigerator and then headed upstairs to my room.

On my bedside table sat a gorgeous assortment of pink roses. My breath caught. I'd never gotten a dozen roses before. Why would my father send me flowers, but not Lindsay? I crossed my room and grabbed the card immediately.

"Do you have your life science notes?" Marc asked as he poked his head in my room. "Who sent you flowers?"

"Yes and my dad, I guess." I shrugged as I pulled the

card out of the envelope. My face paled.

I'm sorry about today. I'm sorry your dad stood you up too.

Love, Chris

"I think I'm going to be sick." I mumbled.

"You okay? Are they from your dad?" I shook my head as I picked up the flowers and dumped them into my trash can. How in the heck had Chris known my father had stood us up? "Brittany?" Marc repeated, walking all the way into my room now. "Are you okay? Were they from your dad? Why do you look like you're going to pass out?" I shook my head again.

"They're from Chris."

"I thought you two weren't together, why is he sending you flowers?"

"That seems to be the question of the day." I sighed. "I really wish Mason never moved."

"Do you want Bret and me to have a talk with Chris?"

"No." I sighed again. "I'll handle him, I got myself into this mess and I'll figure out how to get out of it." Marc nodded before disappearing into the hallway again. I shook my head, went over to my desk and got started on the little bit of homework I had for the night.

Every five minutes I looked over at my trash can and the disgusting flowers that rested there. My cell phone and computer were beeping, alerting me to messages on each. When I finished my homework, I checked both. I had almost seven text messages and five instant messages from Chris. I hadn't given him any of my contact information, at any time.

The next morning when I got to school I went to my locker quickly. Justin was standing in front of his locker with a couple of the Freshman football players, nonchalantly checking the girls out when they walked by. If Chris was anywhere in the building he wouldn't bother me if there were more than a few witnesses, so I would make certain I stuck close to Justin for the day.

"Hey B." Justin grinned as he threw me a wink.

"Hey." I said, smiling back at my friend. "What are you boys up to?"

"Oh, you know." He chuckled. I nodded my head, opened my locker door and stared at the pink rose taped to the inside

88

of the door.

"Who's that from?" Justin asked, hurrying to my side when he saw the blood drain from my face. I didn't need to read the card to know where it came from.

"Chris." I answered quietly.

"He knows your locker combination?"

"No, he shouldn't." I answered confused.

"Then how'd he get into your locker?" I shrugged my shoulders as chills raced down my spine.

Brittany, I'm so sorry about yesterday. I just can't believe you're my girl so it makes me a little crazy when I see you with any other guy. I'll try to be better, I promise. I'll make it up to you on our date Saturday night. I promise. Love Chris

"Love Chris? I thought you were breaking up with him. I guess it didn't go as well as you planned?"

"That's putting it nicely." I mumbled.

"You okay?" Justin asked worriedly.

"Yeah, I'm fine. Just have a lot on my mind, that's all." I lied, shaking my head. I forced a reassuring smile and walked

89

off to my next class.

The rest of my day passed by in a haze, I was constantly looking over my shoulder, afraid Chris would catch me alone. I had avoided my locker all day, terrified Chris would be there waiting for me. We had an away meet after school so I was excused early from my sixth period to dress for our meet. Unfortunately, Chris was waiting for me at my locker; a big smile plastered across his face.

"Did you get the flowers last night? Did you get my note this morning?" He questioned excitedly.

"Yes, how did you get into my locker?"

"Did you get my messages? I didn't think Marc would give them to you." He said, avoiding my question. "Why didn't you respond to any of them?"

"Yes, I did. I'm not interested, that's why I didn't respond to you. Please stop sending me flowers."

"I have big plans for us on Saturday night."

"I'm not going out with you on Saturday night or any night, ever." I hissed.

"Oh that's right, you're babysitting for Joey's little brother and sister, my bad."

"Chris…"I began.

"I hope you know how sorry I am for what I said yesterday…I was just angry and things slip out…I really didn't mean it. Well, good luck at your meet. I know you're going to do great. I'll call you tonight, okay?" My mouth hung open as I watched him in shock. He leaned over to kiss me and I darted out of his way. I was certain I was saying I wasn't interested out aloud, but for whatever reason, he wasn't hearing me.

"So, didn't get up the nerve to dump him?" Haley teased after the meet as the bus pulled back up to the school.

"Huh?" I asked dumbfounded. She nodded towards the parking lot at Chris standing next to his car with a bouquet of flowers in his hand.

"Haley, please don't leave me alone."

"Why?" She laughed.

"Damn it, where is Drake? He's supposed to pick me up."

"I can take you home if you want…not a big deal. But it looks like *that* was Chris's plan."

"Haley, I am *not* riding home with him. He's not right." I replied fearfully, tears filled my eyes. My friend looked back at me worriedly and nodded her head. She looked behind me and narrowed her eyes.

"Hi baby." Chris said trying to kiss me as he met us at the bus. I pulled away and looked at Haley for help. "I called your house and let your parents know I was taking you out to dinner tonight, but I've got to have you home by nine."

"Um, I'm riding home with Haley. She's going to help me understand my pre algebra homework." I stuttered.

"I'm an ace at math. Don't worry Haley, I can help her."

"Sorry, direct orders from Coach Liebermann, my hands are tied." She lied innocently before she turned her back to him and looked at me. "Let's go Brittany, I'm starving, I want to eat before we get too in depth into studying."

I ducked behind my friend, ignoring Chris completely as Haley and I scurried off to her car. He hollered after me, but neither of us stopped.

We were at Haley's car in a hurry, Chris jogging after us. She unlocked the doors and we both climbed inside and shut the doors before he was even close. Haley started the car and I turned to look at her.

"Just go, pretend you don't see him." I begged. Haley grabbed her cell phone as if it were ringing and began talking to an imaginary person as she backed out. I started messing with the radio and within minutes, Chris was in the rearview mirror.

"What's going on?" Haley asked worriedly as we sped away.

"He's just in denial, that's all. I told him I wasn't interested and wanted no part of dating him at all, but he apparently thinks I'll change my mind." I answered rolling my eyes, praying she didn't ask any more questions.

Chapter 14

The football game was away that Friday night and we had a cross country meet the following morning, which also meant we had a curfew, so I stayed at home and listened to it on the radio while I did my homework. It didn't take long to finish what I had due for Monday, so I grabbed one of the new books I'd gotten from the library and started reading it. I was relishing the abnormal silence of our house.

"How's school going?" Michael asked into the phone, halfway into the third chapter.

"It's high school, what do you think?" I lit sarcastically.

"I think it would be better if we were in school together."

"Me too." I sighed. "I miss you guys so much."

"Guys? What about me?"

"I miss you the most Michael. I just…I've never been without you guys for more than a week's time. This is really hard for me."

"Me too. Are you dating anyone?"

"I'm not…there's this guy that won't…"

"You don't get to ask her that question." I heard Mason say in the background. As usual, the two boys got into an argument. I hung up, knowing Michael would call me back later.

The football game ended with Stitlin winning and it didn't take long for my phone to start beeping. I picked it up, thinking it was Michael again.

"We won, I'm so excited, not ready for bed. Can I come over? I want to see you." I was assuming it was Chris, it was the same number from before. My phone started ringing, the same number showing on my caller id. Between my text message indicator and my phone ringing, it was nonstop so I shut the phone off. I went over to the computer and flipped through my social media pages, it didn't take long before I was getting messages from Chris there as well.

I ignored his messages but he didn't stop. He continued buzzing and interrupting despite me not answering and going into hidden mode. Finally, I shut my computer off too.

"Hey, I thought you were going out with Chris tonight?" Marc asked poking his head into my room when he returned from the game.

"No, I have curfew tonight. Not to mention, we're not together. I want nothing to do with him." I answered, not looking up from the book I was reading.

"Does *he* know that?"

"I'm beginning to wonder that myself." I mumbled.

"Well, I'm beat and we've got another early practice tomorrow." He said, dismissing my comment. He said good night and I finally looked up. Marc was leaving my room and Bret was following him.

"I hear *someone* was a big star tonight." I said to Bret as he quietly snuck behind him. Bret stopped but Marc kept going. He crossed into the bathroom and I heard the shower start seconds later. "The broadcasters were raving about you." He smiled shyly and shrugged his shoulders. I started to say something else, but I heard a noise at my bedroom window. I tried to dismiss it, but the sound was persistent and louder each time.

"What *is* that?" I asked Bret nervously.

"I don't know…it sounds like someone is throwing rocks at your window." He laughed.

"Who?" I asked in a terrified voice, knowing the blood had drained from my face. I turned quickly so Bret couldn't see how scared I was. I crossed my room, turned off my bedroom light and peeked outside, dreading what I knew was on the other end of the noises. Sure enough, Chris was downstairs pebbles in hand.

"How does he know which bedroom is mine?" I asked with a trembling voice.

"I don't know. You want me to get rid of him?" Bret questioned worriedly.

"Please." I answered, trying to sound calm. My room was dark, but I didn't miss the way Bret looked at me, he was trying to gauge my response.

A year ago, I wouldn't have hesitated to go directly to the window when I heard noises outside, because I knew then it would have been Michael, Justin or Aaron. I was also living in town and on the first floor back then, Justin would've called before showing up out here.

Bret's stride was wide and determined as he went to the

window. He peered outside, then looked back at me with a raised eyebrow.

"You sure about this? You know what he's going to think, right?" I nodded my head. I didn't care what Chris Kaplan thought, I wanted him gone for good. I was really starting to get freaked out. Bret opened the window and yelled down to Chris.

"Do you need something?" He asked in an irritated voice.

"Yeah, my girlfriend." He answered rudely.

"Girlfriend?" Bret chuckled as he shook his head. "I didn't know you were seeing Lindsay."

"*Brittany* is my girlfriend." Chris spit through clenched teeth. Bret shook his head.

"Does she know that? I'm pretty sure I have a date with her tomorrow, but regardless, you have the wrong room. Hers is that one right there." Bret pointed down to my mom and the Captain's bedroom. "But I think she's already asleep so you might want to knock hard."

My mouth dropped open as I smacked at him playfully after he closed the curtains and backed away. He turned around, flashed his great smile at me, and shrugged innocently.

"You do know whose room that is, right?"

"Of course." He laughed. "Maybe a run in with Mr. Curren will scare him off. Now be quiet and let's listen."

Chris tapped gently on my mother's bedroom window, with each tap he knocked harder until we heard rustling downstairs. The front door flew open and Captain Curren's loud booming voice echoed throughout the country side. I could hear Chris curse, before he ducked down into the bushes. He apparently thought my soon to be step father was an idiot.

"I'll give you to the count of five to step out of those bushes son, otherwise I will assume you're a burglar and pull the trigger on my nine millimeter." Captain Curren hissed in a low, deadly drawl. "One…" Chris stood up slowly, hands in the air as if he were surrendering.

"McHalley told me this was Brittany's room…I was trying to see her, she's not answering her phone."

"There's probably a reason for that young man, so maybe you should take a hint." Mr. Curren growled as he lowered his gun when Chris began slowly walking to the front of the house.

"Furthermore, you will not disrespect my daughter or me and her mother by coming to the window in the middle of the night, do you understand?"

"Yes." He answered, looking down at the ground. "Is Brittany home? Can I see her?"

"I would advise closing your mouth son." Mr. Curren snapped.

"The police will be here any minute." My mother informed her fiancé through the screen door. Mr. Curren nodded and looked back at Chris.

"Your ride will be here soon." Chris nodded his head, but looked up towards my bedroom window. Bret and I stood there laughing. Chris's eyes narrowed as his features grew taut. Bret and I both waved at him before we walked away from the window. I could only hope he could take this hint and stay away.

"Do you think I'm going to get into trouble?" I asked Bret as I fell onto my bed.

"I doubt it, it's not like you invited him over or anything." Bret replied with a shrug. "Just be honest and you'll be fine." I nodded my head and let out a sigh.

100

"Did you talk to him or even tell him you were home?"
I shook my head.

"No, he sent me a text message first and I ignored it. Then he started calling and I shut my phone off. I don't want anything to do with him and he can't take a hint, at all."

"I'm sure he heard Mr. Curren and the nine millimeter loud and clear."

"I hope so." I smiled. "Thanks for helping me out." Bret shrugged his shoulders and nodded his head.

"Anytime." He stood there for a second looking down at the floor, then up at me and then back at the window. I couldn't help but think he was trying to find the right words to say something. I will be absolutely mortified if he believes he needs to clarify that he just told Chris we had a date so the creep would leave me alone.

"You staying the night again?" I asked awkwardly.

"Yeah, my parents and Brian went up north for a wedding so I'll be here until Sunday."

"Lucky us." I lit as I made a face. "Why didn't you go?"

"I didn't want to miss the game, or practice." He

shrugged. I nodded my head and watched as he continued to fidget.

"Shower is free if you need it." Marc said. "And what the Hell happened to make the cops show up? I wasn't in the bathroom that long."

"Chris thought your dad's room was Brittany's." Bret chuckled.

"Nice." Marc laughed. "What was he even doing here?"

"Apparently coming for a visit." I shrugged. "He told your dad he was worried because I wasn't answering my phone."

"Your dad told him to take a hint." Bret smiled. Marc laughed and shook his head.

"Are they still out there?" I asked as I got up and crossed over to the window. The police had gotten here pretty fast. Mr. Curren didn't look happy, but the police officer didn't looked ticked as he held the door open for Chris to climb inside.

"That boy told the police officer you invited him over." My mother said as she appeared in my doorway.

"I did not!" I exclaimed as I reached for my phone on my nightstand. "I didn't respond to any of his calls or messages, you can check my phone."

"He told Mr. Curren that Brittany wasn't answering her phone, ma'am." Bret interjected. She nodded.

"I don't think he'll be coming back, Tom definitely scared him." My mom smiled. I nodded my head. "Why are you boys in here, with the lights out?"

"Bret was in here talking to me about the football game when Chris started throwing rocks at my window."

"And that's when you told him he had the wrong room?" My mom giggled. Bret nodded his head. "He said you were his girlfriend, he's a little old…"

"I went on one date with him mom, before I knew how old he was. The second I found out his age, I ended the date and haven't had anything to do with him since. Unfortunately, he doesn't seem to realize that." My mother nodded her head.

"Excitement is over for the night I hope." She sighed as she looked down the stairs when Tom came back into the house. "I'm sure he realizes you're not interested now, so at least something good came out of me being awakened from a good sleep."

"Sorry mom." She shrugged and smiled at the three of

us.

"You should be getting to bed Britty, you have a meet in the morning." I nodded my head and feigned a yawn.

"Headed there now." My mom nodded before gesturing for the boys to leave. I giggled as Marc and Bret followed her without hesitation.

"Night guys." They murmured good night and were gone without another word. I changed into my pajamas and then climbed into my bed. I felt confident that this was the end of Chris's harassment, hopefully he believed Bret about the date and would move on.

Chapter 15

Stitlin was hosting an invitational cross country meet which meant the football players were able to stop practice for a bit so they could cheer us on. I'm sure they were thrilled with getting a break and bored with watching a meet. I usually try to focus on my running and nothing else, but that's hard to do with a bunch of guys whooping and hollering at you. I couldn't help but laugh as I ran. I wasn't exactly used to having an audience during my running either. In the end, Haley and I finished first and second overall and I was ready to collapse at the finish line.

"Great job sis." Drake said as he met me with a Gatorade.

"Why aren't you at practice?" I asked as I tried to catch my breath.

"When coach saw two of our girls in first place, he let us out early so we could cheer you guys to the win." He grinned with a wink. "And being the best brother ever, I wanted to watch you finish so I skipped changing out first." I laughed and rolled my eyes.

"You just wanted to be the first one to hit on Haley

Jo." I teased. He shrugged his shoulders innocently as he looked around for her.

"You kicked ass, sis. I thought you were going to take Haley."

"Didn't have enough left to catch her." I shrugged. "I'm just shocked I came in second."

"You did great, I'm so proud of you."

"Thanks Drake." I grinned as my brother walked over to where Haley was stretching out.

"I'll catch you at the car." My brother yelled back at me. I nodded my head as I started to stretch out. I looked around to see Bret, Marc and Justin were toting their football gear and had been stopped by a group of girls leaving volleyball practice. My heart sank just a little, I had hoped they'd seen that I took second place. Okay, so truth was, I had really hoped Bret had seen my finish. I wasn't quite sure why I was so determined to impress him. I looked around to see Drake and Haley were flirting, so I grabbed my duffel bag and started towards Drake's car. My brother and the others would follow me sooner or later.

I dug through my bag and pulled out my cell phone and

immediately texted Michael to tell him how I did. He had already

messaged me to ask, I giggled and sent another response to him. I

heard movement on the gravel ahead of me so I looked up. Chris was

standing by Drake's car and he was not happy. I searched frantically

for a way out, for someone to help me. Unfortunately, the parking lot

was uncommonly empty and a knot started to grow in my stomach.

"What was McHalley doing in your room?"

"Excuse me?"

"Why was McHalley in your room last night when I

came by? Is he hitting it too? Am I the *only* guy in this school that

you're *not* giving it too?"

"How do you even know where my room is?"

"Answer the question."

"It's really none of your business. We are not a

couple." I spit.

"Tell me why he was in your bedroom last night and

why you wouldn't respond to my messages or answer my calls." He

repeated, his tone even and deadly. My body was prepping to turn

and run as Chris looked like he was ready to pounce on me.

"I don't have to explain anything to you, Chris. Leave

me alone."

"I am your boyfriend and I deserve to know why Bret McHalley was in your bedroom at eleven o clock last night."

"You're *not* my boyfriend. You never have been. We went on one date, a half a date really. Why can't you comprehend that?" I asked harshly. Chris took a step towards me, grabbed my wrist tightly and yanked me closer to him.

"I will *not* have you making a fool out of me in front of the entire school. You *ARE* my girlfriend and you are *NOT* to be seen with anyone *but* me. Do you understand that?"

"Let go, you're hurting me."

"Brittany, you okay?" Bret asked as he and Justin walked into the parking lot.

"Wouldn't you like to know?" Chris shot. He dropped his grip and got up in Bret's face.

"That was real cute last night, sending me to the wrong window. Don't think I'm letting that slide. Stay away from my girlfriend or *you'll* be the one going for a ride."

"Sorry, my bad, I thought it *was* her room." Bret laughed, obviously not intimidated by Chris's threats.

"I bet you did. You better watch it McHalley, I'm keeping my eye on you."

"Better be keeping an eye on me slick, I'm the one you need to worry about, *not* McHalley." Justin interjected, pushing his way in between the two boys.

"One word Harper and I can have you back in juvee in a heartbeat. But you'd probably appreciate being back with your boyfriend, huh?" Chris threatened. Chris's father is County Sheriff, I guess he thought his ties and threats would scare him off. He obviously didn't know my friend the way I did.

Justin lunged at Chris, but Drake came out of nowhere and grabbed the back of his shirt in an attempt to defuse the situation before it got out of control. Drake squared off to Chris, as he held Justin back with his right hand.

"Get the Hell out of here kid, if I *ever* hear you speak to Harper like that again, you'll be dealing with *me*." Drake said, he turned around and looked at Justin. "This fool is not worth it, Justin. He's just jealous you guys make him look like a fool out on the field."

"I'll see you tonight, Brittany. I'll pick you up at eight." Chris said with a smile, pretending the whole scene had not just taken place.

"No you won't. For God's sake, leave me alone!" I said exasperated. Drake and the others shot me a look; I shook my head and walked to the car.

"Pretty sure I told you last night she has a date with me tonight. Sorry about your luck." Bret called after him with a mischievous grin. Chris glared, but backed off when Drake stepped behind Bret. I didn't miss that Kaplan's angry stares were directed towards me and no one else. So much for Tom scaring him off last night.

Chapter 16

As soon as we got home, I went for a long swim in the pool to clear my head. Marc and Bret tried to join me, but I just reattached my mp3 player to my ears and laid on a chaise lounge, soaking up the sun. No matter how much they tried to talk to me, I would only give one-word answers or pretend not to hear their questions. I was not ready to discuss the argument they saw me having with Chris.

Finally, I retired to the bathroom to take a shower and get ready for my babysitting job. Normally I would wear sweats and pull my hair back into a ponytail, but the Hawkins have a son two years older than me. Joey is a football player at Stitlin and extremely freaking hot. The more I baby-sat, the more I realized Joey and his friends would hang around the house while I was there. Most of the time I tried to ignore the fact that there were five hot guys swimming in the pool or lurking around the house. Unfortunately, I don't think Joey even knows my name or that we attend the same school. He's always polite and well-mannered around me, but most of the time he just treats me like a little girl. But that didn't stop me from trying to look nice, hoping I would get noticed. Since Bret obviously wasn't interested, I should look for someone else. Maybe attention from someone like Joey Hawkins would make Chris leave me alone.

The kids and I were relaxing on the couch watching a movie when the front door opened. My heart stopped, I was terrified Chris would be on the other end. It was a ridiculous fear I know, but it was there nonetheless.

"Sorry, did I scare you honey?" Mrs. Hawkins asked as she walked through the door alone.

"No, I just wasn't expecting you home so soon." I smiled, leaning back on the leather couch and inhaling slowly.

"Alan got called to the hospital, so I just came home. I'm sure it'll be a long night for him, first time mom delivering." She smiled.

"Hey mom. Babies call, I take it?" Joey asked, flashing a smile as he came in from the kitchen. His dark hair was tousled and his muddy brown eyes lit up when his mother spoke.

"You've got it. You want to take Brittany home?"

"Yeah, I was headed out the door anyway." He shrugged as he waited for his mom to pay me and for me to gather my things. He gestured for me to go out the door first and then hurried to open the passenger door of his mom's car for me.

"So do you want to go home or would you like to hang out and see what's going on?" Joey asked as we got into the car, he nodded at the clock so I realized it was only nine.

"I'm up for hanging out." I replied nonchalantly with a smile. My stomach did a flip-flop, Joey Hawkins looks like he walked right off a billboard, a good underwear ad billboard. Every girl at Stitlin High School drools as he walks by her in the hallway and he just asked *me*, to hang out with him tonight. I wanted to scream for joy, but that might make me look like a huge loser.

Joey pulled out of the driveway and headed into town. He messed with the radio for a few minutes before he looked up at me and grinned.

"Sorry, I'm being rude. What kind of music do you like?" I shrugged my shoulders and then remembered reading somewhere that guys like a girl who doesn't shrug all the time.

"I listen to a little bit of everything, I guess." I mumbled.

"My kind of girl. I'm a metal head, but I don't shun

anything but country." He grinned. I forced a smile and nodded my head. I listened to country more than I listened to anything, it also happened to be the genre of music Michael and his brothers sang. He turned the radio to a station and some guy started screaming out of the speakers. I cringed, knowing what he meant by being a metal head now.

"What station is this?" I asked, only so I could avoid it later.

"It's actually my iPod." He grinned as he held up the mp3 player for me to see. I smiled back at him and nodded my head. He thumbed through the playlist as he drove, before settling on another tune in which the guy sounded like he was skinning a cat. "So I hear you kicked some ass at the meet this morning."

"I guess." I giggled. "I placed second."

"I hear Haley is the bionic woman when it comes to running so if you were close to her, it must mean you're pretty awesome too." I nodded my head and gave him a funny look. "So you grew up with Mason and Matt Rhodes?"

"Yeah, they're like my brothers."

"But you dated Mason?" I nearly choked, I turned and

looked at him with wide eyes.

"Umm, no. Why in the heck would you think that?"

"I figured that's why he was telling people to stay away from you."

"Mason and Drake have been best friends since I was born, he's like another big brother. He actually calls me sis. His youngest brother was my boyfriend for two years, though." Joey nodded his head.

"And he didn't want anyone horning in on his brother's girl?" I laughed louder and shook my head.

"Mason is extremely overprotective of me. He doesn't like to see me get hurt. When Michael and I broke up, he beat the crap out of his brother."

"So you and Michael broke up?" He asked, looking straight ahead.

"Yes. He said he wanted me to be able to fully experience high school."

"That sounds like a nice excuse."

"Kind of what I thought." I shrugged. "We're still close though, I talk to him almost every night." He nodded, singing along with the radio as he steered the car down the road.

"It looks like it is dead up here." Joey announced after the second pass through downtown Stitlin. He turned down a side road and headed for the park that sat behind a new subdivision in town. It was too new for the community to realize it needed a curfew, so a lot of the football players had been meeting up there for the last few months. Joey steered towards the park and sure enough there were about ten different cars and trucks in the parking lot, a group of guys gathered around one of the trucks. "You want to go see what's up?" He asked me. I nodded my head. He grinned and pulled into a parking spot. I opened my door and climbed out, Joey was out before me and waited near the hood of the car for me. I looked around nervously, praying Chris wasn't anywhere around. Luckily, I didn't see him anywhere.

"What's up Hawkins?" Trevor Justus asked giving Joey a high five as we walked up. "We're headed out to the cliffs for a major keg…you up?"

"Hell yeah." He answered and then looked back at me. "That cool with you?"

"Sure." I replied, no matter how hard I tried, I still

sounded like the biggest dork known to man. There were no other girls out here so I felt extremely self-conscious, fortunately Joey was polite enough to try and include me.

Chapter 17

Half an hour later, we got back into Joey's car to head out to the party. I was excited but I couldn't get the fear of Chris showing up off my mind. I was also wondering if I was getting excited for nothing, I'm sure I was only still here because Joey was too nice to ditch me.

"You sure you're cool with the cliffs? I mean we can do something else if you want." Joey asked as he started his mom's BMW.

"Of course." I laughed. "My parents think I'm still babysitting, so my curfew is your curfew."

"Atta girl." He grinned, turning in his seat to look at me as he reversed, relying on the back up camera a little too much. Trevor was in the truck in front of us and Joey followed behind closely. "So when we get there you're not going to ditch me for Kaplan are you?"

"Um, no. We're not together."

"Good, that's what I wanted to hear. I would be the laughing stock of the locker room if I showed up with the hottest girl in the freshman class and she ditched me for that freak." He flirted.

"Whatever." I mumbled, turning away to hide my blushing face.

"You did go on a date with him though, right? I heard him in the locker room the other day."

"I did." I sighed, shifting in my seat uncomfortably. "I didn't know how old he was at the time though. I was a little creeped out when I learned he was nineteen."

"You don't like older guys?" Joey asked quickly, his eyes on the road.

"I didn't say that. He's almost four years older than me though." I said. "I guess his age wouldn't have mattered if he didn't creep me out." Joey chuckled and nodded his head.

"He's definitely odd." Trevor turned off onto a side road and Joey followed. Gravel flew up around us and Joey didn't flinch at the sounds of the rock hitting his mom's car. "I'm surprised you have been babysitting on the weekends, I thought you'd have dates lined up for the next month."

"You're ridiculous." I giggled with a roll of my eyes. We pulled up to the cliffs where a large number of cars had already parked. We pulled up beside Trevor and climbed out of the car.

Trevor hopped out of his truck and ambled over to the BMW.

"Brittany, who is your sister dating now?"

"No one in particular." I shrugged.

"Is she here tonight?" He asked awkwardly,

"I don't know, I can text her and see though." I dug in

my jeans pocket for my cell phone and pulled it out.

"Trevor has a huge crush on your sister, he has for a

while but he's too chicken to say anything." Joey laughed.

"You're scared of Lindsay?" I asked with wide eyes.

Joey laughed and Trevor shook his head.

"Jonas still has a thing for her, I just didn't want to

step on toes." Trevor responded with an awkward roll of his

shoulders.

"She's definitely not interested in him anymore." I

sighed and made a funny face. "You know I'm going to tell her you

have a thing for her, right?" Trevor laughed and nodded his head.

"That's why I told you." Joey chuckled as he put his

hand on my arm and led me towards the party. I texted my sister as

we walked, asking her where she was.

"Want a beer or water?" Joey asked as we neared a keg.

"Water, thanks." He nodded his head, reached into a nearby cooler and pulled a bottle of water out, then handed it to me. He grabbed another bottle for himself and then looked around the party. Within minutes, he was leading me to another group of football players. They were all the same age as Drake so I knew the majority of them by name, but I doubted any of them remembered me. I tried not to look like a huge loser, but it's really hard for me. I was so self-conscious as I stood awkwardly and quietly next to Joey. Fifteen minutes after we arrived, my sister grabbed me by the arm and pulled me behind a group of cars.

"I hate you so hard right now!. You've been in high school for a month and you're at a party with THE hottest guy in school, I've been here three years and I find the biggest losers ever."

"I was just in the right place at the right time. His parents came home early and he offered to hang out instead of staying at home and I would've been an idiot if I would have told him to take me home."

"Oohh, I am so jealous. If he kisses you, I'm never

talking to you again."

"He won't kiss me, he was just being polite letting me tag along."

"Whatever sis, I'd ride it as long as you can!" She teased. "Now go back out there and make me proud."

"You're a dork." I laughed. "By the way, Trevor Justus totally has a thing for you."

"Shut up." She gasped. "Who told you that?"

"Joey brought it up and Trevor himself said he was worried about stepping on Jonas' toes." Lindsay rolled her eyes, which was her normal response when Jonas' name was mentioned.

"Should I ask him on a date?" She asked as she gripped my arm.

"Just go talk to him, let him ask you out." I said with a smile. "Come back with me and hang out with us."

"I will in a bit, it would be too obvious if I went now." I nodded my head in agreement. Lindsay walked back to her group of friends and I started back towards where Joey stood with his friends. I looked around and noticed Chris was making out with some girl nearby. Thank goodness, maybe he'll finally stop obsessing over me.

"For the lady." Joey said handing me a bottle of water as soon as I came up next to him.

"Thanks." I grinned back at him. "I'm going to see if I can find Alex or Justin."

"Oh, okay." Joey said with a funny look on his face. "Are you not having fun? We can do something else."

"I'm having fun, I just…I didn't want you to feel like you had to entertain me. I know you were just being nice asking me to hang out." Joey chuckled and shook his head.

"I'm not really a nice guy." He said as he moved closer to me. "I also would not have asked you to hang out with me if I didn't have an ulterior motive." His hand went down to mine and he winked at me. "I was hoping we could double with Trevor and Lindsay."

"You don't have to take me out just so your friend can get a date with my sister."

"Totally not why I want to take you out."

"Whatever you heard from Jeremy Font is not true." I said in a whisper as I looked away quickly.

"I don't believe rumors." He murmured as he reached

up and touched my face gently. "I've wanted to ask you on a date for a while, but I thought you were taken." I was frozen to the spot, shocked by how nice his fingers felt on my cheek. "Why do you think I'm always at the house when you're babysitting?" I shrugged my shoulders, too shocked to open my mouth and answer.

"Hawkins!" A loud voice yelled from behind us. Joey put his finger up in the air behind him, telling the person to wait.

"If you don't want to hang out with me, that's fine. Just know that I do want to hang out with you tonight." He said softly. I nodded my head.

"I want to hang out with you too." I mumbled stupidly. Joey grinned back at me before looking behind him.

"Good. Go say hi to your friends if you want and in the meantime I'll take care of whatever these jerks want and then I'll be all yours." I nodded and turned around. I stood there for a minute, trying to remember what I was doing. I was blown away that Joey Hawkins wanted to hang out with me tonight or any night for that matter. I stumbled off to see if I could find Justin or Alex and found Bret and Marc instead.

"Are you here with Hawkins?" Marc asked in

astonishment.

"Yeah, I guess so." I answered with a shrug.

"Unreal."

"What you don't like him either?" I asked angrily.

"Uh, no. He's a super cool guy, I'm just shocked you didn't stumble upon another loser, that's all." Marc teased.

"We're just hanging out, not dating." I rolled my eyes.

"I'll ask you again next weekend and I bet you have a different answer." Marc answered. "I heard him asking Drake about you during practice the other day."

"You're full of it."

"We'll see." Marc chuckled. "However, now Kaplan knows you didn't really have a date with Bret."

"I saw him making out with some chick." I shrugged. "So, Bret is off the hook for pretending to have a thing with me."

"Totally wouldn't be pretending." Marc said seriously. Bret closed his eyes and shook his head. "He was going to ask you out for real but didn't think it would be appropriate since he's staying at the house this weekend."

"He stays at the house every weekend." I said

awkwardly.

"True, he can't technically date until he's sixteen anyway." Marc shrugged.

"If you want to hit him, I'll pretend I didn't see anything." I said sweetly as I smiled at Bret. He nodded his head and rolled his eyes, obviously embarrassed by Marc.

"I think Joey's looking for you." Bret murmured sadly as he nodded behind me. Joey was headed towards us and I gestured that I'd find him in a minute. I said goodbye to Bret and Marc and went in search of Alex.

Chapter 18

Alex was nowhere around. A quick text message told me she was grounded and stuck in the house for the night. Her parents were extremely strict so she could've sneezed wrong and gotten grounded for it.

I couldn't find Justin either, but I remembered him saying something about having a date with a junior girl. My friend was probably making out with said girl somewhere. I went back to find Joey, who grinned widely when he saw me walking towards him. I grinned back, it was nice to have someone look excited to see me.

An hour later Joey was leading me around by the hand, it felt really nice. I was on top of the world and smiling like an idiot all night.

"I need to pee, I'll be back." I whispered to Joey.

"You need me to go with you?" He asked.

"I think I can manage." I laughed.

"Well if you don't come back in ten minutes I'll send out a search party." He teased with a wink. I giggled and nodded my head as I went in the direction of the woods.

I walked down a path a little ways until I couldn't really see anyone and did my business. I was back on the path again when I heard a noise behind me, just before arms wrapped around me. Fear filled my entire body as cold hands clenched my wrists and whipped me around. I was standing face to face with Chris.

"I thought you were babysitting and instead you're here hanging all over Pretty Boy, Joey Hawkins? You little slut, were you just waiting for the next best thing to come around, is that it? Did you think I wouldn't find out you were cheating on me?"

"Chris, you were just making out with some chick two hours ago."

"That wasn't me."

"Sure looked like you." I replied harshly. Chris's grip loosened on my wrists and he quickly slapped me across the face.

"Don't you *ever* speak to me like that again." He instructed, tears streamed down my stinging face.

His demeanor changed in a split second and he was kissing the spot he had just bruised. And just as quickly, he went back to the angry Chris. I tried to pull away but his grip was too tight. No matter how much I squirmed or pleaded, his actions and words just grew harsher.

"I told you *not* to make me look like a fool, I warned you Brittany, but you wouldn't listen. Everyone else is getting it, so now it's *my* turn."

I tried to pull away again and took a step back; I could feel my ankle twist as I fell to the ground. What happened next was a blur. I heard someone call my name and a split second later, I saw someone rush Chris and knock him off me and pin him to the ground.

"Oh my God! BRET!" I screamed.

Bret was on top of Chris and had already punched him in the face once. He was about to strike him again when the fight was broken up and the two boys were pulled apart, kicking and swinging.

"What the Hell McHalley? What's your deal?" Chris asked innocently.

"Bret, what's gotten into you?" Joey asked.

"He knows." Bret growled, looking at me worriedly.

"McHalley, you get caught fighting again your football season is over." Drake preached. "It's not worth it."

Everyone cleared out a few minutes later and the party died down, I guess the fight was a buzz kill. The two boys were still surrounded by my brothers, Joey and I. I prayed no one noticed the stinging, red spot on my face or knew I was the cause of the fight. I knew Bret was just trying to protect me, but I was mortified and angry. I also didn't miss that Marc's eyes were darting between me and Bret repeatedly.

"Brittany, are you all right? I saw Bret knock you down." Chris lied, grabbing my arm again. I jumped at his touch and shook him off.

"Don't…just *stay* away from me, Chris." I bit icily as I turned around and started away.

"Brittany!" He yelled after me.

"Will you take me home?" I asked Joey, my voice breaking noticeably.

"Sure." Joey said, grabbing my hand. "Are you okay? Did they hurt you? Is that why you're limping?"

"No, I just happened to find a hole in the ground right before, that's all." I lied, looking down at the ground.

"Well, here, hop on. I'll give you a piggy back ride."

"No, I'm fine."

"Sorry, I don't take no for an answer." He insisted,

helping me onto his back. Joey carried me piggyback to his car, opened the door for me and helped me in. He climbed in a few seconds later, started the car and turned to look at me.

"So what did Chris do to set Bret off anyway?"

"I don't know, I was preoccupied getting my face out of the dirt before anyone saw me." I joked. He laughed and shook his head.

"I wonder what's gotten into that kid, I've never known him to have a temper and he's got into a fight twice in the last week." Joey said dismissively as he backed the BMW out of the parking spot and drove away from the cliffs. I looked out the window and fidgeted uncomfortably. The last two fights were because of me, I was causing Bret to act crazy. I was lost in my thoughts and before I knew it we were pulling into my driveway.

"You sure you're okay?" He asked worriedly, I felt his hand rest on my knee. My body tensed up and my mind went blank. What on earth did he just say? Great, I was once again going to look like a huge dork.

"I can help you up to the house if you want. If your parents ask we'll just tell them you tripped playing with Callie and

Cayden."

"No, I'm fine really." I lied. My ankle was throbbing, I think I have a busted lip and more than anything I'm embarrassed that Bret saw me so helpless and had to come to my rescue.

"You're a tough girl, Brittany." Joey said flashing his amazing smile. Suddenly his expression changed to serious. "So, do you want to hang out with me Friday after the football game?"

My heart skipped a beat and my stomach felt like an acrobatic circus was performing inside it. I wasn't sure I heard him right, so an awkward silence had filled the car.

"Umm." I started.

"I'm sorry, I shouldn't have, I'm sorry."

"No, I'm just a little shocked that's all. No, I mean, I have a meet Saturday morning so I have to be in right after the game for curfew. Saturday would work…I mean if you're not busy that is."

"For you…I am free Saturday night." He replied sweetly. In a blur, he leaned in and kissed me gently. I tried to gracefully get out of the car, but that didn't work. Instead, I fumbled nervously for the door handle, when I found it I realized it was locked.

"I am such a dork." I mumbled embarrassedly. Joey laughed and leaned over to open it.

"You're not a dork, you're absolutely adorable." He offered as he kissed me again. I limped up to the house, up the stairs and collapsed into my soft bed.

Chapter 19

"You witch." Lindsay hissed as she exploded into my room. "He kissed you...I saw him kiss you. Oh my God, I can NOT believe THE hottest guy at Stitlin High School kissed my bratty little sister."

"He did." I said dreamily. "I can't believe he did. And he asked me out for Friday night."

"OMG! He didn't. What did you say?"

"No." I answered, Lindsay's jaw hit the ground.

"Are you insane?"

"No. I told him I had curfew after the football game but I was free on Saturday night. So I have a date with Joey Hawkins on Saturday night." I screamed excitedly.

"Well, I happen to have a date with Trevor Justus on Saturday night as well." Lindsay grinned.

"He asked you out? OMG" Lindsay giggled and nodded her head.

"I was beginning to think you were crazy because he barely said two words to me, but I started talking to him anyway and about twenty minutes in, he asked me out."

"I'm so excited for you!" I squealed as I hugged her quickly. She rolled her eyes and laughed at me.

"I am dying of thirst, you want to go downstairs with me and get a drink?" I nodded my head and limped behind her and down to the kitchen.

"Drake, you will never guess who put the moves on our little sister. Brittany has a date with Joey Hawkins next Saturday." Lindsay announced.

"I really wish you wouldn't date my friends. It makes things a little awkward in the locker room."

"I didn't realize you and Joey were friends." I said, shooting him a weird look. "Besides, Lindsay failed to mention she is going out with Trevor on Saturday as well."

"Why couldn't I have all brothers?" Drake lit as he looked over at Marc. "I don't want to deal with having to beat the Hell out of a guy for breaking my little sisters' hearts or doing something that should only be done on your wedding day."

"Yeah, usually Mason took care of this stuff for you." I teased.

"I should probably call him and ask him to be on call for the clean up after Saturday."

"What does that mean?"

"Nothing." Drake said as he shrugged his shoulders and pulled microwaveable macaroni and cheese cups out of the pantry. "Anyone else want some?" The boys were all over it but Lindsay and I shook our heads. My sister grabbed two water bottles out of the fridge and handed me one.

"Two fights in one week Bret?" Lindsay asked with a raised eyebrow. "I didn't peg you as a guy with a temper, you taking steroids or something?" She was teasing but Drake looked back curiously.

"No." Bret responded evenly. "I just don't like it when people run their mouths about my friends."

"Everyone just ignores Kaplan, you should learn to do the same." She said with a smile as she gave him a half hug. "He's just upset Britty doesn't want anything to do with him."

"I know. He crossed the line though."

136

"How?" Drake asked with a raised eyebrow. Bret shook his head.

"I took care of it, that's all you need to know." I rolled my eyes and limped into the living room. Drake nodded his head, he really was a lazy older brother when I thought about it. Sure he looked out for us like any brother would, but all his life he had the Rhodes boys do most of the dirty work. Mason or Matt were always the ones to keep guys in line around us and now he was letting Bret take over the job.

The boys and Lindsay followed me into the living room with their snacks. I plopped down on the large leather couch closest to the remote control and flipped on the television. There were requests of course, but I went to the guide and started surfing through the channels to find something decent to watch. When I couldn't find anything I handed the controller over to Lindsay.

I sat back quietly and thought about how much my opinion of Bret had changed in the last few months. Bret was so different from what I had originally believed. Aaron was always telling me I should give Bret a shot, that he was a really great guy. Unfortunately, I was starting to realize Aaron had been right, but I couldn't tell him that.

I'm sure he was gloating up in Heaven though and if there were any way possible for him to throw it in my face, he would be doing it right now. I smiled at the thought of Aaron and looked back at Bret.

Every time I hung out with Bret, I began to like him even more. He just doesn't seem like normal guys my age, he's so sweet and genuine most of the time. We hadn't known each other for very long, but most of the time I had felt like he had grown up with me like Michael and Justin.

I shook myself out of my daze and realized Drake and Lindsay were no longer in the living room. Marc was passed out and snoring on the couch across from me. Bret and I were both awake, both mindlessly staring at the television screen.

"So, I guess you'll be dressing varsity at Homecoming?" Bret looked over at me questioningly and nodded his head.

"Oh. I was just kind of hoping you would be my escort, that's all."

"I don't have to; I would love to be your escort. I can ask coach…"

"Bret, no!" I exclaimed, hitting him playfully. "There

is no way I would let you do that. I will find another escort, it's just that you are, were, my first choice."

"Thanks." He blushed.

"Well, I guess I should get to bed." I replied as I started to get up from the couch. "It's been a long day and I am beat." I said, yawning and stretching as I stood up completely.

"Wait, Brittany?" Bret grabbed my hand and then quickly let go.

"What's wrong?" I asked concerned by the torn look on his face.

"Nothing…I just, I just wondered if you were okay. I saw…"

"I'm fine Bret; I'm just a klutz that's all."

"A klutz that gets slapped across the face?" He pried. "Why haven't you told anybody what he's been doing to you?"

"He didn't mean to slap me, he was drunk and upset."

"*Brittany*, I saw your arm after your argument in the parking lot. I see how terrified you are when he's around."

"You're wrong *Bret*. That's the first time he's ever hurt me." I lied. "Besides I'm a big girl, I can take care of myself."

"What if I'm not there the next time?" He asked worriedly, he looked down at the ground and closed his eyes.

"I don't *need* to be rescued, Bret. I've been perfectly fine all my life without you in it. Besides, I can take him." I joked, hoping he would lay off.

"You act like it's not a big deal, but it is. I don't think you realize how serious of a situation it really is. Kaplan isn't normal; ever since his brother died he's...he's not right."

"He never said anything about his brother dying."

"I don't think he knows." He answered seriously; I shot him a weird look. "I've heard him talk like he's still alive. It's like he repressed it or he still sees him, I don't know. He's a psych ward's dream patient."

"Whatever." I said blowing his words off. "I'm going to bed, I'm exhausted."

"Please be careful, I care about you..." Bret began, and then realized what he said. "I mean, you're my friend and I don't want to see you get hurt anymore. I didn't like the look I saw on your face earlier tonight. It scared me. Just stay away from him, okay?"

"Okay." I answered quietly; I leaned over and gave

him a big hug. "Thanks for earlier."

Bret turned to me, a little shocked and nervous at the same time. Our eyes locked for a second and I just wanted to stay right there for the rest of my life. I was lost in his deep blue eyes, in his arms and in his lips. I mean, his lips were millimeters away from mine, I felt his hand brush gently against my cheek and I heard someone coming down the stairs. I quickly came back to reality, turned and raced up the stairs. I fell onto my bed and screamed into my pillow. I'm such an idiot, I can't have feelings for Bret, he's like my brother. Well he was anyway; he'll probably never talk to me again. I just made everything super awkward between the two of us. Why on earth would I think Bret McHalley would want to kiss me? Why would I try to kiss him? What the freak is wrong with me?

Chapter 20

Bret

I am an idiot, an absolute freaking idiot. I thought to myself as I fell back onto the couch and buried my face in my hands. I should've kissed her so she wouldn't doubt how I felt about her, but seeing how she just sprinted away I was more confused than ever. Did she run away because she didn't want me to kiss her or because she did and that terrifies her?

I should go up and talk to her before she closes herself off to the rest of the world to figure things out. No, I need to go discuss my feelings with her before she goes on a date with Joey Hawkins. I really can't say a whole lot of bad things about Hawkins, he's a nice enough guy and that's what scares me. I had heard he and Makenzie Yarden had a thing, a mutual agreement, I guess you would call it. I'm sure she wouldn't be happy to learn he had a thing for Brittany now.

I've been so close to asking her out so many times and then she says something that deters me or she is already busy. It doesn't

142

help that I'm not sixteen yet and technically can't take her on a real date unless my parents allow it. I don't want our first date to be in the back of Drake or Lindsay's car either.

I guess I'll just watch from afar for the time being and keep an eye on the situation with Chris. Maybe once he learns she has a date with Hawkins, he'll back off. I didn't like the look on his face when he was talking to Brittany and the more I learned about him, the angrier I was with myself for even allowing her near him. I made a promise and I should've kept it better. If he hurts her again, it's all on me.

I would be sixteen in less than a month and the first order of business is to take Brittany on a date. Therefore, I could only pray that her date with Hawkins goes exceptionally bad. It's very possible he'll turn out to be a creep like Font and Kaplan. I prayed she didn't have to go through that crap anymore but, honestly, I just wanted her to realize how amazing we would be together.

Chapter 21

Brittany

I woke up the next morning a bundle of nerves. Bret would be at my house all morning. I was terrified and trying to figure out how I was going to act around him. Does he know how badly I wanted him to kiss me?

I went downstairs midafternoon to eat lunch with my family after mom, Mr. Curren, Bret and Marc had returned from church. I padded down the stairs and stopped in my tracks when I saw the boys carrying plates and silverware into the dining room. I stared back at Bret, too stupid to think of anything to say. Marc raised his eyebrow in question and then shook his head.

"Hey Brit." Bret smiled. "Are you just waking up?" I shook my head. Do I look like I just woke up? Crap, do I look that bad?

"We're going to go horseback riding after lunch, you want to go with us?" Bret asked. I shrugged my shoulders, eyeing him carefully.

"You lose your voice over night?" Marc teased with a chuckle. I rolled my eyes and walked into the dining room. Everyone was scurrying around. I just sat down and took it all in. Bret handed me some plates, gesturing for me to pitch in. I rolled my eyes and took the plates from him.

"What's up with you today?" Bret asked as he eyed me carefully. I shook my head, stood up and started putting the plates down on the table. How can he act as if nothing happened, or almost happened, between us last night?

"Maybe I just don't have anything to say." I muttered. My siblings and Bret roared with laughter.

"I think that would mean the world is ending." Drake teased.

"You guys are mean, maybe that's why I'm not talking." I said as I stuck my tongue out at my older brother.

"Stop picking on your sister." My mom scolded as she walked into the room, her arms loaded down with dishes of food. Captain Curren was directly behind her, carrying just as much food. I stuck my tongue out at them again and sat down to eat.

145

After lunch was finished, the dishes cleared and the kitchen cleaned the boys headed out to the stable. I followed. I hadn't been able to ride as much as I wanted to, so this would be amazing. I won't lie, being out alone with Marc and Bret had me nervous for the simple fact that I was afraid Bret would try to kiss me again. That wouldn't be a bad thing by any means, I was just terrified of my reaction, or his.

Bret and I both started towards my saddle, he grabbed it first and turned around with it in his arms. I shot him a funny look as he passed by me.

"I can do that, you know?"

"I know." He chuckled. "I'm just trying to be polite." I eyed him carefully. What is this polite thing he speaks of?

"Why?"

"Do I have to have a reason, other than I want to?" He asked, as he ignored me and threw the saddle over my horse's back. He tightened the straps and made sure it was secure before he moved out of the way. I hurried past him to where the extra saddle rested, grabbed it and lugged it to the horse Bret usually rode when he was

146

here. I wasn't as graceful as he was, of course, and could now remember why he was doing it for me.

"Need some help?" Bret asked, hiding a smile. I shook my head, got the saddle up and tightened before I turned around and gave him a smug look. "Thanks for helping me."

"You're welcome." I said haughtily as I crossed back over to my horse. I felt like an idiot because I hadn't thanked him for being thoughtful. At this rate, I was never going to get him to kiss me again.

"Need some help?" Bret asked as he came up behind me.

"Huh?" I was so deep in thought about Bret kissing me that I was now staring at the saddle, not moving. I felt my face grow red when I turned and almost locked lips with him. He didn't back away, just smiled.

"I can help you up." Bret murmured. I was lost in his baby blue eyes, fighting the urge to just lean in and kiss him, to take charge and see what happened. I could kiss him, but if his interest in me was all in my head then it would make everything really awkward from this point forward.

"Thanks." I breathed as I quickly looked away. Bret hesitated for just a second before he bent down and looped his hands together so I could use it as a foothold. I closed my eyes as soon as I was up. I was such an idiot.

"Are you sure you're okay?" Bret asked softly, his hand on top of mine. I looked down, right into his eyes again. "If I did something…" He stopped, looked down at the ground quickly, and then looked back up at me again. "If I crossed the line last night, I apologize. I care about you Brit and sometimes I forget how fragile you are."

"Fragile?" I repeated.

"I just…I don't mean." He inhaled and exhaled as he looked down and shook his head. "Just don't second guess what you're feeling, okay? Or what I'm feeling…"

I nodded my head, removed his hand and trotted off. Running away from the issue seemed like the easiest answer. I was too terrified of the end result if I thought about my feelings or Bret's, for even a second. I couldn't risk everything turning awkward when it didn't work out between us. I was not ready to feel anything for anyone. Because as soon as I develop feelings for someone, they tend

148

to disappear out of my life and I was not ready to lose Bret McHalley

in any way.

Chapter 22

It was all over school that I had a date with Joey Hawkins on Saturday night. Luckily, the news had been spread to Chris, as well, and he was not making surprise appearances at my locker anymore. In fact, he was blatantly avoiding me and then talking about me when I was nearby. I felt terrible for obviously hurting him, because that wasn't my intention at all. However, the way he was acting so childish made me definitely not regret my decision.

On Friday, two dead roses showed up in my locker. Later, after cross country practice I found a dead squirrel in my duffel bag. Haley tried to tell me it was someone playing a joke on me, but I had a gut feeling Chris was behind it.

"Dinner and a movie sound good?" Joey asked Saturday night as we drove into town.

"Yes, it does." I grinned.

"I was thinking about that steakhouse on Main Street?"

"Sounds good. What movie?"

"Whatever you want to see."

"You might regret that." I giggled.

"I doubt it." He chuckled. "I heard you kicked butt at the cross country meet today."

"Top five." I shrugged nonchalantly.

"That's awesome! Did you beat Haley?"

"No, I finished two behind her." Joey just nodded but didn't say anything. He leaned forward, messed with the radio until someone was screaming from the speakers. He started singing along and my eyes widened. I leaned back in the seat and took it all in.

Dinner and a movie was entertaining but there were a lot of awkward spots in the conversation, which was something I was not used to. On the way home, I stared out the window and thought about Aaron and Michael. I missed them both a lot, but I also knew I was meant to move away from the safety of our group.

"Do you have a date for Homecoming?" Joey asked as we sat in my driveway at the end of the night.

"No, it's still a few weeks away." I mumbled embarrassedly.

"Good, you have a date now."

"I do?" I queried, shooting him a funny look.

"Yes ma'am, I would love to be your date for the dance."

"I would like that too." I murmured softly with a smile.

"Do we have a date next weekend then?" I nodded my head. Joey leaned over and kissed me gently. "I'll see you at school on Monday." He breathed as he winked at me. I nodded dumbly and exited the car with as much grace as I could.

I had a date for Homecoming and finally found a perfect guy to be my escort. Blake Allerton was someone I've known for a long time, but he didn't fall in my close knit circle. We have a few classes together, he's a freshman football player, a big teddy bear of a guy and he's the funniest person I've ever met in my life. He's also the only person I know, my age, who is also absolutely insane about eighties hair bands too! I have a feeling I'm going to have a blast with him through all the boring parts.

Another week had passed and I was on top of the world. Joey and I were getting along really well. He would stop by my locker to see me once or twice during the day and then he'd wait to walk with me to the locker rooms before our practices. He gave me just enough distance that I wasn't freaking out about being in a relationship with someone different.

"We need to watch movies more often." Joey said, kissing the top of my head, as I snuggled closer to him on the couch. I was babysitting his little brother and sister again, but the two kids had fallen asleep an hour ago. Joey would usually hide in his room until they were fast asleep and then come downstairs to spend time with me. We figured if his parents found out we were dating, I wouldn't be asked to baby sit anymore and these were our best dates.

"Why's that?" I asked coyly.

"I wonder." He leaned down and kissed me sweetly.

"Yeah, well you better hope Callie and Cayden don't come down here, because we will *so* be busted. Plus Cayden would probably beat you up…he wants me to be his girlfriend, you know?"

"Oh really? I was hoping you would be *my* girlfriend, but obviously I'm just good for kissing and nothing else." He teased.

"That's not true, you're good at football." I laughed.

"Ouch." He chuckled as he grabbed me up in his strong arms and pretended he was going to pick me up and throw me. Instead, he pinned me against the couch and grinned. "Are you avoiding my question?"

"I wasn't aware there was a question." I breathed, unsure of how I felt about the position I was in.

"Will you be my girlfriend?" He asked with a raised eyebrow.

"I suppose I have nothing better to do." I sighed as I winked at him. He laughed and leaned in to kiss me hard.

"Good." He smiled as he dropped his arms from around me, kissed me quickly and stood up. "I'll be right back." I shot him a weird look as he hurried out of the room. My stomach was tight, wondering if I'd done the right thing. I like Joey, but I'm pretty certain I'm not ready to be in a relationship.

Chapter 23

It was absolute luck when the front door opened and Joey's parents walked through. Five minutes earlier and we would've been busted no doubt. I stood up and crossed over to the breezeway where they were standing, removing their jackets.

"Hey Brittany." Mrs. Hawkins smiled. "The kids already asleep?"

"Yes ma'am, for a few hours now. They played hard."

"I bet." She laughed. "I think Joe is coming down with something." She said frowning at Mr. Hawkins, who looked as though he might pass out.

"I'm heading up to bed." He mumbled as he waved good night, turned on his heel and disappeared up the stairs.

"Heeyyy dad." Joey said as he came around the corner. "You look rough."

"Thank you son." His dad mumbled. Joey padded down the steps and grinned at his mom.

"You didn't go out tonight?" Mrs. Hawkins asked her son in shock.

"No, I have a big history test on Monday and it's just hard to remember all those dates. I haven't done very well on the last few quizzes so I figured I'd stay in and cram. I don't want to miss out on a scholarship because of my grades."

"You are the smartest person I've ever met, Joey. You worry too much." His mom said, patting him on the shoulder. "Can you take Brittany home? Your father and I had a rough couple of shifts."

"Not a problem." He said smoothly as he grabbed the car keys off the breezeway table. "Although, Brittany may think it's a pain to be seen with me." I rolled my eyes and turned around to get my backpack from the couch.

"I hope not. I think she's a good influence on you." She smiled as she called over her shoulder. "I haven't seen you stay in this much since you were in grade school and studying? Pretty certain I've never seen you do that."

"Busted." Joey chuckled. My eyes were wide, but Mrs. Hawkins turned around and threw me a wink.

"Pretty obvious when she's your date to homecoming." Joey nodded his head and laughed again.

"I guess it is." He called after her before he waved good bye and ushered me out the front door.

"It would have been a little more believable if you would've told her you were studying anatomy or something." I teased as we climbed into his car and started towards my house.

"Yeah, but when I fail that class they would become suspicious." Joey admitted with a laugh.

"And they won't when you fail history?"

"I warned her I had trouble remembering dates." He lit.   He started the car, adjusted the radio and pulled out of the driveway.

"Does that mean she's fine with us dating?" I asked awkwardly.

"I believe so." Joey grinned as he leaned over and squeezed my hand. "Were you worried?"

"A little."

"What THE?" Joey said, as I felt a jerk to the car. I started to turn around, but we were jolted again, this time harder. The next few minutes were a blur, but I think a black car with tinted windows hit us a few more times before finally running us off into a ditch. My head hit the windshield and agonizing pain shot through my right arm.

I looked over at Joey whose head was resting on the steering wheel. Lights panned over us in the ditch, the car was coming back! The black sports car backed up, jarring us again. More lights shined across, I was terrified the car was making another run at us, but this time it sounded like a horn honking. A semi pulled off to the side of the road and the driver jumped out to assist us.

"Don't worry, I called 9-1-1, an ambulance is on the way." A bearded, older man said.

"Joey? Joey?" I kept repeating, but he didn't answer.

"Are you okay, little girl? Are you all right?" The man kept asking, but I had passed out already.

Chapter 24

"Brittany? Brittany?" I heard my mother's voice whisper. I opened my eyes and tried to focus on her.

"Where…what…"I mumbled.

"Sssshhh," She whispered. "You were in an accident, you're in the emergency room, but you're okay."

"Where's Joey?" I asked, sitting straight up in the bed.

"Honey, he's fine. Your dad is with him right now, he'll be okay."

A few minutes later, my dad, an emergency room doctor who I rarely see, walked into the curtained area and engulfed me in a hug. I sobbed into his shirt as if I were a two year old little girl again. I missed my father so much and it took something like this for me to get to see him. I could only imagine what was going through his head when I came off that ambulance on a stretcher.

"What happened to Joey?" I asked.

"He's fine, sweetie. He was knocked unconscious, I gave him a few stitches, he has a little concussion and some whiplash, but he's more worried about you. How's your arm feel?"

I looked down and realized my arm was in a pink cast. I hadn't noticed the pain that was shooting throughout my entire body, I was too confused and freaked about everything else. I scanned the room, trying to focus on who else was there, but just my mother stood at my bedside.

"Dr. Hoffman, we need to have a few words with your daughter." A lanky police officer interrupted as he moved into the doorway of my room. My mom and dad cleared out of the area and I was left alone, staring back at a tall, dark headed man in full uniform.

"I know you've had a rough night ma'am, so I'll try to make this quick. Do you remember what brought you here tonight?"

"No." I began. "I mean, I remember a jolt…" I filled the police officer in on everything I remembered, including the car coming back to hit us again and again.

"I think the license plates had HTHK or something." I replied groggily.

"Had you and your friend been drinking or anything else tonight?"

"No!" I exclaimed. "I was babysitting his little brother

160

and sister; he was home all night with me."

"Do you know of anyone who would want to hurt you or Mr. Hawkins?"

"No." I lied. I wanted to scream Chris Kaplan's name, but I couldn't prove anything. It was just a feeling I had in my gut, which really wouldn't fly in court. My mother and the Captain were talking quietly with Joey's parents when my father walked me out into the waiting room. Mrs. Hawkins surrounded me in a hug and apologized profusely.

"It's not your fault. You couldn't have known this was going to happen." I assured her. "Can I see Joey before we leave?"

My mother nodded her head and my father led me to the room he was in. Joey was lying on the bed staring up at a television set. He tried to jump up when I walked in, but I put my hands out to stop him. He sat up in the bed and when I got next to him he wrapped his arms around me tightly and kissed the top of my head.

"Brittany, I'm so sorry. I've been so worried about you, no one would tell me anything. I'm so sorry."

"Joey, stop." Tears streamed down my face. "You didn't do anything wrong, there's no way you could've stopped what happened."

"I wasn't paying attention, I didn't see what happened. I don't know what the car looked like or anything." I just shook my head, pretending I couldn't remember very much either…maybe it was all in my head but the more I thought about it, the more I could picture the driver grinning as he came at us.

Chapter 25

A few minutes later, my father knocked on the door and led me back to my mom and the Captain. The ride was quiet and long and I couldn't wait to fall into my bed. Everyone was waiting up for me in the living room when we walked in though.

"Oh my God, are you okay?" Lindsay gasped as soon as my feet hit the hardwood floor. She rushed and engulfed me in a hug. "A broken arm?"

"I'm fine." I murmured. "I'm just really tired."

"Don't you have to stay awake for another hour or something?" Lindsay asked worriedly.

"They put me to sleep to fix my arm, I think I'll be fine." I said with a small giggle. My whole body was starting to hurt and I looked at the couch longingly.

"Sit down for a minute sis." Drake offered as he jumped off the couch and gestured for me to take his spot. I was grateful, I'm pretty sure my legs were about to fold underneath me.

"Do you need a drink or anything, Brittany?" My mom asked as she put her purse down and hovered worriedly.

"Water. I'm feeling kind of nauseous." She nodded her head and disappeared into the kitchen.

"Do they know who hit you guys?" Bret asked, his eyes were full of concern and I knew he was blaming the same person I was for tonight's events.

"No, I don't really remember much." I mumbled softly. "No one really saw anything."

"How's Joey?"

"Concussion and whiplash is really the extent of it." I murmured. "I'm sorry, I'm really tired. I think I'm going to bed."

"Here, I'll help you up." Bret stated, jumping off the couch immediately as he stood in front of me.

"Thanks, but I'm fine." I said, standing up slowly. Bret followed behind me as I made my way towards the stairs. My mom met me just outside of the kitchen.

"Here sweetie, your dad sent you some pain and nausea meds. You're supposed to take them before bed to help you sleep." I nodded, took the three pills and the bottle of water that she gave me. I swallowed the pills and some water before I said good night and headed up the steep stairs. Once I was in my bedroom, I changed into a tank and a pair of shorts. Adding and removing clothes with only one arm is not very easy at all. I crossed over to my bed and pulled the pink comforter back.

"You okay?" Bret asked, poking his head into my room as I climbed into my bed.

"I just want to go to bed and forget about it all." I replied quietly as I tried to snuggle under the covers. Yikes, I was sore.

"Did you tell the police about Chris?" Bret questioned worriedly as he came directly to my bed and tried to help me pull the covers up. I shook my head aggressively. "Well, maybe you should have. Maybe he'd back off."

"He has backed off, he hasn't bothered me since Joey and I started dating."

"Until tonight."

"What makes you so sure it was Chris and not some drunk asshole who thought we were someone else? The cops even said it could have been a jealous guy or girl." Bret cocked an eyebrow.

"Do you *really* believe that?" He asked, sounding a

little aggravated.

"I don't know what to think right now, Bret. And I definitely don't want to listen to you lecture me about what I *should* have done. You weren't there, you didn't see Joey laying lifeless against the steering wheel. I thought he was dead." My voice broke and I stared down at the carpet.

"You're right, I'm sorry. I don't mean to lecture, I just worry about you so much and I guess I tend to sound like my father sometimes." He said, forcing a laugh.

"Well, thanks for your concerns. I'll be okay. I'm just glad it wasn't any worse than this, that's all. And as for Chris, I really don't think it was him. I mean, I didn't recognize the car and the license plates were like h-something. Chris may have issues with me but I don't think he'd take it that far."

"I hope you're right." Bret mumbled, he hugged me awkwardly and then walked out of my room. He was probably thanking God for the fact that we didn't kiss after all, if we had, it's very possible he would be the one sitting in the hospital right now.

My stomach was in knots as scenarios flipped through my mind on overdrive. I couldn't stop thinking about that car coming at

166

us, couldn't stop thinking it really had been Chris attacking us. If that were true, was he satisfied or would he attempt worse? I tried so hard to sleep, the medicine tried even harder to pull me under, but my brain wouldn't shut off and the nightmares would not give up.

Chapter 26

Unfortunately, my freshman cross country season was over because of the cast, which hurt worse than the broken arm. I was not happy to be sidelined at all, especially not when I was doing so well. I may have been more upset about the fact that I wouldn't be getting out of school early for the last few meets too, though.

Homecoming week arrived and everything that came with it was keeping me pretty busy and helped to keep my mind off things. Joey and I hadn't been able to spend much time together and when we talked on the phone it was usually pretty short. I didn't blame him though, I would avoid me as well, if Chris was the one behind the car accident.

All the homecoming candidates were excused from classes while the voting took place and to take pictures for the yearbook and newspaper. After the pictures were taken, I followed behind the other Freshmen girls as we headed back to our lockers. None of them wanted anything to do with me. It was a competition, right? Were they just hateful because they thought I had a shot of winning? I shook my head and cleared the crazy thoughts. I stood in front of my locker, a weird smell permeating the air around it. I opened it slowly

to find a dead, bloated, black cat hanging where my backpack was. I

screamed just as the bell rang and people poured out of classrooms.

"Brittany!" Justin yelled, grabbing my arm and

shaking me out of my shock. "What the Hell?" He took one look into

my locker, ran to a trash can and vomited. He was a lot of help.

"What's going on?" A teacher asked as he came out of

his room. I pointed to the dead animal. "Jesus." He cried, gagging

before he turned around to flag down the janitor. "Mr. Harper, why

don't you escort Miss Hoffman to the nurse's office?" The teacher

closed the locker door so no one else could see what was going on.

Justin nodded, his face still a green tint.

"What in the Hell was that?" Justin asked in a rough

voice as he pulled me close to him. He slid his arm around my

shoulder protectively. "And why was it in your locker?"

"A cat, I think." I mumbled. "I don't know, I certainly

didn't put it there. There was a note on the door though.

"A note? Did they sign it?" I rolled my eyes and

shook my head, but I pulled the tattered paper out of my back pocket

before we turned down another hallway. I opened it slowly and Justin pulled me off to the side of the hallway, tucking us away so no one would run us over in their hurry to get to the next class.

Brittany,

You think you're so much better than everyone else, but soon you will be exposed to all. The other night was NO accident and unfortunately, it did nothing for your ego. There is more damage to be done, you won't be so lucky then. You will pay for the pain you have caused.

Fear gripped my entire body as I dropped the note to the floor. I looked up at Justin, who was looking back at me with wide eyes. The hallway had cleared out and I looked around nervously.

"We should get to the nurse's office before they're looking for us." Justin stated, protectively holding me closer to him. I nodded numbly.

"Why would someone send that to me?"

"I'm sure it's just some jerk trying to be funny."

"They put a dead cat in my locker." I said drily.

"Yeah, there is that." He replied with a funny look.

"It's probably just some stupid girl messing with you because of the Homecoming vote."

"Some sick girl." I sighed. "I would gladly give them my spot if it means so much to them. I sure don't want it that bad." Justin led me into the nurse's office.

"Can I help you?" A woman in pink scrubs asked as she came out of another room, followed by the baseball coach.

"Mr. Klien sent us. Brittany had something in her locker that um, kind of…she had a dead animal in her locker. I puked and she is in shock so he sent us here."

"A dead animal?" Coach Goodwin repeated.

"A dead cat to be exact." Justin added slowly, he shivered at the memory.

"Someone put it there?" Mrs. Hefner, the part time school nurse asked.

"I don't think it climbed up there itself." I answered. Mrs. Hefner's eyes narrowed and her hand went to her hip.

"Don't get sassy." She warned. I nodded my head and mumbled an apology. "What happened to your arm?"

"My boyfriend and I were ran off the road Saturday

171

night." I replied softly. Her eyes flashed as she looked me up and down carefully.

"You were with Joey Hawkins?" I nodded my head, feeling uncomfortable under her scrutiny. Her eyes traveled over to Justin and she smiled sweetly.

"I'll pop in later." Coach Goodwin said as he grinned and waved. She barely paid attention to him as she looked Justin over.

"Are you feeling okay? You look a little pale sugar." She crossed over to Justin and felt his forehead.

"I'm fine." He said with a shy smile, realizing the thirty something woman was flirting with him. I really almost puked too, but she probably wouldn't notice. "I was just shocked I guess."

"I bet, you poor thing. Why don't you lay down?" She asked. Justin shook his head, his eyes darting towards me uncomfortably.

"It was in Brittany's locker. Not mine. She is the one you should be concerned about." The nurse nodded her head, looked at me dirtily before she shook her head.

"If there's nothing physically wrong then you'll have

to collect a tardy and head to your classrooms."

"Excuse me?" Justin asked. She repeated herself and hurried us out of her office.

"That chick has issues." Justin said with a shake of his head as he pulled me into him again. "She was probably screwing Coach Goodwin and if you wouldn't have been there she probably would've tried to mount me."

"That's illegal."

"I don't think she cares." He chuckled. I nodded in agreement as he held the office door open for me and gestured for me to go ahead of him. We explained what happened, Mr. Klein was already in the Principal's office explaining his findings. We were given passes to enter our next classes without any issues. At this point though, I really just wished they would send me home.

Everything in my body screamed accusations towards Chris Kaplan. I tried to push it out of my head, but he had placed a rose and note in my locker before, who is to say he hadn't done it again. I was terrified as I tried to think of what the words in the note meant.

Chapter 27

My locker was completely cleaned up, destenched and everything put back in its place as if nothing ever happened. However, I couldn't bring myself to go back to my locker the rest of the day, so I carried my backpack with me. When the bell rang signaling the end of the school day, I ducked my head and rushed out of study hall before anyone could ask me about what was in my locker. I rushed to catch the bus but realized I'd forgotten my French book and I had a test tomorrow. I turned and hurried back to my locker, grabbed the book out and sprinted out the front doors just in time to see the bus pulling away.

"Crap." I muttered as I dug in my pocket for my phone. Hopefully, I could get a hold of my mom before she left work and she could swing by to get me.

"Miss the bus?" I heard Chris crack behind me.

"I guess so." I mumbled as I walked down the hallway and towards the offices so I could call my mom and have witnesses around. I trembled with fear and could barely dial the phone from my hands shaking so much.

"What? You're too good to acknowledge me?" He asked angrily, apparently today wasn't my lucky day.

"I…I thought you weren't talking to me." I stumbled innocently as I tried to keep walking.

"Nice try, you've been a snotty bitch to me since we started dating." He replied hatefully. My eyes grew wide as he grabbed my arm and pulled me into him. "I'm just kidding." He laughed. "I've missed you. I tried to call you after your accident. I went to the hospital but they said you weren't allowed visitors."

"How did you know I was even in the hospital?" I asked meekly as I pulled away from him.

"My father is the county sheriff, Brittany." He answered quickly. "I heard your name over the scanner and I was freaking out. I was worried you were hurt, so my brother drove me to the hospital."

"How many brothers do you have?" I queried, changing the subject as I moved further away from him.

"One. My older brother Heath, he's in college. He's going to be at Homecoming, he doesn't believe we're dating. He thinks I'm making you up." He rambled, looking around nervously as

175

he moved closer to me. I had never noticed how fidgety he was before, but he couldn't keep his hands still. It was almost like he was worried someone was going to come after him.

"Chris…" I sighed. How could he still not understand that we weren't together and never have been?

"Hey babe." Joey said as he slid beside me, kissed me on the cheek and then leaned in and whispered hi into my ear.

"Hi." I said softly, smiling back at him gratefully.

"I think we were in the middle of something." Chris snapped rudely to Joey.

"Sorry man." Joey offered, putting his arm around me.

"*Sorry man?* That's all you can say when you walk up to some other guy's girlfriend and kiss her?" Chris yelled angrily, his eyes darting to me. "Is this how it's going to be Brittany? You can't even tell me we're through; you just blatantly throw it in my face?"

"Chris, I have told you repeatedly there is nothing between us."

"And let me tell you now." Joey smiled as he took a step towards Chris. "There is nothing between you two, there never has been."

"You can't do this; you can't play games with people, Brittany. It's going to come back to hurt you." He threatened as he walked away. "It won't be my fault when it does, either."

Chapter 28

"Forget about him." Joey breathed, kissing my forehead sweetly as he pulled me closer to him. "He has issues." I nodded my head as I looked up at him.

"Joey, can we talk later?"

"How about now?" He asked. "Early day remember? And I don't have practice until three."

"Will you drive me home then? I seem to have missed the bus." I lit with a small giggle. He chuckled and nodded his head, before sliding his hand down to mine.

"Did you hear what was in my locker today?" I asked quietly.

"No." He said drawing out the o as he looked at me sideways. He led me through the hallways and towards the back of the school, where his car was parked.

"Someone put a dead cat in my locker. I found it after Homecoming court pictures."

"What?" He asked, his mouth gaping open. "Are you kidding me?"

"No, I found a note attached to my backpack too." I said as I dug the notebook paper out of my jeans pocket. Joey took it from me the second we were outside of his car. His eyes widened while he chewed the inside of his cheek.

"You should probably look at this then." Joey sighed as he unlocked the car, opened the passenger door, pulled something out of the console and handed the notebook paper to me. "I found it under my windshield wiper on Monday."

Joey,

You think you're so much better than everyone else. Soon you and   Brittany will be exposed to all. The other night was NO accident;   unfortunately, there were only minor damages. The next time you won't

*   be so lucky. Stay away from Brittany Hoffman or you will pay for the   pain you two have caused.*

"Why didn't you tell me?" I asked. "Is that why you've been so distant?"

"No…no, Brittany." He responded quickly as he moved in front of me, his eyes pleaded with me to understand. "I didn't want to scare you. I feel so responsible for what happened, I didn't know what to say or do. And then when I got this, I didn't think I should worry you with it."

"Joey, the whole thing is obviously because of me, the note says to stay away from *me*. Just take me home…I don't want you to get hurt again."

"I'm not going to get hurt again. It was probably some drunk asshole that hit us and someone's playing a joke, trying to scare us, that's all."

"I don't think it's a joke. I think we should show it to the principal, the police, or *at least* our parents."

"You're overreacting." I shook my head and pushed away from him.

"Please just take me home." I murmured crossing my arms in front of my chest to hug myself. "I don't think we should see each other anymore, Joey. It's obviously because of me that this is happening. If we're not going out then they won't hurt you again." I announced, near hysterics.

"Brittany." He breathed, putting his hands on my face. "We are *not* breaking up. Nothing is going to happen, sweetie. This is *not* your fault. It's probably just Kaplan, he's pissed we're together and this is his way of dealing with it. That's what he wants Brittany, for us to break up. Don't give in to him."

"I'm scared Joey. If it is Chris…I think he might do something."

"He doesn't have the balls."

"He's not all there, he's not…"

"Ssshhh," Joey began, placing his finger to my lips. "I will not let anyone hurt you again, Brittany. I promise." He wrapped his arms around me and hugged me tightly. I relished the warmth, but I didn't feel safe there. There was an incredibly horrible feeling in the pit of my stomach, clawing it's to my brain and telling me to run and not look back.

I knew without a doubt Chris was responsible for the car accident, but I couldn't prove that. I was positive he had threatened me with the dead cat and the note, but I had no physical proof, so it meant nothing in the grand scheme of things.

I pulled away from Joey and moved to climb in the car. He looked back at me with a hopeful smile. He was certain he'd eased my fears, but he was wrong. Joey was clueless as to the issues I've had with Chris over the last few months. He didn't know about his temper or his split personalities. Bret was actually the only one who knew everything. I contemplated showing him the note, but I really didn't want to hear an 'I told you so'.

Chapter 29

Joey dropped me off at home and I buried myself in my homework until dinnertime. As usual, Bret took his seat at our table for another family dinner. I was obviously distracted throughout the entire meal, Marc just teased that I was nervous about the Homecoming vote.

"You okay?" Bret asked me later as he was leaving the house and I was coming in from the stables.

"Fine, why?" I lied, hoping he couldn't see the truth.

"You're just acting a little jumpy."

"Marc was right, I'm nervous about the vote. I act like I don't care, but I guess I do."

"Nope, that wouldn't make you jumpy." Bret pried.

"Seriously, can you just drop it?"

"No. Is it Chris?" Bret snooped. I let out a loud sigh and handed Bret the note I had been carrying in my back pocket.

"It was in my locker this afternoon after pictures. Joey had one left on his car Monday." I explained.

"I think you should show your parents or even the

principal. I don't think it's a good idea to pass it off as an innocent prank."

"What if I'm just overreacting? I don't want to accuse Chris of something and it is someone else being stupid."

"It's Chris doing it and you know it."

"Yeah, I have a feeling it's him, but I don't have any proof. Why would some guy get so upset over *me*, anyway?

"He's not right in the head." Bret stated rudely.

"Thanks." I said sarcastically.

"That's not what I meant, Brit. I'm sure you're a very hard girl to get over." He said, touching my cheek gently.

"I don't think I'm ready to tell anyone else about this, I mean I just don't have enough proof." I sighed, backing away from his touch quickly. As much as I longed for Bret McHalley to touch me and even kiss me, I knew we could only be friends. I think that's how he feels anyway, I'm sure I'm reading too much into his touches and glances. Besides Joey Hawkins was my boyfriend, I really shouldn't be exploring feelings for another guy, it wasn't fair to anyone. I sighed in exasperation, I really should stop allowing myself to be torn between two guys. I need help. Honestly. Do you think they have self-help books for this sort of thing?

"I'll go with you, if you want me to."

"No, Joey doesn't think we should worry about it."

"But he also doesn't know the whole story, *I do*."

"I'm just not going to worry about it right now, Bret. But thanks for being such a good friend and listening to me.

"A friend?" He asked, obviously a little hurt by my choice of words.

"Uh, yeah? I thought we were anyway. I'm sorry."

"No, I just…Never mind, it's not a big deal." He said, stopping his sentence and shrugging it off. Bret jumped on his four-wheeler and headed back to his house without another word. I just watched as he left, standing there like an idiot, thoroughly confused. Bret McHalley sent me so many mixed signals, I didn't know which way was up or down with him. I really thought he was my friend, but apparently, he didn't feel the same way, which kind of hurt my feelings.

Chapter 30

"Hey Bret?" I yelled as he passed by my room a few days later.

"Yes your highness?" He teased as he came inside the doorway.

"You said Chris had a brother that died, how old was he?"

"In college, I think. There are pictures of him in the trophy case; he broke a few football records when he was here."

"What was his name?"

"Heath. Why?"

"Chris never really talked about him, that's all. Does he have another brother?"

"Nope, it was just Heath and Chris." He answered.

"If his brother died, why would he have told me he was coming home from college and he wanted me to meet him?"

"After his brother died his parents pulled him out of school for a while, a lot of people said it was because he had to go to a mental hospital." Bret responded with a shrug.

"Did he?"

"He never talks about anything from his brother's death or the time he missed from school. When he got back he just said his family moved to Montana for a little while, but realized they missed Stitlin too much and came back home."

"You really need to steer clear of him. He still acts like the two of you are together." He added.

"I'm well aware." I quipped rolling my eyes. "I wish Michael wouldn't have moved, the first guy I date after him is a psycho. I knew I wouldn't find anyone who could hold a candle to him or Aaron."

"Well, if Michael was *so* great he wouldn't be posting pictures of him making out with some other girl." Bret remarked harshly. I shot him an odd look. I had seen the photos and Michael was definitely making out with some chick. It didn't hurt as bad as I once thought it would though. I quickly changed the subject.

"So, you got a hot date for Saturday night?"

"Not really." Bret answered awkwardly.

"I thought you were going with Makenzie Yarden."

"I am."

"Don't sound so excited." I replied. "Are you okay? Did I do something to make you mad?"

"I'm just not into the whole dance thing, that's all."

"But Makenzie is super cute."

"Yeah, but she wasn't my first choice. I don't want the attraction to be strictly physical, I want more than that. I want someone who I can talk to and have fun with." He stated honestly.

"I never realized you were so deep. Besides, I find it hard to believe that *you* can't get your first choice." I teased with a laugh.

"I was too late. She was already going with someone before I got up the nerve to ask."

"You can't honestly tell me you get nervous about asking a girl out. Any girl who would turn you down is certifiably crazy. You're the sweetest guy I've ever met."

"Thanks." He chuckled, as he shook his head. "Sweet doesn't exactly get you very far. Especially not when stupid stuff falls out of my mouth around the girl of my dreams."

"Oh puh-lease, you are one of the HOTTEST freshmen guys, you're smart, funny, an extremely talented football player and…sorry I'm embarrassing you. I just find it hard to believe you're self-conscious, that's all. I used to think you were so cocky."

"I don't know if that's a compliment or not." He laughed awkwardly.

"Sorry." I smiled.

"Don't apologize; it's actually kind of nice to know you don't think I'm a huge jerk anymore."

"Yeah, well I do apologize for that. I guess I was so wrapped up in my little circle that I didn't think there could be anyone out there as great as my guy friends are." I said, and then immediately regretted it as I watched Bret's face turn red in embarrassment. I had just admitted to thinking that he was as great as my ex-boyfriend, as Justin and Aaron, who I practically placed on a pedestal on a regular basis. Marc poked his head in my room and pulled Bret back to reality.

"You going to help me with the project or what?" Marc teased. Bret rolled his eyes, threw me a wink and was gone before I could say anything else. Once my room was empty, I buried my face in my hands.

"I'm such an idiot." I mumbled.

Chapter 31

It was Homecoming weekend and things were absolutely crazy at school because of it. As if that weren't stressful enough, Chris was dead set on getting back at me for not being interested in him. First of all, I'd been told by a few people that he was saying I only started dating Joey so I could win the Homecoming vote. When people weren't offended by this, he proceeded to tell everyone that I slept with the entire cross country team and the freshman football team to boot. He apparently didn't know that I've lived here all my life and that I grew up with the majority of the people in this school, very few people were believing his lies.

"Rumor has it, all the candidates are pissed at you." Justin advised with a shake of his head. "Chris has been saying you've been spreading shit about them."

"I don't even know most of them." I defended in a tight voice. "What was he saying?"

"I don't know exactly." Justin shrugged apologetically. "Lena Torres caught me earlier to warn me away from you, because you were a witch. She also said it was pretty ballsy of you to tell everyone that she was a lesbian."

"Like I care if she likes girls, Kristy…"

"I didn't tell her that, but I told her there was no way you would bad mouth someone, especially someone you barely knew."

"Did she believe you?"

"Possibly. I'm pretty convincing, you know?" He said as he winked at me. He bent down in his locker and grabbed his books out. "I'll walk with you to class. Lena did tell me that Chris pulled her off to the side yesterday and thought she should know what you were saying. I tried explaining to her that he's just trying to get back at you for not being interested, I think she understood that, because then she told me Chris had basically told any and every girl who would talk to him something similar. He laid it on super thick with the candidates though." We headed in the direction of our next class and I could feel the dirty looks people were throwing my way.

"Lovely. That explains a lot. It doesn't matter what I say either, they'll probably believe him."

"Probably, because that's just what girls do." Justin chuckled. We were in front of the classroom door when he gestured for me to go in first, as soon as I walked in the room most of the conversation stopped. I stopped dead in my tracks and looked back at Justin for help.

"Ignore them." He whispered in my ear. "They don't know you the way I do and if they believe his lies, they don't deserve to know you." I closed my eyes and took a deep breath, Justin slid his hand into my mine and tugged me behind him.

"Bitch." Someone whispered loudly.

"Whore." Another female voice cackled.

"Says the girl who has slept with more guys in the last few months than a prostitute does in a week." Justin threw over his shoulder. The girl's jaw dropped to the floor and she turned forward angrily.

"Apparently Brittany has slept with the entire freshman football team." Someone interjected.

"And if you believe Chris Kaplan's lies, you're an idiot. He doesn't know the difference between reality and the shit he makes up in his head. Brittany wouldn't sleep with him and he thinks that is grounds for ruining her life."

"She's the one running her mouth."

"No, I'm not." I mumbled, sitting down in a desk and looking out the window.

"I've known her all my life, she doesn't run her mouth about anyone or anything." Justin growled. "And you, Tori, should know that because you've known her all your life too." Tori rolled her eyes, shot me a dirty look and turned around. Tori had always had a thing for Aaron growing up but he was not interested in her at all, mostly because Ashley didn't like her. I somehow got blamed for that though and Tori hasn't been very nice to me for a long time.

Despite Justin defending me, the rest of the day played out with snide comments being muttered as I walked by. I had been shoved, tripped or had my books knocked out of my hand in between each class and even in some of my classes when the teacher's back was turned. How could all these people, who didn't know me, form such a hateful opinion from the words of one person?

I walked into the last class of the day, study hall. My arm was throbbing from being jostled so much and I just wanted to lay my head down on a desk and forget about the horrific day. I stepped foot into the cafeteria just as Hillary Cleep stood up and got up in my face, she was another freshman homecoming candidate.

"Hey bitch, you should watch who you run your mouth about." She snarled as she reached out, grabbed my books out of my hand and threw them in the floor.

"I don't even know you." I responded in a flat voice.

"Exactly, so you shouldn't be spreading lies about me." She hissed as she shoved me, making sure to hit where my cast was.

"Maybe you should take your own advice." Bret spit as he came up behind her. "Maybe instead of attacking someone you should see if the lies others are spreading about her are even true. I know for a fact, they're not."

"Only because you're screwing her."

"I assure you I am not." He chuckled. "She is better than that. Don't act so innocent either, I'm positive just last Saturday you offered yourself to me and I told you no." She harrumphed, spun around and stormed back to her seat.

"Are you okay?" Bret asked sadly as he bent down and began helping me pick up my books. I nodded my head, trying to hide the tears falling down my cheeks. "Aw Brit, don't let them get to you."

194

"Easier said than done, I've been getting this all day. Not to mention, my arm is killing me." Chris walked into the cafeteria just as we stood up. He took one look at my tears and started roaring with laughter. Justin came out of nowhere and shoved him into a wall.

"You better back off her now." He growled. "I will end you, if you don't stop tormenting her."

"She needs to learn not to toy with people's emotions." Chris hissed back. "She deserves everything she's getting, and more."

"Spreading lies about her, telling people she's spreading rumors about them? She does not deserve any of this. She told you from the beginning that she wasn't interested."

"They are only lies if no one believes them." He chuckled. "Fortunately, the girls in this school let their insecurities make them believe anything." The rest of the room started buzzing with conversation at Chris's admission.

"Justin, Coach is coming." Bret warned quickly as the assistant football coach was headed down the hallway. Justin pulled back and Chris laughed again.

"Another time, another place Kaplan and I won't hold back."

"Don't hold back Harper, I would love to see your ass end up in prison." Chris remarked with a weird smile. Justin lunged as Bret grabbed his shirt and pulled him back.

"He's goading you. Let it go before you get expelled." Bret advised calmly, just as Coach Cal walked into the room.

"Get in your seats kids." He said lightly as he barely paid attention and walked directly to the table at the front of the room.

"You okay?" Bret asked again as he walked beside me to our table. I nodded and held my head high, doing anything else would make Chris think he had won. I couldn't allow that.

Chapter 32

"I really just wish this day were over." I grumbled as Alex and I waited for everyone else to leave the cafeteria.

"I know." She murmured softly. "It almost is."

"No, it isn't. We have the parade now, the game tonight and then the dance tomorrow so I can't even get a break from this crap."

"Maybe after what Chris said people will back off."

"I doubt it." I sighed. "Especially since Justin and Bret both insulted two girls, in front of everyone, to defend me."

"If it's just two girls though, it's a lot better than ninety percent of the female population." I nodded my head as I stood up.

"I didn't bring my pain pills and my arm is killing me."

"I have Tylenol in my bag, do you want some of that?" Alex asked sympathetically. I nodded again and the two of us followed the last few people out of the cafeteria. Bret, Justin and Marc were waiting at the doors for us. They looked like bodyguards

197

waiting for someone to make a move or say something to me.

"You going to change out for the parade?" Justin asked. I nodded my head.

"Yeah, with Alex's help. I don't know that I can get my dress on by myself."

"I'll be more than happy to assist you." Justin flirted. I giggled and smiled back at him.

"No thanks." I leaned in to him and put my head on his shoulder. "Thank you for defending me today. Just be careful with Chris, I don't want you to get in trouble because of me."

"I don't care if I get in trouble baby girl, I'm not going to sit back and let people hurt you." I nodded my head, reached up and kissed him on the cheek.

"I love you Justin." I sighed.

"I love you Britty." He grinned. "Go get dressed so you can piss the girls off even more. You know they're all just jealous because you're so much hotter than they are."

"Thank Justin." I laughed as I rolled my eyes. I was lucky to have him in my life, he always knew how to make me feel better.

"Do you want us to wait for you?" Bret questioned as he looked around worriedly.

"No thanks. We'll be fine. You guys need to meet up with the rest of the football team, don't you?"

"I'm riding in the car with you, remember?" Bret asked with a smile.

"I forgot. We'll be fine, we'll just meet you out there in about twenty minutes."

"Are you sure?"

"I don't need to be babysat." I sighed. "I'm positive, I'll be fine." Bret nodded his head and the three boys headed off in the opposite direction. Alex led me to the Spanish classroom where my dress was hanging in Mrs. Garcia's closet so it didn't get wrinkled.

"I pulled everything out for you sweetie." Mrs. Garcia smiled as she gathered her things and left the classroom, pulling the door shut and locking it behind her. We moved to the back of the room and Alex helped me to slide my clothes off and pull the strapless, light blue sundress on. She brushed through my long hair and then pulled the curling iron through it, making ringlets all over my head. I pulled on a pair of strappy low heels and I was ready to go.

"Thanks Alex. You did amazing with my hair."

"You look amazing." She grinned. "Thank goodness the weather held out for that dress, it's perfect."

"I agree. I'm in love with it." I smiled as I twirled in the mirror. The two of us cleaned up our mess and left the room. The convertible was parked behind the school so we headed in that direction.

"Shit." I heard Alex mumble as she grabbed my hand and tried to tug me into a bathroom just as I saw Chris turn the corner.

"Well, well, well, don't *you* look beautiful?" Chris said icily, looking me up and down. "Can't I get a kiss from my girlfriend before she goes out to meet her adoring fans?"

"Get away from me. I'm *not* your girlfriend and I don't even want to be in the same time zone as you." I stated angrily, trying to push by him.

"What did I do *now* my little drama queen?" He asked drily.

"I know you've been spreading rumors about me."

"Truth hurts?" He replied innocently.

"Everything you said is so far from the truth…maybe in your little world they happened, but in reality you're WRONG." I said angrily, glaring back at him.

"In *my* little world, you would've been knocked off your high horse a long time ago." He stated hatefully. "You've gotten brave, haven't you?"

"I'm not scared of you Chris; I know you need mental help."

"*I DO NOT NEED MENTAL HELP*!!" He screamed, throwing me up against the lockers. Alex darted away, but he tripped her as she was going. When she landed with a thud on the cement, he then kicked her in the stomach.

"See what you've done, Brittany. You run your mouth and someone gets hurt. Your boy toys aren't around to help you now, are they?" Chris's hands were wrapped tightly against my throat, tears streamed down my face but I could see Alex slowly trying to crawl away. I tried to scream, to keep his attention away from her, but his grip was so tight that no noise would come out.

"You know, you're pretty sexy when you're so

helpless." He whispered into my ear with a laugh. I felt his hand run up and down my thigh, and then his fingers went up under my skirt, making their way slowly to my panties. Out of the corner of my eye, I realized Alex had made it up the steps; she had picked up a wet floor sign and hurled it at Chris, distracting him from me. When he realized what was going on he threw me down to the ground and sprinted after Alex. She had rounded the corner and I could hear her yelling for help. Chris turned around and glared at me icily, knowing that if he didn't leave he would be in a lot of trouble.

"This isn't over." He said before darting out the double doors. By the time the teachers ran outside, he was long gone.

Chapter 33

"Brittany, are you okay?" Bret asked breathlessly as he rushed up beside me. "I was coming in to check on you guys and saw Chris attack you. I couldn't get to you. I couldn't get in the door." Frustration pulsed through him and I just nodded numbly. I was shaking, tears rolled down my cheeks again as I thought about what could have happened if Alex hadn't been with me. Bret took a step towards me, but Alex grabbed me into a hug.

"What happened?" Coach Cal asked as he hurried up to us. "What was all the commotion about?"

"Chris Kaplan attacked us." Alex explained quickly. "Brittany and I were going out to the parking lot, he grabbed her and threw her up against the locker and…he threw me down to the ground and started kicking me. I was yelling for help and trying to get him away from Brittany because he had his hands wrapped around her throat." Coach looked me up and down for marks, I'm guessing.

"I was outside, coming back in to check on the girls because it was taking them too long. I saw Chris attacking from the window, I couldn't get inside until now." Bret said.

"I saw Chris Kaplan sprint out the front doors." Mrs. Garcia said as she came up behind us. "He knocked down Mr. Sprague on his way out, didn't even stop to check on him."

"Follow me." Coach Cal said, gesturing us to move behind him as he lead us to the office. Dr Yarden, our superintendent, was standing outside her office door talking to Mr. Leighton, the Principal.

"Wait right here." Coach Cal advised as he asked to talk to the two school administrators in private. Two minutes later, Alex and I were called into her office.

Dr. Yarden sat behind her large mahogany desk with a sour look on her face. She rarely smiled and today was no different. She questioned us rudely, but she wasn't listening to what we had to say. She rolled her eyes when I confessed about my run ins with Chris in the past and shook her head with a deep sigh.

"Ma'am?" The secretary said hesitantly through the intercom. "Bret McHalley would like to come in to speak with you about what he saw. He also says he knows, and has witnessed, the situation in the past."

"Absolutely not, Miss Jones." She hissed into the

phone. "It's all just hearsay and I don't need him to rush in here trying to make himself look like a hero by bashing someone else."

"Okay." Miss Jones said hesitantly before she hung up. Dr. Yarden closed her eyes, took a deep breath and exhaled. When she opened her eyes she was glaring at Alex and me.

"Miss Hoffman, I realize high school is a very tough time, it's a learning experience for everyone." She began in a fake, sweet voice as she stood up and motioned for us to do the same. "When you break up with someone, there's always a chance they'll be upset and spread rumors. It's not very lady like for you to accuse Mr. Kaplan of such wild lies. He and his family are *very* well respected members of this school and community. I will not sit back and allow you to ruin their good name, because you're jealous that he's moved on. The next time you make such accusations about a member of this student body, you had better have hard evidence or I will suspend you for gossiping. Do you understand me?"

"Yes ma'am." I said softly.

"What?" Alex gasped. "You can't be serious?"

"Unless you want to be suspended right now, I suggest you close your mouth and leave my office right this instant." She hissed. I grabbed Alex's hand and tugged her away.

"What a bitch." Alex grumbled once we were completely out of the office and down the hallway.

"No one believes me." I mumbled, tears rolling down my cheeks again. That did not go at all how I hoped it would. How could all this be used against me? It was clear Chris was harassing me and instead, Dr. Yarden made me out to look like the psycho.

More than anything, I was a little bitter towards Bret. He had told me to tell the truth, that people would believe me, if I did it then Chris couldn't hurt me anymore. Boy was he wrong. Now I looked like a stupid, immature school girl trying to get back at an ex-boyfriend.

It didn't matter that I was extremely shaken up by everything, I was still expected to ride in the parade. I had asked Coach Cal, Mrs. Garcia and Coach Lieberman if I still had to participate. I just wanted to go home and forget about this day, this life. They all thought I was being too dramatic.

Bret and his dad had been rebuilding a 1967 Ford Mustang Convertible for Bret to drive when he turned sixteen. When he learned I was one of the attendants he offered it to me, to ride in during the Parade and before the game. I graciously accepted, I was flattered he would allow me to use something so sacred to him. It was beautiful and the site of the fresh black paint and beautiful body, made me feel a little better.

Coach Axson assured us that Chris Kaplan was not allowed at the football game until he was questioned and cleared. Fortunately, a student teacher had seen him run out the double doors and had contacted the school security guard. Despite Dr. Yarden's orders, he contacted the city police, who took statements from us.

Mr. McHalley was in the passenger seat, Bret was driving. Blake, Alex and I were in the backseat, with me sitting up on the back of the convertible. We were in the middle of the parade, tucked in between the cars with the other candidates riding in them.

"We got the Mustang done in the nick of time." Mr. McHalley grinned, looking at the car admiringly.

"It's absolutely gorgeous." I breathed as I ran my hand across the dark leather seats. "I can't believe you guys did this yourself."

"We had help, but we did a lot of it together." Mr.

McHalley said proudly. "I'm afraid when Bret gets his license I won't hardly get to see the car again."

"I'll still take you for rides pop." Bret teased.

"Careful son." He chuckled. "Don't say anything that'll make me embarrass you in front of the girls."

"I'm all for hearing about embarrassing things sir." I lit. "I could definitely use some ammo against him and Marc."

"We'll have to talk." He said with a wink.

"I'll make sure that doesn't happen." Bret laughed as the procession started moving. "Get that smile ready Brit, you're fans are waiting."

"Fans? I'll be lucky if they don't throw crap at me."

"They won't throw anything at me, so you'll be okay." Bret teased.

"Yeah, I'll protect you Brittany." Blake grinned back at me. "I'm like an impenetrable wall." I laughed and shook my head. Between Mr. McHalley, the boys and Alex, I was grinning from ear to ear and had forgotten about Chris and his craziness.

However, I still didn't want to attend the football game tonight. And especially didn't want to attend the dance tomorrow. I was terrified Chris was going to show up to either one of the events with a gun and mow everyone down like you see on the news. I didn't want to be the reason for so many innocent people dying. I didn't want to die either.

"Don't be scared of this kid, Brittany." Mr. McHalley said as he put an arm around my shoulders. "I've seen a lot in the Marines, seen many men with the same psychological issues that this young man seems to have. The fact that you reported him is a step in the right direction. If you change your life, go into hiding because of your fear, then you're just fueling him."

"Yes sir." I said with a nod. "I know that in my heart, but it's hard to tell my head to listen."

"I imagine it is. Bret will take care of you though, you just have to let him."

"I don't want him to get hurt." I sighed.

"He's more worried about you than he is himself. Nothing you or I say will change that."

"I'm learning that." I smiled.

"Tom and I will keep an eye on you tonight. Tomorrow, Marc and Bret will." I nodded my head. "You need a ride home now?" I nodded again. "Your chariot awaits."

Chapter 34

"Freshman attendant, despite all of Chris's hard work." Lindsay lit as we climbed back into the stands after half time. "Won't he be pissed?"

"I hope not." I mumbled, grabbing the flannel blanket from my mother as we sat behind her, The McHalley's and Mrs. Harper. I received hugs from all the women and then the Stitlin High football team took the field again.

"Bret and Justin look as though they've played football together their entire lives." Alex said.

"They are pretty amazing out there." I agreed proudly. "Their names are all you hear over the radio." The Stitlin team was pretty solid, every player contributed in some way. Joey had a touchdown, Bret threw three perfect passes to help score touchdowns and Justin ran for some unbelievable amount of yards. We won the game, of course, because our boys were unstoppable.

We made our way down from the bleachers just in time for the team to be walking towards the locker room. Justin instinctively grabbed me in a huge hug.

"Congratulations on attendant." He said as he picked me up and spun me around.

"Congratulations on an amazing game." I giggled as I hugged him tightly. "You guys were phenomenal." Bret, Marc and Drake came up behind us, all three giving me quick hugs and congratulations.

"Oh my God Bret, you were awesome! I'm always so in awe to watch you move out there." I exclaimed giving him a big hug.

"Thanks." He replied, blushing.

"What did you think of that baby?" Joey interrupted, pulling me away from Bret and picking me up and spinning me around.

"Pretty great game." I smiled.

"I am so pumped right now." He said, excitedly hugging and kissing me again before he ran with the rest of his teammates to the locker room. He stopped halfway there and ran back to where we were standing.

"I forgot to say congratulations." He stated with a smiled before he kissed me sweetly.

"Thank you." I answered dreamily.

"Now, you girls don't go too far. I want to make sure my girl still looks this good when I come out and that she hasn't found someone else by then." He teased, before he headed back to the locker room with his teammates.

"He is SO sweet." Haley teased.

"He is SO freaking hot." Alex said. "I hate you."

"Shut up." I laughed as we walked out to the parking lot with a group of people. I hadn't seen Chris since the incident that afternoon, but I was positive he wouldn't cause any problems when I was in a crowd.

"He's not coming around tonight Brittany." My escort, Blake assured me. "My dad is the Chief of Police for the city, and on the school board, he said they were all over Chris's house today. They put the fear of God in him; his father took it very seriously."

"I know I shouldn't worry, but I can't help it." I admitted, shrugging my shoulders as Blake jumped off the truck and made his best Superman pose.

"No one is getting through the man of steel!"

"You are such a dork!" I laughed.

"But you laughed and that's what I was going for." He smiled. I nodded my head and gave him a half hug. Chris may be putting me through Hell and that definitely sucked, but he was also showing me how many amazing people I had in my life.

Chapter 35

Fifteen minutes later, Joey and most of the team made their way out to the parking lot. They were all screaming and yelling, obviously pumped up from their victory. Joey picked me up, threw me over his shoulder and carried me to the car.

"Joey put me down!" I laughed. He sat me down next to his car, leaned me against the door and kissed me passionately.

"Whoa." I murmured as I looked up to see he was grinning down at me. I smacked at him playfully. "Next time you decide to go caveman, check and see if I'm wearing a dress, you just made me moon everyone!" I laughed hiding my face in his chest.

"Look, they enjoyed it." He teased as he pointed at the group that was whooping and hollering at us. He winked as he pulled away from me and let me in the car. He crossed over to the driver's side and within minutes we were out of the parking lot and headed towards town.

"Oh, I almost forgot." Joey said, digging behind the front seat as we cruised down the road. He presented me with a bouquet of beautiful red roses and smiled back at me proudly.

"Congratulations on getting attendant."

"What if I would've lost?" I asked with a laugh.

"I would've given them to you anyway, just for being you." He answered sweetly. I leaned over and kissed him on the cheek.

"Thank you." I sighed as I rested my head on his shoulder as we drove. Joey's phone beeped and I went to grab it to hand it to him but he snatched it up quickly. He looked at the screen, then showed it to me.

"Trevor says there's a house party at Jonas's house to celebrate our victory. Does that sound good to you?"

"Of course." I smiled. Joey kissed the top of my head and turned towards Jonas's house. He knew how nervous I was about Chris showing up so he didn't leave my side all night long. If I went to the bathroom, he waited outside the door for me. I had a few beers, but stuck with water for the most part. As the night went on, Joey became pretty intoxicated. He was staying the night with Jonas, something he'd failed to tell me before, so he didn't have a cap on his alcohol intake.

"Why don't you call and tell your parents you're

staying at Alex's tonight?" Joey asked seductively, pulling me into an empty bedroom.

"Have you met Marc's dad? He would send the National Guard out to bust me if I did that. I wouldn't get away with it." I answered quickly.

"Can't you just try? I want you to stay the night with me." He begged, kissing me passionately.

"Joey, I can't. I'm meeting my dad for lunch tomorrow, besides Drake would NEVER let me stay."

"Alex will cover for you."

"Are you kidding me? Alex is the worst liar in the world, especially when she's trying to lie to Drake." I laughed.

"Don't you *want* to stay the night with me?" He pouted.

"I'm not ready to…" I began.

"We don't have to do *that*, I just want to hold you all night long, that's all." He answered innocently. I wasn't an idiot though.

"Aww." I began, as I kissed him quickly. "There will be other times, Joey. Just not tonight, okay?"

"Tomorrow night?" He asked hopefully.

"No." I laughed. "My mom and Captain Jerk are making it mandatory for us to all attend church Sunday. They think it'll make us a stronger family or some crap. You know I *will* be babysitting Callie and Cayden sometime soon."

I was coming up with every excuse I could think of because I really just didn't want to be put in that position. I wasn't ready to go to the next level with Joey and I didn't want to make him think I was. I had lost my virginity to Aaron before he died and he was the only person I had ever been with. More than anything, it was hard for me to think of doing that with anyone else, just because of the emotional ties it held to Aaron's memory. The truth was that my mom and Tom had left immediately after the game for some Marine thing in Virginia, but I didn't want anyone else to know that.

"I know. Tonight's been so great already I just wanted the whole weekend to be awesome."

"Let's go back downstairs before Alex and Haley send out a search party." I said, pulling him out of the bedroom. Chris was walking up the stairs just as we were coming out of the bedroom.

"You slut!" He exclaimed, lunging in my direction.

Joey stepped in front of me and grabbed Chris by the shirt.

"Apologize to her, right now." He threatened.

"Get your hands off me Hawkins, this doesn't concern you."

"I think it does." He drawled, pushing him against a door.

"Am I not good enough for you Brittany? You can sleep with everyone else but me? You can cheat on me without any guilt?"

"She's not cheating on you, Chris. Brittany is *my* girlfriend; the two of you went on one date and she has ended it, repeatedly. Why can't you get that through your head?"

"We did *not* break up. She's lying to you. Everything that comes out of her mouth is a lie. She's a fucking whore!"

Joey slammed Chris against the door harder this time and tightened the grip on his shirt. Joey's teeth were clenched as he stared angrily at Chris.

"You *will* apologize to her now, Kaplan."

"I'm not scared of you Hawkins; you're just a rich pretty boy who acts like a bad ass. I know you're a big pussy. I don't think you have the balls to hit me." Chris taunted.

"Joey, he's not worth it. Let's just go."

"NO!" Joey yelled. "He's done tormenting you. He's going to apologize, then he's going to walk away and leave you alone for good."

Chris began laughing. He slowly grabbed Joey's hands and pulled them off of him. Chris was like a monster as he picked up Joey and threw him against the wall. Fear gripped my entire body as I watched the tables turn. I was frozen in fear, unsure if I should run downstairs or lock myself in the nearest bedroom.

"Brittany, go downstairs, go find Drake and don't leave his side." Joey instructed without taking his eyes off Chris.

"What's the matter Joey, you scared? Don't think you can handle me on your own?"

"I just don't want Brittany to see me beat the Hell out of your crazy ass." Joey answered icily as he stood up and went for Chris again.

"I AM NOT CRAZY!" Chris screamed, attacking Joey the second that he stood up. In one fluid movement, he threw him against the wall and then down to the floor as if he were a rag doll. I lunged past the two boys and went for the stairs screaming for help, but Chris grabbed me by my broken arm and flung me against the wall, slamming my head against it. I fell down a few steps and lay against the banister, trying to get my bearings. The music was so loud; no one could hear what was happening. I felt as if I were in a bad dream, screaming but no noise would come out. Joey started to get up as Chris punched him in the stomach. I tried to stand up but I was woozy from the pain in my arm and head. Chris grabbed me before I could take a step and pulled me back up. My arms were pinned behind my back and I screamed and writhed as excruciating pain shot up and down my broken arm.

Chris pulled me into an empty bedroom and tossed me onto the bed. I screamed and kicked, but nothing I did seemed to faze him. His eyes were empty, but focused on me. It was almost as if someone else had taken over his body.

"BRITTANY!!" I heard Joey yell as he pounded on the locked door. I was defenseless against Chris Kaplan, fear and pain took over my body and paralyzed me. Chris pinned me down on the bed and began groping.

"You just had to play hard to get, didn't you Brittany?"

He breathed, kissing my neck. "You give it up so easily to everyone else, but for me, I have to work for it?"

"You didn't have to make it so hard, you know? You've known what I wanted all along, but you had to pretend to be daddy's little angel, didn't you?" Chris repeated, as he kissed me harder and ripped my panties off. Out of nowhere, rage took over. I was not about to let Chris ruin something so sacred to me.

I raised my knee up quickly and nailed him between the legs. He cried out in pain, his body loosened, giving me another opportunity. I kneed him in the stomach and pushed him off me with superhuman strength. I leapt towards the door and got it unlocked.

Chris grabbed my leg and pulled me down to the ground before I could get the door opened. I felt his greasy hands on me, as adrenaline and rage overtook me again and I kicked at his face and chest, trying to loosen his grip. Finally, the bedroom door flew open and Joey lunged at Chris.

Two seniors pulled Joey and Justin off Chris, who lay on the floor bleeding profusely. They had to remove Justin from the room, because he kept going after Chris. I sat curled up in the corner, quietly watching everything that was taking place. Everything around me sounded like a roaring train, people were talking but I couldn't understand what they were saying. Chris was lying in the floor still, motionless. Suddenly his eyes popped open, his head turned towards me and he smiled devilishly.

"It's not over." He mouthed, before closing his eyes again. Tears streamed down my face, I still sat against the wall, sobbing. Alex sat next to me, rubbing my back as she tried to get me to talk to her. I stood up quickly, I needed to get the Hell out of this house.

Someone grabbed my arms; I screamed and fought to get away. I would not let Chris come after me again. He was talking to me, but I couldn't tell you what he was saying. I was screaming hysterically at this point, fighting to get away.

"Brittany." He said calmly, moving so he was in my face and looking into my eyes. "It's me. It's Bret. It's okay. I'm going to take you out of here, okay?"

I nodded my head slowly, barely able to focus on anything but his deep blue eyes. I took a deep breath, tried to take a step, but I couldn't.

"I'll help you." Bret said smoothly as he put his arm

around my waist. He started to pick me up, to carry me out, but he shook his head. "I don't want to make a big scene, if I'm carrying you out then people will start talking. There's a back way out, we'll take that okay?" I nodded my head and leaned into him.

Drake and Marc were waiting at my mom's SUV, they had the door open and Bret ushered me inside quickly. He had barely gotten the door closed before Drake was tearing out of the driveway. I didn't know where we were going, I just knew that I wanted to go to sleep and wake up from this nightmare, without any memories, as soon as possible.

Bret was holding me in his arms like I was a baby, holding me tightly as I sobbed quietly. I could hear Drake yelling into the phone, but I couldn't make sense of it, he seemed so far away from me.

Before I knew it, we were pulling into the hospital where my father worked. I didn't want to go in, but I didn't have any fight left in me. I was exhausted and kept drifting to sleep every few minutes.

"I think she's in shock." Drake admitted in a panicked voice as everything went dark.

Chapter 36

I woke up in a strange bedroom and panic set in. I closed my eyes tightly, took a deep breath and reopened my eyes. I looked around the room. I'd never stayed the night here before but I recognized a few of my father's things.

Why was I at my father's house? I looked down to see a brand new cast covering my arm. As I moved to get out of the bed, my entire body hurt and my head felt as though it weighed a thousand pounds. I moaned but forced myself up and out of the bed, slowly making my way to the bedroom door.

"How ya doin' princess?" My dad asked as he stood on the other side of the door.

"My whole body hurts."

"I'm sure it does." He said softly. "Are you all right?"

"You're the doctor, you tell me." I teased, forcing a laugh. "What happened?"

"I was hoping you could tell *me* that." He said, his voice full of concern. The scenes from last night flashed through my head, I closed my eyes and shook my head no. I couldn't describe the terror I had felt last night, especially not to my father.

"I don't remember." I lied.

"Well, the boys are asleep in the living room. I'll let them know you're awake. Unfortunately, I have to get back to the hospital."

"Thanks daddy." I mumbled, slowly reaching up to kiss him on the cheek. He flinched, but allowed me to do so.

"Take it slow, sweetie. Y'all can stay as long as you need to. I called and told your mom you were staying with me tonight."

My eyes grew wide. He was rarely a father figure to my siblings and me; it was weird that he chose this moment to be one. In all honesty, this was the most I had seen my father since he and my mother had announced their divorce.

"Your mother doesn't know anything." He stated. "I told her you tripped down the stairs at the house and re broke your arm."

"Why?" I asked.

"I made a promise to your brother and that's all I'll say." He replied as he gave me a quick hug and started away. "Take

226

it easy today, okay?" He said over his shoulder as he walked into his bedroom to take a quick shower.

Drake and the others were already awake and milling around when I walked into the living room.

"There she is." Drake announced, smiling at me worriedly. "How ya feelin'?"

I shrugged my shoulders and walked into the kitchen to grab a bottle of water. I could smell pancakes and eggs, but I didn't see any left.

"We saved you some food. You hungry?" Lindsay asked, putting her arm around me. I was, but the smell of food was making me nauseous. I shrugged my shoulders and stared at the ground awkwardly. Everyone was now in the kitchen, all staring at me as if I would fall apart at any second.

"I'll eat later," I began.

"You should really eat something." Drake interjected.

"I'm not hungry right now." I said testily.

"You should at least try."

"No, I'm not hungry. I hurt too badly."

"Brittany." Drake began.

"Dad grabbed these for you before we left last night, why don't you take one now, but you have to eat something with it, okay?" Lindsay interrupted, handing me a bottle of painkillers. I agreed, took the pills and then ate half the pancake on the plate before I stood up from the table and made my way into the living room. I fell onto the couch and was asleep within minutes.

I woke up around three o clock that afternoon because of the doorbell. I sat straight up and looked around, my heartbeat quickened thinking Chris had found me. The room was empty and I prayed I would wake up from my bad dream sometime soon.

"It's all right, we just ordered pizza." Bret said, as he came up behind me and put a hand gently on my back. "You want some?"

I shook my head no and tried to calm my breathing. I took a deep breath and stood up from the couch before I made my way to the bathroom. I was groggy and really out of sorts, but I thought the warmth of the shower would make me feel a little better. It eased my sore muscles but I really just wanted to go back to sleep.

"Hey sweetie, you ready to go back home?" Lindsay asked when I came out of the shower fully dressed in sweats.

"Why?"

"To get ready for the dance. Everything we need is at the house and it's where everyone is meeting us at."

"I'm NOT going to the dance." I said, shaking my head. "There's no way in Hell I'm going anywhere in public until Chris Kaplan is dead."

"Brittany, you have to go."

"No I don't."

"Yes, you do." Drake stated. "You are the freshman attendant, you *have* to be there. They'll do another ceremony and take more pictures tonight. You will look like an ungrateful snob if you don't show up."

"I don't care how it looks, I'm not going. Joey and I were attacked last night by a psycho asshole! He'll probably come back tonight!"

"Kaplan won't bother you tonight." Bret replied quietly.

"How do you know?" I questioned angrily.

"He's in the hospital. Dad made sure he wouldn't be released for a few days." Drake explained quickly.

"Joey probably doesn't want to come anywhere near me."

"He'll be at the house at seven, Brittany. I talked to him this morning. And you're wrong about him sis, he would've been over here before you even woke up but his parents wouldn't let him leave."

"You don't have to lie, Drake. Joey Hawkins is an idiot if he still wants to be with me. This is the second time he's been hurt because of me."

"Well I guess he's an idiot then, Britty. When I called to check on him and see if he was still going tonight, he acted like I was stupid for even questioning it." Drake replied irritably.

"Look at me....I'm broken and bruised. There's no way."

"Haley and Alex will be at the house after a while. We're going to help you get ready. We'll do your hair and makeup; you don't have to worry about anything." Lindsay said as she hugged me. "Now let's eat something and then head to the house."

"Don't worry about Chris anymore, okay?" Marc said

walking into my bedroom an hour later.

"Huh?" I asked as I snapped out of the trance I had
been in.

"Chris won't be coming around anymore. I overheard
his parents talking about sending him away to a hospital. They think
he's been purposely hurting himself to get attention lately. Of course,
they don't know what he's done to you, either. He lied and told them
he was jumped last night by some football players from Chauncey,
the same ones that attacked Joey."

"What are you talking about?"

"Joey and Chris would've gotten into a lot of trouble,
had we told the truth. We didn't want to risk Kaplan filing charges
against Justin or Joey for what they did to him last night. He told
your dad he would remain quiet, if they did."

"So, no one knows what Chris did to me, to us?" I
asked in shock. Marc shook his head no and looked at me
apologetically.

"Sorry, but we had to protect Joey and Justin and
ended up protecting Chris too, unfortunately." He answered.

"Marc, promise me you won't leave me alone until

Chris is for sure gone."

"Bret and I don't plan on leaving your side for a long time, sweetie." He answered with a smile as he stood up.

"Who is ready to be a princess?" Haley asked, exploding into my room.

"I think you're already one." I commented, noticing that her hair and makeup looked perfect as she dropped her dress and overnight bag down on a chair.

"That's my cue to leave." Marc laughed as he hurried out.

Chapter 37

Alex, Haley and Lindsay pampered and spoiled me as they made me up for the dance. They did everything they could to help me forget about last night and to keep my mind off Chris. They were doing a great job of it, too.

Around seven o'clock Joey hadn't shown up yet, but everyone else's dates and parents were there. I was obviously nervous, because my boyfriend was nowhere around and we were all taking couple's pictures.

"Brittany?" Mrs. McHalley called, awaking me from my self-pity. "Why don't you and Bret get together for a picture? The two of you are just so cute together."

"Mom, do you wake up every morning thinking of ways to embarrass me?" Bret teased, obviously mortified by her comment. She laughed and nodded. She was right though, we did look cute together and it felt extremely natural to pose in pictures with him.

"What's this?" I asked pointing at the limo pulling into the driveway a few minutes later.

"We changed our plans so we could all go to the dance together." Drake answered with a smile. "We've still got a few stops to make, so let's hit the road."

"What about Joey?"

"Change of plans...we're meeting him somewhere." Lindsay answered. Haley and Drake were going together, Alex and Justin, Lindsay and Trevor were coupled which just left Marc and Bret's dates. We went to Makenzie's house to pick her and her friend Ashley Johnson up.

"You're not going with Joey, Brittany?" Ashley asked in shock.

"We're meeting him." Marc answered quickly.

"Too bad you still have your cast on and those horrendous stitches." Makenzie commented, rudely pointing at the five stitches in my forehead. I nodded and looked out the window. The two girls made a few more rude comments, I tried to be polite and bite my tongue, but it was so hard to do.

"You know, I had a horrible night and I really don't even want to be here right now, so if you two aren't going to be nice, just don't talk to me." I stated icily.

234

"Yeah, so horrible, you were voted freshman attendant. I bet it was the worst thing that could've happened to you." Makenzie replied sarcastically as her and Ashley laughed and rolled their eyes.

"Makenzie, I only agreed to be your date tonight because Marc wanted to go with Ashley, so I had to take one for the team. I don't want to be here as it is, you being incredibly rude to my friend is not helping matters at all. So please keep your snotty comments to yourself, before I leave you dateless."

Makenzie's jaw hit the ground and she looked like she was about to cry. Ashley moved awkwardly and the entire limo became silent. Luckily, we pulled up to a restaurant a few minutes later and everyone started to get out.

"Thanks." I murmured to Bret as we walked into the restaurant, he just rolled his nonchalantly.

"No big deal. I really didn't want to go with her, she's just making things worse." He advised me. I made a sad face and gave him a half hug.

"I really wish you could've went with the girl you wanted to go with." I mumbled. "I'm sure she won't have as much fun being someone else's date." Bret chuckled.

"I wish that too. I hope you're right though, I worry that she'll fall for this guy and I'll never get a chance."

"I'm pretty certain if she knew your feelings, there wouldn't be another guy." I smiled as I reached down and squeezed his hand. He looked back at me thoughtfully, before he nodded and shrugged.

"Sometimes I think you might be right and other times, I don't know." He mumbled.

"Want me to talk to her?" I asked. Bret's eyes widened. "Okay, so maybe I'm just dying to know who the lucky girl is. Do I know her?"

"Seriously?" He questioned, his face moving into a confused frown. Did I say something wrong? He let go of my hand and shook his head.

"Sorry, I..."

"How can you not know?" Bret almost seemed mad or sad, I couldn't quite tell as he watched me closely. I shrugged innocently and looked down at the ground.

"I...I..." I was an idiot, I don't know what I said to

upset him, but I should learn to keep my mouth shut, I guess. Was it wrong that part of my heart was screaming for him to say he wanted me as his date, that I was the girl he was crushing on? I knew it wasn't possible though, no matter how badly I wanted it to be true. I had enough issues to deal with though. I had a crazy, obsessive stalker and a Homecoming date who was a no show, so far.

"Brittany, it's…" Bret began, just as Alex grabbed me and tugged me away.

"Sit by me, okay? I will chew my arm off if I have to be near Ashley and Mackenzie." Alex whispered. I forced a laugh as I nodded and sat down next to an empty chair. Everyone else was pretty much coupled off and I was all alone. This sucks.

"He'll be here, don't worry." Lindsay leaned over and whispered to me. A few minutes later, a waiter came to our table.

"Miss, the chef is requesting your presence in the kitchen." The young man smiled.

"What?"

"I was just told to go get the most beautiful girl at the table." He answered with a shrug, as he made a gesture towards the kitchen. I looked back at my table and Marc nodded to me that it was okay.

"Sir?" The waiter said into the kitchen. "Your guest has arrived."

The waiter turned and walked back through the double doors as Joey walked around the corner with a single rose for me. His face was battered and bruised and he moved slowly, but he looked amazing in his white tux.

"Uh, I'm confused."

"I wanted to make tonight extra special, so *I* did a little rearranging." He answered with a smile as he kissed me on the cheek. He took my hands and led me to a table for two that was lit with candles and had more beautiful roses placed on it. "This is my uncle's restaurant, he let me do this for you. I made dessert, it's about the only thing I can get right in the kitchen."

"You cook?"

"Not really." He laughed nonchalantly, as he pulled a chair out and gestured for me to sit. "I wanted to surprise you."

"You did…I thought you were standing me up." I answered quietly as I slowly sat in the chair.

"I would never do that." He stated sadly, leaning down

to kiss me again. He moved over to the other chair and sat down.

"Please eat and eat a lot, I'm pretty certain my uncle is watching." He teased with a wink. I giggled and dug into the plate before me. Dinner and dessert were absolutely amazing. We talked and laughed and it was as if last night had never happened. Joey's parents met us outside afterwards to take pictures and then we all piled into the limo to head to the dance.

For a few hours, I finally forgot about everything that had been going on. I focused on having fun and spending time with my friends. I couldn't stop smiling as Joey held me close while we danced. I was surrounded by my siblings, by my friends and my boyfriend and I knew they would all keep me safe tonight. I felt like a princess and I didn't think even Chris could steal that feeling away from me today.

"So, did you have a good time tonight?" Joey whispered in my ear on our way home from the dance.

"I did." I replied with a big smile. "It couldn't have been more perfect."

"Good. You deserve it." He responded, kissing my forehead as he put his arm around me and pulled me close. I snuggled up to him and closed my eyes, hoping to imprint the perfect memory into my mind. Despite the drama with Chris, things were definitely starting to look up and I actually began thinking that my heart was healing. The only problem with that though, was it meant that I was falling for Joey Hawkins. After all, Bret McHalley had it bad for someone else.

Chapter 38

I awoke the next morning feeling invincible. All the terrible things were in the past and today was the start of a brand new, beautiful day. I walked downstairs around one o clock to see that Lindsay was the only one home.

"Where is everyone?" I asked, that invincible feeling slowly slipping away.

"Some silly pick up football game at the school." Lindsay answered, rolling her eyes. "Mom called way too early this morning and said they won't be home until tomorrow afternoon."

"It's weird being in this huge house all alone, isn't it?" I asked nervously.

"Don't worry, the boys will be back soon. They left at like nine this morning…seriously way too early on a weekend."

I went back upstairs and took a long, hot shower. I was so excited about taking a shower that I forgot to grab a change of clothes from my room. I wrapped a towel around my hair and one around my body, and then darted across the hallway to my room.

"BRITTANY!!!!" I heard Marc scream as I looked for

clothes in my room. "Close the freaking door!!!"

"Sorry! I didn't think anyone was home!" I exclaimed with a giggle. "That's a little embarrassing."

I pulled on a pair of yoga pants, a tank top and went downstairs to find something to eat for lunch. Everyone was already downstairs eating delivery pizza and sandwiches.

"Thanks for the show!" Marc teased throwing a plastic cup at me as I went to the refrigerator.

"Sorry, sometimes I forget I have another brother. At least I had a towel on." I replied innocently.

"Barely." Bret blurted out, shooting me a funny look. I could feel my face grow red with embarrassment as I looked back at him, humiliated.

"You saw too?" I squeaked. "Oh my God."

"It wasn't *that* bad, I kind of enjoyed it." He teased.

"Yeah well, *I'm* probably going to have to see a psychiatrist later in life, just so you know." Marc announced, shaking his head.

"Whatever." I laughed rolling my eyes.

"Mom wants you guys to come over for dinner

tonight." Bret announced, his eyes directly on me. "And be warned, if you don't come she'll bring dinner over here to you guys."

"That's nice of her." I said with a smile.

"She's worried about you being here alone." Bret admitted. "She knows about Friday night and doesn't think you guys should be here by yourself. So don't be surprised if she asks y'all to stay the night at the house, either."

"Marc said Chris's parents took him to a mental hospital or something."

"She's still nervous." He shrugged. "She's a mom, she can't help it." I nodded my head. There is no way I would stay the night at the McHalley's house. They were extremely nice people, but it would be weird to sleep at Bret's house.

"We'll be fine." Drake shrugged. "I won't let anything happen." Bret nodded his head and watched me carefully.

"Did you guys order something for me?" I asked, looking through the pizza boxes and sandwiches.

"Turkey on wheat." Drake responded, digging through the bag and producing a wrapped sandwich for me. "Heaven forbid you eat too much pizza on the weekend."

"Thanks Drake." I giggled. "I'm not able to work out, I have to watch what I eat."

"You're perfect the way you are." Bret mumbled shaking his head. I ignored him and went into the living room with my bottled water and sandwich. The others followed and we flipped through the football games on television until we agreed on one.

The five of us goofed off for a while and then separated to start homework or watch more football. I was still sore from Chris's attack, but I felt I was, surprisingly, healing emotionally from it all. I wouldn't be feeling this good if it weren't for my siblings and Bret, though, they were amazing.

Marc had been right, Chris's parents had taken him out of Stitlin and placed him elsewhere. There were rumors that he had been placed in a mental hospital, others stated he was helping out at another school until things died down.

Jeremy Font was telling everyone that Chris had told his parents I was spreading rumors and causing all my friends to begin bullying him. His parents felt removing him from the harassment for a short period, would help him out tremendously. I was offended by the rumors about me, but I could handle it as long as Chris would be out of my life for a while.

Chapter 39

The next few months flew by and it was already December and my birthday. I was more than surprised when I came home from shopping with Lindsay one Saturday afternoon to realize that my mom and Captain Jerk had arranged a birthday party for me.

The entire Rhodes family and Ashley were in my house when I walked inside, which was the best present I could've gotten from anyone. It had been a long time since the five of us were able to hang out. It was nice.

However, it was extremely uncomfortable for me to have to introduce my old boyfriend to my new one. But I think I worked myself up over it for nothing, because the two of them were extremely cordial to one another. Mason, on the other hand, had played football with Joey and knew him well, but he was giving him the third degree. I was shooting him dirty looks but he wasn't paying attention to me.

"Mason, give it a rest." Ashley said flippantly as she grabbed my arm and tugged me out of the room.

"Not that he's not freaking hot, but I really thought

you and Bret would've hooked up by now." Ashley whispered to me as we walked through the kitchen where all the parents were.

"We're just really good friends."

"Yeah well, friends don't look at each other the way he looks at you." She smiled.

"Whatever, he treats me like his bratty little sister." I protested, rolling my eyes.

"Sure, if that's what you want to believe." She shrugged with a giggle. "Too bad we're not in the same high school, we would be getting into so much trouble together."

"No doubt." I giggled. "How is Cali?" I asked as she led me upstairs to my bedroom where we were away from everyone else.

"It has perks, but no one is as awesome as you guys. I hate bringing new people to my house, because they see pictures of Aaron and ask questions and I hate having to explain everything. Or then, people will ask if I have any siblings and I don't know how to respond without depressing the Hell out of myself and everyone else." She admitted as she grabbed a brush off my dresser and pulled it through her long, blonde hair.

"Yeah, at least here you wouldn't have to explain because everyone already knows. That would be tough." I said giving her a quick hug before we headed down to the basement where the others had congregated to play video games.

The rest of the night was fantastic, I never wanted it to end. Haley, Alex and Ashley all spent the night with me. My mother was adamant that Marc couldn't have a sleepover at the same time and actually kicked him out of the house. So, for once, Marc was staying the night at Bret's house. Of course, Bret had invited Justin and Michael to join them.

As I heard my cell phone go off later that night, I was transported back in time. It was just like the old days, whenever we had a sleepover my guy friends would always harass us by phone or in person the entire night. I half expected Aaron's sweet voice to be on the other end.

"Meet us outside in five minutes." Marc said into the receiver.

"What?" I laughed, realizing he was trying to sound like he was involved in covert operations.

"No questions. Just do it." He instructed, I could hear

the other boys laughing in the background.

"We're being summoned to meet the boys outside later." I turned around and informed my friends.

"Sweet." Ashley said excitedly. "Have I mentioned your new brother is hot? Or that our boy Justin Harper is starting to look *damn* good."

"You're unbelievable." I laughed, looking back at Alex nervously. The two girls always had a rivalry when it came to Justin. Usually, Ashley was the one who always came out ahead though. My thoughts were interrupted by my cell phone ringing again, this time it was Joey.

"What are you girls up to?" He asked.

"Just hanging out, gossiping." I answered.

"And what are you gossiping about?"

"You."

"Oh really? What about?"

"How I think I can do better than you, I'm just trying to figure out how to cut you loose." I teased.

"Ouch." He whispered with a laugh. "I guess it's a good thing I'm drinking beer then, at least I can drown my sorrows."

"Oh I see how you are. Instead of being miserable without me on a Saturday night, you go out partying."

"I'm just celebrating your birthday…uh, without you." He laughed. "Besides, you girls could sneak out and meet up with us. I would *love* to be alone with you tonight."

"I bet you would." I flirted. "You'll get your chance, but not tonight."

"Ouch." He said. "Well, I guess I'll let you girls get back to your night and I'll just go miss you in my beer."

"That sounds like a country song." I laughed.

"Yeah, maybe your friend Michael could use it." He joked. I hung up a few minutes later and my friends and I snuck outside the house to meet Michael and the others.

"What in the heck took you so long?" Michael asked exasperated.

"Brittany was talking to Lover Boy." Ashley laughed, rolling her eyes.

"You chose *him*, over us?" Michael scoffed, again sounding a little irritated. I shot him a dirty look and turned around to talk to Justin.

"Not that you kids aren't great, but I was really hoping to hang out with Drake tonight." Haley admitted, flashing a smile at me.

"I know you're just using me to get to my brother Haley, I already texted him and told him to meet us outside." I teased.

"I didn't think I was doing a good job of hiding it." She laughed as she winked at me. Drake, Mason and Lindsay joined us outside about an hour later and the ten of us hung out, extending my birthday party until late into the night.

Chapter 40

"So, you really like this Joey guy?" Michael asked, sounding a bit hurt, as he pulled me away from our friends. I shrugged my shoulders.

"I guess. Why?"

"I don't know, I guess it just hurts that you moved on already."

"Michael, I saw you making out with some chick two weeks after we broke up. What was I supposed to do?"

"That was just for publicity, our agent made me do it."

"Well, it didn't look like you hated it all that much." I said, rolling my eyes.

"I miss you Britty. It sucks not being around you guys all the time, it's like we're going two totally separate ways."

"We are." I admitted quietly. "But it doesn't mean we won't always be friends or that we won't end up in the same place in the end."

"I hope you're right." He shrugged; he put his arm around me and hugged me tightly. He tried to kiss me but I pulled away quickly as I shot him a dirty look.

"Michael, what has gotten into you?"

"I don't know, I just…"

"Don't do it again, I can't be your friend if you're constantly testing me." I warned. I loved Michael, I really did, but I was not in love with him any longer. I probably never really was.

"Whatever." Michael snapped angrily as he shrugged his shoulders and stormed off towards the others. I shook my head and hugged myself. I probably shouldn't have snapped on him. He was probably just feeling sentimental because of the situation, I know he misses Aaron as much as I do, he was probably just looking for a little familiarity to help with the pain.

"I'm beat." Justin announced a few hours later.

"Wuss." I teased with a smile. The boys started to go back to Bret's house, but Justin really couldn't leave Ashley. As much as he tried, he kept going back to flirt or try to kiss her. I could see Alex was fuming. I hated seeing the two of them still fighting over a guy.

"Hey Bret?" I asked.

"Hey Brit?" He mocked with a flirtatious smile.

"Would you do me a favor?" I asked, motioning for him to come closer to me.

"Anything for the birthday girl." He stated.

"It's not my birthday anymore."

"Then no, I won't do you a favor." He teased. I gave him my best puppy dog face, batted my eyelashes and waited for him to cave.

"Sometimes, you're evil."

"I try." I shrugged.

"What's up?"

"Well, I have a little problem. You probably don't know this, but Alex has a thing for Justin and sometimes he acts like the feeling is mutual, unless Ashley is around. It causes a little bit of a riff between Ashley and Alex, of course. I was just wondering if maybe you could occupy Alex, or something?"

"What exactly are you asking me to do?" He asked, sounding a little upset by my request.

"I'm not asking you to make out with her, I was just hoping you could talk to her and put her mind elsewhere."

"So, you want me to hit on her so she and Ashley don't get into a fight?"

"I guess." I shrugged.

"Isn't that just going to make matters worse?" He retorted, his face dark with anger.

"No."

"Brittany, I'm not going to lead her on and make her think I like her. Because I do not. Alex is a great girl but she's not the one I want." He answered honestly.

"It's just harmless flirting Bret."

"Not to me."

"Whatever, you flirt with me all the time and it doesn't mean anything."

"Maybe not to you." He muttered softly. I took as step back and shook my head. Did I hear him right? Surely, I'm imagining things.

"What?" I asked confused.

"I said, maybe not to you." He repeated angrily.

"And what does that mean?"

"Nothing, obviously it doesn't mean anything." He

said, shaking his head sadly.

"Bret, I thought we were just friends. I didn't mean to…that's just how I am. I flirt with everyone, I didn't realize…"

"I get it Brittany; it's not a big deal. I tell you what, Marc actually has a thing for Alex so I'll tell him to man up and go flirt with her. How's that? Will that make you happy and hopefully make you forget what I just said?" He asked drily, before he hurried off towards Marc and the others.

"Bret!" I yelled after him. Was I the girl he was talking about having a crush on at Homecoming? Certainly not, I was reading way too much into things. I had to be. My heart jumped and screamed excitedly at the thought of Bret liking me though. I was completely confused and torn between two guys, again. I had never thought in a million years that Bret McHalley would have any type of feelings for me. Why would he? We're so different, he's perfect and I'm not. I couldn't understand why he hadn't told me this sooner either. If he had feelings for me, why was he waiting until now to let me know?

My overactive imagination flipped back to the reasoning behind Aaron finally revealing his feelings for me and I panicked that

Bret was dealing with the same situation. An hour later, I had worked myself up into a frenzy. I was sitting in a circle on the back porch with Michael, Mason, Lindsay, Bret, Marc and Alex. Justin and Ashley had coupled off somewhere and my brother and Haley were nowhere to be found. I jumped up and stood in front of Bret.

"Can we talk?" I asked quickly, staring back at him, trying to calm the craziness rushing through my head. He looked back at me nervously and shrugged his shoulders. I extended my hand and helped him off the ground, then pulled him into the stables with me.

"What's your deal McHalley?" I asked coldly.

"You're the one who asked me to talk; obviously you're the one with the problem." He shrugged, kicking at the ground nervously before he walked over to one of the stalls to pet my horse, Ginger.

"Why did you tell me that earlier? Is something wrong with you?"

"What?" He laughed.

"Last time someone told me how they felt about me it was because he was dying. Is that why..." I asked tearfully.

257

"No." He laughed as he rushed over to me, grabbed my hand and squeezed it. "I'm just an idiot with bad timing, that's all."

"It's not funny."

"No, it's not but it's cute. You were actually worried about me." He shrugged.

"No I wasn't." I lied quickly as I looked down at the ground. Bret smiled as he moved down so he could look up at me.

"You know, you have a very overactive imagination." He stated with a laugh.

"Aaron used to call me a drama queen." I pouted as a tear slipped down my cheek.

"I could see that." He laughed softly, before he took a step closer to me. "Sweetie, just because someone makes a confession to you, it doesn't mean they're dying. I'm actually sorry that thought would even cross your mind."

Bret grabbed me in a hug and smiled back at me. I felt like an idiot for thinking something could be wrong with him, but I began to wonder if deep down, I had let myself get so worked up so I had an excuse to talk to him. I really wanted to know if he seriously had feelings for me. Suddenly, Joey's face popped into my mind and I instantly felt guilty.

"I feel so stupid." I whispered.

"Don't. I feel pretty stupid myself."

"Why?" I asked in bewilderment.

"I don't know…" He started with a shrug. "I guess because I just sit back and think all the good things will just happen to me."

"Um, they do." I laughed. "Everything you touch is gold, Bret. Every guy at Stitlin, in the state, wishes they had a third of your athletic ability."

"Yeah, but that kind of thing isn't what matters to me." He replied as he looked directly at me. He took a step towards me, pulled me to him and kissed me passionately. I felt my entire body go weak, my stomach jumped and my heart raced. So many emotions exploded in my heart and mind. I didn't know what else to do but continue kissing him. I didn't want him to stop.

I flashed back to my birthday party last year, when we played truth or dare. Marc had made it his responsibility to make Bret and I kiss as much as possible and Aaron had sent the two of us into a closet for a game of Seven Minutes in Heaven. I felt the same crazy things then but pushed them off as I had caught the flu or something. Now, I realized they were caused by something much more.

I cursed myself for having the feelings and once again being torn between two guys. I couldn't do it again though. I couldn't let myself fall for Bret, when I was already falling for Joey. What kind of person would I be if I did that twice in a row? All these thoughts were rushing through my mind, my conscience was telling me I had a boyfriend but my heart was telling me not to stop.

Unfortunately, Bret pulled away and looked back at me worriedly. He exhaled quickly and searched my blue eyes for a response and I searched his for the meaning. I wanted to smack him for waiting until I had a serious boyfriend to make a move, but more than anything, I wanted to kiss him again.

"Wow." I breathed. Bret smiled back at me and I felt his hand gently caress my cheek. Without another thought, I pulled him back to me and kissed him again. I would've kissed him all night too and dealt with the consequences later if Marc wouldn't have barged into the stables.

"Oh, shit. Sorry." He cursedd, his eyes were wide

with excitement and disbelief. I watched as he shook his head and smiled back at Bret. "My bad."

My face flushed with mortification. Then guilt shot through me and I buried my face in my hands. I was still ensconced in Bret's arms and I could feel his eyes boring into me. He watched me for a minute, before his hand went my face and he tipped my chin up so I was looking back at him.

"That sucked, I mean, Marc coming in here sucked." He admitted nervously. I nodded my head and felt tears stream down my face. "I'm sorry, I shouldn't have done that, I...I just thought you wanted me to. I had the opportunity and I usually blow them but I don't know, something told me not to miss this chance. I'm apologizing, but it doesn't mean I regret it."

"I did want you too." I sobbed.

"Then why are you crying?" He questioned worriedly.

"Because I have a boyfriend. Why does this always happen to me? It's just like Aaron and Michael all over again." I babbled emotionally.

"No, no it's not. I mean, I'm sorry, I didn't mean to put you in this situation Brittany. I'm an idiot."

261

I shook my head in disagreement and stared back at Bret helplessly. Everything inside me was telling me to stay and see what happened next between us. Aaron's words to me about opening my heart to Bret and seeing where it went, were echoing through my ears, almost as if he were there repeating them. I shook my head trying to block out Aaron's ghostly voice and began to cry harder. My heart was even betraying me by telling me to stay, to forget about Joey and accept Bret.

"I'm sorry Bret. I can't...I can't do it. I want to, I just can't." I babbled, before I ran out of the stables and into my house. I dove into my bed, buried myself under my comforter and pillows and sobbed.

"What in the Hell just happened?" Alex asked, racing into the bedroom after me.

"What's wrong Brittany? Why are you crying?" Ashley asked from where she had been sound asleep in the floor.

"Bret kissed me." I sobbed.

"Again, why are you crying?" Ashley asked with a giggle.

"I have a boyfriend."

"Why is it that you always get to be torn between two guys? Seriously, I would just like *one* hot guy in my life." Ashley commented.

"So are you crying because he kissed you and you feel guilty, like you cheated on Joey? Or are you upset you have feelings for him *and* Joey, but don't know what to do?" Alex asked wisely. I nodded my head tearfully.

"What's going on in here?" Haley queried, sneaking into my room. Ashley filled her in quickly and Haley's eyes grew wide with surprise. "Dude, I always miss the good stuff."

"I don't know what to do. I ran away crying and I told him I had a boyfriend, but I just wanted him to kiss me again. Does that make me a horrible person?"

"No baby, it doesn't." Haley answered, hugging me quickly. "It just means that you're human."

"Bret and Joey are both amazing guys, I personally think Bret's more suited for you though." Ashley said. "Aaron even said it and that means something coming from him, considering he was madly in love with you."

"Brittany, I wish I could tell you what to do, but you're

the only one who knows what your heart wants. Honestly though, I agree with Ashley, you and Bret are perfect for each other. I just think that next year, you and Joey are going to go your separate ways and it might be too late for you and Bret. If Aaron taught me anything, it was to follow your heart and not live with any regrets. Unfortunately though, I can say that but I have a hard time acting on it." Alex shrugged.

"What do I do?"

"Don't freaking cry about it!" Ashley exclaimed. "You have two amazingly hot guys before you and *you're crying*? You're unbelievable! Milk it for all it's worth."

"I can't do that again."

"Again?" Alex asked, confused. I shook my head and looked back at Ashley.

"We can't tell you what to do, Britty. We can just support your decision and be extremely jealous." Ashley laughed.

"OMG." Haley sighed. "Is that the sun?" She giggled as the sun started to rise behind the trees. "Let's go to bed."

"Excellent idea." I said sadly. I fell asleep and dreamed about dating five guys at once. I woke up a few hours later, more confused than I had been when I went to sleep. The truth was, I wanted Bret McHalley but anytime I found myself getting too attached to a guy, they walk out of my life. My grandfather did it, my father, Michael and his brothers, Aaron and even Justin for a bit. I could survive if Joey left me high and dry, I don't think I would if Bret did. Honestly, his father was a Marine, who is to say he won't get orders tomorrow and get shipped across the country? I could not take that chance with my heart. Not ever again.

Chapter 41

For the next week and a half, Bret continuously tried to talk to me, but I never gave him a chance. I knew if I was alone with him that I would listen to my heart and nothing else. I couldn't do that. And yes, I ducked into rooms, turned around dramatically and went the other way and sometimes even pretended to fall asleep to avoid him.

"Bret doesn't deserve to be ignored, you know? He was just telling you how he felt and you're being a complete bitch about it." Marc stated icily as he barged into my room one night. My mouth dropped open in shock. Marc rarely raised his voice, let alone called anyone a name, unless it involved Bret.

"I know, I'm not doing it on purpose."

"Then what's the deal, do you like him or not?"

"Why do you think this is so hard for me, Marc? If I didn't have feelings for him, I would've just told him that and we'd be friends again."

"Then why are you ignoring him and putting him through Hell?"

"I have a boyfriend."

"I don't understand what Joey has to do with this. You and Bret kissed, you both like each other, why can't you just be together?"

"It's not that easy. I have feelings for Joey too."

"You can't have feelings for two guys, Brittany. It's not possible."

"Obviously it is. Are you forgetting that last year when you met me I was in a similar situation? I mean, at the time I thought I was madly in love with both of those boys and I wasn't. I was physically and emotionally in love with Aaron and my love for Michael is more on a spiritual and friendship level. Unfortunately, I don't know how to decipher my feelings for Bret and Joey."

"I'd like to be able to tell you that Bret won't wait around forever but that'd be a lie. He's waited this long, I'm sure he'll wait another thirty years if he has to." Marc grumbled.

"Does he hate me?" I asked quietly as I looked down at my bedspread uncomfortably.

"No, *I would*, but he couldn't." He laughed. "Could you please talk to him? If nothing else Brittany, just tell him you want to be friends and figure out your feelings later. The current situation is absolutely killing him."

"I don't know what to say. I'm afraid."

"Well, you don't have a choice." Marc said, as he started out of my room. "I'm sick of listening to him cry about it."

Marc pulled Bret out of his bedroom and threw him into mine. Marc shot both of us a firm look and nodded towards me. Bret stood in my doorway, staring at the ground. He was obviously mortified and I thought at any minute he might bolt.

"This is awkward." I mumbled, forcing a laugh. I heard Bret chuckle a bit and then he looked up at me with sad, blue puppy dog eyes. My heart melted instantly, I just wanted to run and hug him.

"I'm sorry Brit, I didn't want this to happen. I didn't mean to ruin our friendship, or put you in such an awkward position. And I definitely didn't want you to feel like you had to ignore me because you were afraid of hurting my feelings."

"Bret, that's just it, I'm not ignoring you because I don't like you. I'm ignoring you because I *do* like you." I whispered quietly.

"What?" He asked, looking up at me excitedly.

"I like you Bret, but I'm with Joey. I like him too and it's not fair for me to just throw him to the side and explore this." I gestured between the two of us and took a deep breath. "What if tomorrow you decide you want someone else? I can't tell the difference...I don't know how to decipher my feelings. I'm completely confused."

"Apparently, it's not the same thing that I feel, because you would know."

"I didn't say I didn't feel anything." I said, wishing I could retract the statement immediately after. It was almost as if someone else was talking for me. Bret smiled back at me and started towards the bed.

"Bret, please stop." I whispered, "I can't. I won't, I'm too scared that if we explored this further it would just ruin our friendship. I think you're only interested in me because I'm taken."

"What?"

"Seriously, if that wasn't the case then why would you wait until *now* to tell me?"

"Because I'm an idiot? Brittany, what do I have to do

to show you that I'm for real?"

I shrugged my shoulders and looked back at Bret's sad face. My heart, my mind and my body were screaming to stop talking and just fall for him. I started to speak, but nothing came out. Suddenly my cell phone rang and I breathed a sigh of relief, realizing I had really been saved by the bell at that moment.

"It's Joey." I whispered, looking back at him sadly. Bret looked back at me questioningly, as if answering the phone would tell him who I chose.

"Bret I like you, *a lot*. But I'm with Joey and what kind of person would I be if I threw five months away because of a kiss?"

"Obviously not the girl I thought you were." He mumbled sadly, before he walked out of my bedroom to let me answer Joey's call.

Chapter 42

"Brittany, please? Please, please, please." Joey begged as we lay on his parents couch, making out. I was babysitting his little siblings, something that hadn't happened in a while because of our relationship. His parents were in a bind though and Joey was ecstatic to know we were going to have the house, somewhat, to ourselves.

"What?" I asked coyly as I kissed his neck.

"Baby, please, you're killing me. Look what just kissing you does to me." He whined, taking my hand and placing it on the outside of his jeans.

"Joey." I gasped, ripping my hand away quickly.

"Please baby, I love you, I just want to show you." He pleaded. If you haven't figured it out yet, Joey was begging me to sleep with him. The school year was almost over, prom was a week away and Joey and I had been dating for seven months. We still had not had sex, I am not ready.

I sat up quickly and looked back at Joey sadly. He tried to pull me back down to the couch and continue kissing me, but I pushed him away. I hadn't told Joey about my past and I thought I should before we took our relationship any further.

"Joey, I'm not a virgin." I whispered.

"So? Neither am I." He stated, kissing me again. He realized there was something bothering me, so he stopped and looked back at me questioningly.

"What's wrong baby?" He asked. "Are you scared? Did you and Kaplan sleep together and you're afraid I'm going to turn into a jerk too?"

"No...*no*, it's a lot more complicated than that." I whispered.

"You can tell me, Brittany. I'm your boyfriend, whatever you say, isn't going to make me turn against you." I looked back at Joey through tearful eyes and began explaining my relationship with Aaron and how I was seeing Michael at the same time. I could only imagine what he thought of me once he realized I had cheated on Michael with his best friend, but if it bothered him, he didn't let it show.

"Brittany, I'm not going to push you to do something you're not ready to do." He admitted. "I love you and I'll wait, if you

272

want to. It's just really hard for me, that's all. I'm sure it's hard to think of making love to someone else, especially with such an emotional tie to the memory. But someday, you're going to have to let him go. I'm not saying forget him honey, but you can't let his memory haunt you and keep you from living your life."

I nodded my head and looked back at him tearfully. I didn't know what to say or do, but I felt incredibly vulnerable. I wanted to take our relationship to the next level, but I was also afraid that in doing so it would tarnish Aaron's memory or cause a whole lot of untouched issues to come rushing back.

"Come here." Joey whispered, pulling me close to him and hugging me tightly. "I love you Brittany. I'm sorry if I've been pushing you."

"No Joey, if I didn't want to do it, I wouldn't have." I admitted. Joey had been telling me that he loved me for the last few months, but I never repeated it. In all honesty, I was still torn between him and Bret, but I couldn't admit that out loud. And if you're wondering, Bret backed off and the two of us have gone back to being friends with no awkwardness between us.

"Joey, when we do…for the first time, it's not going to

be on your parents' couch or in your bed while I'm babysitting. It's not going to be in the backseat of your car either. " I admitted. Joey nodded his head and smiled back at me.

"I can handle that, I would rather it be that way. Sometimes, I just get caught up in the moment and can't think straight though." He stated, kissing me sweetly. "I've really got to stop doing that, you drive me crazy."

I kissed him again, teasing him a little bit. At that moment, I knew next weekend would be when I wouldn't tell him no. I know, I know, it's super cliché for our first time to be after prom, but it just seemed perfect to me. Maybe, all the young adult novels and movies have influenced me, but I don't care. Joey knew my secrets and he wasn't judging me, how could I not take the next leap?

Chapter 43

So many things were flipping through my mind. Aaron had been at the forefront a lot lately; sometimes, I felt as though he was standing right beside me and I would feel at peace. Other times, my stomach would hurt so bad from missing him that I couldn't breathe. The only way to clear those feelings was to run; the longer, the better.

I needed to clear my head. Mostly, I'm terrified I won't be able to fit into my prom dress or that it'll look horrible on me. I'm very self-conscious, especially around Joey, and I just wanted to look amazing. I had my mp3 player attached to my ears and I was off on an amazing jog through some trails behind my house. Out of nowhere, something jumped in front of me. I screamed and jumped back.

"Sorry, I didn't mean to scare you." A familiar voice apologized. I stared back into Chris Kaplan's dark eyes. There was something different about them though, they seemed calm and sincere, it was something I'd never seen before.

"Chris? What are you doing here?" I asked nervously.

"I just live a mile or two down that way." He

explained with a laugh. "I was just taking a walk, how weird that I'd run into you."

"Yeah weird." I repeated.

"I'm glad I did run into you, though. I've been wanting to talk to you, to see you." He stated. I eyed him carefully as I pretended to fumble for the volume to my mp3 player as I secretly checked to make sure my cell phone was accessible. I slowed my breathing, trying to calm my heart and pray Bret decided to come through the woods at this time.

"I just wanted to apologize for everything. I was horrible to you and I shouldn't have been. I've changed Brittany." He began. "I was really hoping you could find it in your heart to forgive me and maybe we can be friends again."

"Chris." I began.

"You don't have to say anything now." He laughed. "It's a lot and it's probably really scary for you to see me right now, especially alone. I'll leave, my parents will get worried before too long anyway."

Without another word, Chris waved and was gone. Tears filled my eyes as the realization of my terror hit me. I took a few deep breaths before I turned around and sprinted back towards my house. I should've called someone and told them exactly where I was, knowing none of them would think to check the GPS function I had enabled on my running app.

I wouldn't be taking those trails anymore, that's for sure.

Chris wasn't back at school and no one else had mentioned they'd seen him around town. I just kept telling myself he must have just been home for a visit. I couldn't let myself worry about him, especially when I was freaking out about prom and semesters already.

Chapter 44

Prom finally arrived and I couldn't believe how nervous and terrified I was about the whole situation. There was a deep pit in my stomach about the decision to sleep with my boyfriend, it felt like guilt and dread, but he had been right when he said I needed to get on with my life.

Joey had decided we would have our parents sign the permission slips stating we would be attending the after prom party hosted by our high school, but it was a decoy. He had went to great lengths to forge, copy and paste or whatever, for us to turn in slips to the actual high school stating we would not be attending the after party.

Mr. and Mrs. Hawkins were out of town for some ob-gyn classes and he had arranged for us to stay the night in their pool/guest house. Joey had rented a limo and a few of his friends would be joining us for the night. I was nervous because I was rarely around him without my friends, which made me even more self-conscious. Drake and Lindsay were going with other people but my mom made sure we were all leaving at the same time so she could get in her photo opportunity.

I hadn't told Joey I was ready to sleep with him, in case I chickened out. Instead, I just told him I wanted to stay the night with him and nothing else. We hung out during the fast songs and danced to every slow one.

Finally, we all headed back to the limo and the driver dropped everyone else off before he took us back to Joey's house. We were snuggling in the back seat while everyone else was in the vehicle with us, but as soon as they were all gone, he was all over me.

"Oh Brittany, you look so beautiful tonight. I love you so much." He said breathlessly between kisses. Our kissing had gotten so intense that I didn't notice the limousine had stopped. I could hear the chauffeur clearing his throat, hinting for us to get out. Joey helped me out of the vehicle and the two of us rushed to the backyard and snuck into the pool house.

We began kissing again, I felt Joey's hands moving to the back of my dress, and he started to unzip it. I didn't stop him, I just followed his lead and began helping him out of his clothes. Before I knew it, we were lying in the bed making out, barely clothed.

"Brittany, look what you do to me." He whispered,

kissing my ear lobe as he moved my hand down to his boxers. I felt

his lips move down my neck and then to my chest as he began to

unhook my bra. There was no turning back now. Within minutes, we

were both naked and I felt him go inside me. He finished quickly,

kissed me sweetly and fell into the bed next to me.

Well, that was disappointing. The guilt and grief hit me like a

tidal wave and I could feel the depression starting to pull me under.

What had I just done? I didn't love Joey and I should not have given

him something so sacred to me.

It wasn't at all what I had imagined it would be like. When he

rolled over and faced the opposite way, I wanted to punch myself in

the face. I was an idiot and I felt tears stinging my eyes, but a shadow

by the window caught my attention. At first, I thought I was

imagining things, but as I strained to get a better look, I realized there

was a figure watching us outside the window.

"Joey, there's someone outside." I whispered, my

voice trembling in fear as I yanked the covers up over my naked

body.

"No there's not, it's probably just the way the trees are

casting shadows." He mumbled drowsily.

"No Joey, no there's someone there. I can see the outline of a body." I mumbled nervously, my eyes not moving from the window. Joey flipped over and breathed an exasperated sigh. Suddenly, he saw it too. He threw his boxers on, jumped out of the bed and raced outside. By the time he got to the door though, the figure was gone. Joey sprinted outside anyway and searched around the house, but there wasn't anyone there.

"Whoever it was, took off." He announced with a shrug. "Probably just some perv."

I nodded my head and settled back under the covers. Tears streamed down my face now, as thoughts raced through my head. In my gut, I knew Chris Kaplan had been spying on us, he hadn't changed at all. Joey thought I was crying because I was scared. I would let him believe that was the only issue I was having at this moment.

"Baby, it's okay." He whispered, kissing my forehead. "I won't let anyone hurt you, I promise."

I nodded my head and let him wrap his arms around me and hold me until he fell asleep. I stared out the window nervously the rest of the night.

The thoughts and scenes rushing through my head were ridiculous and freaking me out. I wanted to call Bret and tell him what I just saw, because he would take seriously. He knew what Chris was capable of, Joey should've too, but he didn't seem at all worried about it.

Chapter 45

A few nights later after track practice, my mother dropped me off at the McHalley's to baby sit for Bret's little brother, Brian. Usually when I babysat, Marc and Bret would be lurking around the house, pretending not to be there. Brian had gone to bed early so I sat on the couch, trying to study for my upcoming finals. The boys had been out for part of the night but came home early.

"You okay?" Bret asked, sitting down on the couch next to me.

"Yeah, why?"

"I don't know, you've been acting kind of distant, that's all." I could feel tears stinging my eyes, but I shrugged my shoulders and didn't look up.

I wanted to tell him how I'd slept with Joey and it was horrendous, that I realized I didn't love him. I needed to tell him, to tell someone, that I missed Aaron so bad sometimes that I couldn't breathe and how I felt like I had ruined the sacred moments my best friend and I had shared by letting Joey have that part of me too.

"If you think ignoring me is going to get me to leave

you alone, you're wrong." He announced. "I'll just sit here and ask twenty questions until you tell me what's bothering you."

I gazed up at him and shot him a nasty look. Bret just smiled back at me, as if my looks couldn't kill. I tried to call his bluff, but he was relentless and continued to bombard me with questions.

"Bret, *nothing* is wrong with me. I'm just worried about finals and freaking about the conference track meet, that's all."

"Nope, that's not it." He decided, shaking his head and eyeing me carefully. "You know when you lie you can't look me in the eye, it's a dead giveaway."

"Why do you care what's wrong with me Bret?"

"Because you're my friend and I hate seeing you sad like this."

"I miss Aaron, is that what you wanted to hear? It's been a freaking year and I'm still not over it!" I cried.

"No one said you had a set time frame to grieve, Brittany." He stated sadly. "Unfortunately, it's probably something that you'll never get over. You just have to learn to let it help you become a better person."

"Easier said than done."

"I get that, I wish I could tell you how to deal, but I can't." He shrugged. The room fell silent and Bret still pressed on with his inquisition.

"You know, if there's something else bothering you, you can talk to me about it. You don't have to keep everything bottled up inside." He murmured. I wanted to tell him everything so badly, but it would be wrong.

"Please stop."

"No Brittany, I won't. You're falling apart right before my eyes, you're terrified about something and it's killing me that I can't help you. I just wish I could make it all go away, comfort you or something. The last couple of weeks you've been jumpy and you barely smile or laugh anymore. Heck, you're practically becoming a recluse."

"You're exaggerating."

"Am I?" He asked, scooting closer to me on the couch. I felt him grab my hand and squeeze it tightly; I looked back at him questioningly. How could he see all this, but no one else did? My own boyfriend hadn't even noticed.

"Yes." I lied, trying to continue looking him in the

285

eyes, but it was too hard. The front door opened and Bret sighed sadly. He didn't let go of my hand, I did that. He didn't move away either.

"Brittany, please talk to me." Bret begged as his mother was waiting for me in their entryway, I shook my head and repeated that I was fine. Mrs. McHalley took me home and I jumped on the computer before I went to sleep. I was instant messaging Michael when someone else popped up on my screen.

"Hey, did you have a good night?" The person asked.

"Yeah, I guess." I typed back.

"How long have you been babysitting for the McHalley's, I thought the Hawkins was full time?"

"Who is this?"

"Sorry, it's Chris. I didn't mean to freak you out."

"How did you know I was babysitting?"

"Oh, my mom told me. She was out with the McHalley's tonight."

"Are you back?"

"No, still at school." He typed.

"I should get going, I've got a long day tomorrow."

"Night." He typed. Panic filled my entire body at the thought of Chris knowing my whereabouts. I didn't like that he was still trying to be my friend either. I didn't trust him and I'm pretty certain he's just playing nice until he decides what to do next. You can't change crazy.

"I'm sorry if I was pushy. I just worry about you." Bret typed, popping up on my screen.

"You worry for no reason though, I'm fine." I typed slowly.

"I still don't believe you, but I know you'll come to me when you're ready. At least, I hope."

"I'll make something up if it means you'll back off. ☺*"*

"Funny. I just hope you know I'm always here if you need me."

"I do, I don't understand it, but I do."

"You're my friend."

"Thanks." I typed back. Bret's words eased my fears temporarily, but when I finally logged off the computer, I was scared again. I climbed into bed and lay wide awake, staring at the ceiling

and jumping at the shadows playing on my walls.

Chapter 46

The following weekend, Joey and I joined our friends at the Cliffs for a huge party to ease our struggles with the upcoming final exams. My emotions were all crazy, I was jumpy and grieving constantly. My chest always felt tight, as if my heart would beat out of my chest or as though I couldn't breathe. I think I was having anxiety attacks, but I hadn't told anyone about my fears or issues. I steered clear of Bret when I could, only because he apparently could read me better than anyone else. I was so caught up in everything going through my head that I was throwing back alcohol as if it were water.

"Brittany, maybe you should slow down a bit." Bret warned cautiously. I shook my head.

"Nope, I need to relieve my stress."

"Do you really think alcohol is the way to do it?"

"Yup." I answered sharply. "It's this or sex, which would you prefer?" Bret's eyes widened and his face filled with hurt to realize I was sleeping with Joey. I instantly felt like crap. I chugged another beer.

"What happened to you running to relieve your stress?" He questioned.

"A girl can't run alone when she has a stalker." I stated without thinking. Bret looked back at me in surprise.

"Excuse me? Stalker? Is Chris back?" He asked angrily as his voice fell to a whisper.

"Maybe I'm talking about you." I hissed as I stormed off to get more alcohol. It didn't take long for Bret to find me again, pull me off to the side and start questioning me again.

"Back off Bret!" I warned angrily. "Maybe if you dropped the holier than thou attitude and had a little fun every once in a while, *you* would have a girlfriend right now!"

Bret stared back at me with his sad blue eyes and I instantly felt guilty, but I squashed the urge to apologize. I was honestly sick of him always lecturing or prying into my life. Yup, that was exactly what my issues were.

"I am a big girl. I can take care of myself. And I definitely don't need you to pretend to be my father. That bastard bailed a long time ago." I slurred, eyeing him angrily. Bret put his hands up in surrender and walked off, shaking his head in disbelief.

Joey chose that moment to come back from talking to a group of people I didn't know. He wrapped his arms around my waist and kissed my neck sweetly.

"We should just get out of here." He growled low in my ear. I could barely stand or see two feet in front of me, but it sounded like an excellent idea. I took my boyfriend's hand and let him pull me towards his car.

"You need a ride?" Bret asked worriedly, as he realized Joey was in no shape to drive and I had no business walking.

"No, we're cool." Joey slurred.

"Are you sure? Drake's leaving in a few minutes; it would just be easier if you rode with us."

"I'll ride with my *boyfriend*, thank you." I snapped icily.

"Do you really think that's a good idea? Joey can barely walk, let alone drive. And how are you going to get up the stairs without Mr. Curren busting you?"

"We'll be fine."

"Marc and I will wait up for you." He offered with an exasperated sigh.

291

"Don't bother." I shot coldly. "I don't plan on being home for a while." I smiled wickedly back at him, ignoring the pang of guilt I felt when I saw sadness fill his eyes.

Bret knew me better than anyone, the same way Aaron always knew something was wrong, without me telling him. It terrified me to think I could have that kind of relationship with someone other than my late best friend. I already ruined one cherished memory Aaron and I had shared, I couldn't do anything else to dishonor my friend. Being so horrific to Bret McHalley was not the answer, however, it was the only one I had.

"Well, we'll still wait up for you." He shrugged, trying to hide the sadness in his eyes. I looked back at him, trying to look like a tough girl and knowing I probably wasn't doing a very good job of it. "Just be careful."

Joey and I climbed into his car as Bret watched. I pulled Joey towards me and kissed him passionately wanting to push Bret as far away as I possibly could. He had no business liking me, knowing me so well or anything. I glanced outside, praying for a reaction that would justify my actions. Instead, two junior girls came up to Bret and started flirting with him. I wanted to punch them in the vaginas.

And then, I wanted to punch Bret in the stomach for talking to them. Alcohol was not my friend, jeez.

Ten minutes later Joey pulled off on a side road and pulled me into the backseat with him. We drunkenly made out and proceeded to have sex. I stupidly thought the second time would be better, but I was wrong, I think it was worse. I chalked it up to the excessive amounts of alcohol we consumed and continued kissing him in the backseat. We still had a little time to kill before I had to be home for curfew and I was adamant I would make Bret as jealous as possible, by coming in with only minutes to spare.

"Joey." I gasped, as I looked out the back window of his car.

"Yeah baby?" He asked, not really focusing on anything but my body. Suddenly, I began to scream when I saw Chris standing behind the car watching us with a wicked smile playing on his lips.

"What? What's wrong?" He asked frantically. He pushed me off quickly and looked out the back window, trying to focus on whatever I was looking at.

"Chris. It's Chris." I stammered.

"I don't see anything." He grumbled. I stared in horror at the spot where Chris had been standing, but Joey was right, he wasn't there anymore. My breathing grew rapid as I looked around frantically, waiting for him to jump out from anywhere. We were like sitting ducks. Scenes from every horror movie I'd ever seen flashed through my mind.

"He was there."

"Are you sure? Are you sure, it was Chris? Are you sure it wasn't just a shadow or something?" He questioned. I shook my head vigorously. He didn't believe me.

"I know what I saw." I whispered tearfully.

"Well, he's gone now." He shrugged, trying to kiss me again. I pulled away from him, put my clothes back on and climbed into the front seat without getting out of the car. I remembered an urban legend about a car breaking down, the guy goes to get help and later the girl hears scraping against the car roof, her boyfriend had been murdered and was hanging above the car. I shuddered and almost puked at the thought. I would not get out of this car until we were safe in my driveway.

"Take me home." I mumbled. Joey was frustrated, but

I didn't care. I was terrified and he thought I was being ridiculous. Chris Kaplan was following me and I was going to end up in a loony bin if I didn't do something about it.

"Are you going to be okay?" Joey asked, moving my hair out of my eyes when we finally pulled into my driveway. I nodded, nervously looking back at my large, dark house before us. Drake's vehicle was home and Marc's bedroom light was still on.

"I'm sorry about earlier. I guess...I don't know, I guess it probably was just the shadows. Sorry, you probably think I'm a freak. It all ended too easily, you know? I just keep thinking he's going to jump out of the shadows and get me."

"Brittany, baby, he's gone. He's not coming back and if he was, don't you think we'd know about it? I'm not going to let anyone hurt you, okay? I'll protect you, sweetie." He whispered, kissing me sweetly. I nodded my head and stumbled out of his car.

Chapter 47

I was trembling as I staggered inside the house and up the stairs. Bret and Marc were waiting for me at the foot of the steps, knowing I couldn't conquer them on my own. Bret took my hand and pulled back. He could see I was shaking and looked back at Marc for help. I wouldn't look either of them in the eyes and just stumbled up the steps slowly, by myself. The two boys followed, ready to catch me if I took a diver backwards.

"What's wrong?" Marc asked. "You look like you just saw a ghost."

"Nothing." I mumbled as I shrugged my shoulders and fell into my bed fully clothed. I tried to pretend as if I couldn't keep my eyes open. Maybe I really couldn't, but they didn't need to know that I just wanted to be alone, because they would never leave.

"It's hot." I grumbled as I tried to grab the hem of my sweatshirt and pull it off. It was as if the thing were made out of grease and both boys took pity on me and hurried to help. Marc helped with my sweatshirt, while Bret tried to take my shoes off.

"Did something happen between you and Joey?" Bret

asked quietly, almost as if he really didn't want to hear my answer. I shook my head again, praying they would just leave me alone.

"Are you asking if we screwed Bret?" I snapped. "Because the answer is yes. I had sex with my boyfriend."

"Did you want to? Did he...force you?" I shook my head and laughed. Bret looked back at me worriedly. "I realize you're drunk but you act as though something bad happened. Did you...did you lose your...?"

"Oh my God, shut up!" I exclaimed. "No, I didn't lose my virginity to him tonight. Joey didn't do anything I didn't want him to do. It's stupid. *I'm stupid.*" I rambled.

"You're not stupid Brittany, you're far from it." Bret stated as he pulled my shoe off and set it down on the ground softly. He held my other foot in his hand gingerly as he looked back up at me worriedly. I shook my head and looked down quickly. I felt the tears stinging at my eyes. Marc finally got my sweatshirt over my head, which wiped the tears away in the process and I lay back in my bed. "What happened, Brit? You look like you're really shook up. Like maybe Joey did something you didn't want him to do."

"I just thought I saw something and it freaked me out,

that's all. Joey probably thinks I'm psycho and I'll be surprised if he ever wants to see me again."

"You're so dramatic, Brittany." Marc laughed.

"What did you see?" Bret asked.

"Nothing. I just thought I saw someone in the shadows, watching us." I rambled, looking away quickly. I didn't want to say the last part and I couldn't figure out why my dang mouth wouldn't close like I wanted it too.

"Who?"

"I don't know, I couldn't tell." I lied with a shrug. "It was stupid; I'm drunk and probably just imagined it. I don't mean to be rude but I'm just ready to go to sleep."

"Me too, we've got church in the morning." Marc shrugged. Bret was reluctant to stop his inquisition and eyed me curiously. I shook my head and fell back on to my bed. Bret began to get up and walk out of the room. Without thinking, I shot straight up and grabbed his arm, pulling him back down to my bed. That was not a good idea, because the whole world and all its problems went rushing through my ears and body. Bret grabbed a trashcan and caught my regrets before I could make a mess.

"I'm sorry about earlier." I whispered tearfully, when my stomach had calmed down. "I was horrible to you and I shouldn't have been."

"I'm over it." He shrugged.

"I hate it when you say that. Please don't be over it, don't be over me. I'm just stressed out and that combined with alcohol makes me a little irritable. I had no right to jump down your throat or be so hateful to you." I said apologetically. "I shouldn't have…told you I was…that Joey and I…I was trying to hurt you and…"

"It's not the first time you've yelled at me Brittany and I'm sure it won't be the last. You're so thickheaded sometimes, it's frustrating. I guess I tend to be a little over protective of you and I'm sorry for that."

"Why do you always give in to me so easily?" I asked with a coy smile. Bret shrugged his shoulders.

"Because I'm a sucker for a pretty girl." He laughed. I rolled my eyes and hugged him quickly.

"I think it's just because you want me to hug you."

"You're right." He joked. He lifted his hand, brushed

the hair out of my face, and stroked my cheek. I looked back at him and got lost in his beautiful blue eyes, all I could think about was kissing him.

"I know *something is* going on in that pretty little head of yours Brit, I just wish you would tell me what it was. Unfortunately, I'm certain you're not ready to trust me completely." Bret whispered, looking back at me sadly. I nodded my head and smiled, realizing that maybe it wasn't so bad he knew me so well.

"It's nothing." I answered quietly. Bret nodded his head and I watched as he leaned towards me and kissed me tenderly at first, but then it turned harder, hungrier. I don't know if it was the alcohol or just my yearning for him to kiss me again, but I think this time the kiss was better than all the times before.

"Bret." I breathed, as he pulled away and hugged me tightly. "Please don't stop."

"Are you sure?" He asked.

"No." I answered shaking my head tearfully. "But I don't care; I don't want you to stop kissing me. It just feels *so* good, *so* amazing. I don't love Joey and."

Without hesitation, Bret leaned in and began kissing me again.

Tomorrow, I probably wouldn't remember any of this, mostly out of embarrassment for taking the step towards Bret McHalley that I was nowhere near ready to take.

My heart had ultimately chosen to fall for Bret, but was it only because I didn't have him yet? I questioned myself, unsure if I was doing the right thing. Did I not feel anything for Joey because he was the first person I slept with after Aaron or was it because I was too confused and wanted what I didn't have? Nothing made sense except that I want to kiss Bret forever and forget about everything and everyone else.

He did nothing but kiss me, until he realized I was about to fall asleep on him. He left my room a few minutes later. On the other side of the wall I could hear Bret and my soon to be stepbrother talking, if I had the energy I would've eavesdropped, but my drunken eyelids were way too heavy.

I fell asleep with a huge smile on my face. Somewhere in the dark, I heard breathing and a noise, followed by a curse word.

Chapter 48

"Bret?" I questioned, unsure if I was still asleep or not. No answer. I repeated his name and nervously peered into the pitch black of my room. I heard another noise; rustling in the corner of my room, by the window. I prayed for a mouse to be there, too terrified of what I knew was lurking in the shadows. It was then that I noticed my curtains were floating in the moonlight. I had not opened my bedroom window, I wouldn't when the air conditioner was on and neither would Bret. I slowly moved my hand towards my bedside lamp and flipped it on. I screamed as I saw Chris standing in my bedroom, smiling at me.

"Hey Brittany." He whispered. "I was just making sure you made it home safely."

My screams echoed throughout the entire house and jarred everyone out of their dreams. I heard commotion in Marc's room, knowing the two boys would be in my room and find what I was looking at.

"Guess I better go." He laughed, before he began climbing out the window. Within seconds, Bret and Marc raced into my room.

"What in the Hell?" I heard Marc curse as he stopped dead in his tracks trying to make sense of Chris standing near the window. Chris laughed again.

"Thanks for tonight, Brittany. I'll see you around." He was grinning as he went out the window. Marc and Bret raced after him, just as Drake came skidding into the room wearing only a pair of flannel boxers. My mother and Captain Jerk shot up the stairs and into my bedroom next. I definitely noticed the gun my mother's fiancé was carrying in his hand.

"What is going on?" Captain Jerk exploded as he saw everyone standing in my room, just as confused and startled as they were. I couldn't speak, I just screamed.

"Brittany, Brittany, stop sweetie." Lindsay said, rushing to hug me. I exploded into tears once I realized he was gone, but I was terrified that he had been in my room and I hadn't known he was there or even how long.

"Chris was here." Bret announced, looking back at me angrily.

"What? Who?" My mother asked.

"Chris Kaplan, we saw him go out the window." Marc explained.

"Why was there a boy in your room, Brittany?" My mother questioned, not catching on that I didn't invite him there.

"Did you know he was back in town?" Bret interrogated, forgetting everyone else in the room. I looked away quickly and nodded my head.

"I'm lost, who is this guy and why would he climb in your bedroom window?" Mr. Curren asked.

"Kaplan is the guy who showed up outside one night and left in the cop car. You know the one that attacked her at Homecoming." Drake explained, forgetting the school had contacted my father, and not my mother, for whatever reason. They were clueless as to the problems Chris had given me.

"What?" My mother asked in shock. "When were you attacked?"

I looked back at my brother helplessly, hoping this whole thing was just a nightmare. Drake shrugged his shoulders apologetically and began telling my mom and Mr. Curren some of the details of Chris's harassment.

304

"I'm calling the police." Mr. Curren announced, rushing downstairs to grab the house telephone.

"No, we can't." I protested.

"Are you kidding me, Brittany?" Bret yelled angrily. "He was in your bedroom while we were all asleep and you don't think we need to call the police?"

"He said he was just making sure I made it home okay." I stammered, realizing how stupid it sounded after I said it.

"Normal people would've called, not snuck into your bedroom. You have no idea how long he was even in here, Britty." Drake replied worriedly. I looked back at Bret nervously, wondering if Chris had seen the two of us kissing. I immediately grew worried he had and would run and tell everyone, just to ruin my life.

"How long have you known he was back, Brittany?" Bret questioned again, his jaw tightening with anger.

"A few weeks." I shrugged nonchalantly. "I was running on the trails behind the house and he came out of nowhere."

"Why didn't you tell anyone?"

"Because he said he'd changed and I wanted to believe him." I sobbed, again realizing how stupid and naïve I sounded.

Within an hour, the police arrived, asked questions and left. I told them everything, from the beginning, but again I felt like the authorities didn't believe a word I was saying. Mostly because, it was their boss's son. Thirty minutes after they left our house, the police returned. I sat at the bottom of the stairs, eavesdropping on their conversation with Mr. Curren.

"The Kaplan's informed us that their son is away at a college in Georgia, the school assured us that he is still there. Are you sure that is who your daughter saw in her room?"

"Positive, the boys saw him too."

"Well, maybe it's just a case of mistaken identity. The Kaplan's did inform us that your daughter has caused a lot of trouble for their son, which is what caused him to move in the first place. They think maybe she's lying to get attention." An older police officer explained to Mr. Curren. My mouth dropped open and I felt Lindsay's hands on my shoulders, holding me down as I tried to jump up and defend myself.

"I'm sorry, but they have to be mistaken. I know my children and they are far from the bullying type. I also saw the look on my daughter's face and it wasn't something anyone could fake. She was terrified and the boys saw him too, that should tell you something."

"Regardless sir, Mr. Kaplan's whereabouts have been confirmed. There's nothing we can do about it."

"It's a sad, sad world when you can't depend on the people who are sworn to keep you safe, to do so." Mr. Curren stated, shaking his head as he slammed the door in the police officers' faces. He walked into the kitchen and saw me sitting there crying.

"Sweetie, that boy won't be back. I'll make sure of it." Mr. Curren stated, wrapping his arms around me awkwardly.

"They don't believe me." I sobbed.

"What matters is that we do. It's going to be all right, Brittany. I promise. Now, why don't you two go sleep in Drake or Marc's room for the night. In the morning, I'll work on making this place a little more secure, okay?" I nodded my head and followed Lindsay upstairs. Apparently, Lindsay and I weren't the only ones who were freaked out by the incident, because Marc and Bret were already sacked out in Drake's room too. My older brother gave Lindsay and me his bed and joined the other two boys on the hardwood floor.

"I wish you would've told us Brittany." Bret whispered, as Drake turned the lights off.

"What would that have accomplished Bret? The school didn't believe me and now the police don't either. Nobody believes me; Chris can do whatever he wants to me and nobody will stop him."

"That's not true." Drake interjected. "He won't come near you again, Britty."

Chapter 49

It was the last day of my freshman year and I had promised
Marc I would meet him at his locker so could head to the baseball
diamonds to watch Bret's baseball game. Over the last two weeks,
my family and Bret had not left me alone. Captain Jerk had upgraded
the security on the house by installing an alarm system and cameras
so we would have proof if Chris was lurking anywhere near the house
again.

Thankfully, no one else knew about the incident. I hadn't told
Joey, even though it would validate what I told him I saw both times
we had slept together. I had become distant from my boyfriend
because I was so terrified of Chris coming back at any second. Not to
mention, I was trying to decipher my feelings. I also wasn't too
happy about the fact that Joey didn't ever believe me when I told him
Chris was somewhere in the shadows.

I walked to my locker and opened it to get out my backpack.
My last final of the day was a tough one, but I felt extremely relieved
that it was over. I replayed some of the questions in my head, second
guessing myself, as I bent down to get the excess stuff out of my

locker. A single red rose lay amongst the trash, with a note attached.

Brittany,

I see how disappointed you are after you and Joey are together and it makes me laugh. If only you would've thought I was worthy of what you have to give, you would never have that look of regret on your face after I finish.   There's still time for you to change your mind though, I'll wait for you, forever. I hope you know though, you're playing with fire and you will get burned. Two guys at once, even you can't pull that off. You can't lead so many guys on, someday soon you'll find a guy who won't put up with your crap and then it'll be the end of Brittany's perfect little reign.

Love Chris

I shuddered at the thought of him rummaging through my stuff and watching my every move. I looked around nervously, expecting to see him peering around a corner, but I didn't. I threw the rose onto the floor and tucked the note in my back pocket before anyone else could see it.

"Someone leaving you love notes, besides me?" Joey

asked, wrapping his arms around my waist and kissing me in the hallway. I shook my head as I leaned in to him.

"You mean, that wasn't from you?" I joked.

"Wanna head back to my house? Some of the guys are coming over, I thought we could have a little pool party and unwind together." He asked suggestively. I shook my head and made a sad face.

"Sorry, I already promised Marc I'd go to the baseball game with him. I told you that."

"Oh come on, blow it off, he'll understand." He begged.

"No, I can't. My mom's really on me to accept the whole new family crap." I lied with a shrug.

"Okay, but promise me that tomorrow I get you all to myself."

"Deal." I said, kissing him quickly before I escaped to find Marc.

"Why are you still with him, if you like Bret so much?" Marc questioned irritably, glaring at Joey.

"Who says I like Bret?" I asked nonchalantly.

"Bret. At least that's what you told him, more than once. Seriously Brittany, you can't keep making out with him and then run back to Joey as if nothing happened."

"I never made out with Bret."

"You can't honestly think I believe you were so drunk that night Chris came into your room, that you don't remember making out with Bret." He accused angrily. My eyes grew wide and I shrugged my shoulders again.

"I really don't remember that, are you sure Bret's not making it up?"

"Any other guy would, but not Bret. He's crazy about you Brittany, if you keep toying with him like this; you're going to make a huge mistake."

"I'll apologize to him, if that's what you want. But honestly, I don't remember *ever* making out with Bret McHalley. I definitely think that's something I would remember." I lied. Marc shook his head disgustedly.

"Bret's my best friend and you're going to be my sister soon. I just…I just don't know what you see in Joey. I guess I'm a little biased, but Bret is definitely the better guy."

"Maybe he is." I shrugged. "But Joey and I have been together for eight months. It'd be kind of unfair for me to dump him because my brother says so."

"No, it's unfair that you obviously have feelings for Bret and act on them when the two of you are alone and then deny them later on."

Marc and I were finally at the baseball field behind our school. I looked out onto the diamond and saw Bret warming up at first base. Our eyes locked and my heart stopped when he smiled and waved at the two of us. Marc stopped lecturing me and we cheered on our team.

"Drake's taking us to a house party later tonight, you wanna go?" Bret whispered, as his parents drove us back to my house after the ball game. I shrugged my shoulders.

"Chris won't show up in a public place, obviously, or he would've done it by now." Marc replied. "Besides, we'll be there to watch out for you."

"Come on, you've been hiding in your room for the past two weeks, you need to come back into society." Bret laughed.

"Fine, I'll go." I caved. The McHalley's followed the

three of us inside the house, visited with my parents for a while and ate dinner with us. After dinner, I ran back up to my room to change clothes before we all left for the party. I emptied my pockets and pulled out Chris's note. I stared back at it, somehow I had forgotten all about it. Bret walked out of Marc's room at the same time and I hollered for him to come into my room. I handed him the note without a word and watched his expression as he read it.

"He was at school?" Bret began. "How could we not have known?"

"I don't know." I shrugged. "But I've caught him twice when Joey and I...were together."

"Did you show anyone else?" He asked worriedly.

"No, it's pretty incriminating on all accounts. It wouldn't take much to figure out who the two guys are, my mom would ban you from the house."

"Is that really the reason or you just don't want Joey to find out?"

"That too." I answered honestly, looking down at the ground shamefully.

"We need to show Mr. Curren."

"No, then they won't let me go tonight. And you're right, I really need to get out of this house."

"I know I'm going to regret this later, but fine. Promise me that you'll show them tomorrow."

"I promise." I lied. I had no intention of showing anyone else the note, ever. His words were pretty explicit about my sex life and no one else could know about that.

"I won't let you out of my sight tonight, Brit." Bret said, taking my hand in his. "Just have fun and don't worry about anything else, okay?"

I nodded my head and stared back at Bret. I wanted him to kiss me again, but Marc's words echoed in my ears. I couldn't continue to lead Bret on, if I was still with Joey. It wasn't fair to anyone.

"Thanks, but I'm sure Joey won't let me get too far away from him." I laughed nervously as I began to walk out of my room.

"You look really pretty tonight." Bret commented, pulling me back to him. I was just wearing a pair of khaki shorts and a dark green tank top; I actually thought I was a little underdressed.

"Thanks." I blushed. I wanted to tell him that he looked amazing too, because he did, all the time actually. He was just wearing a t-shirt, jean shorts and a baseball cap but honestly, everything looked good on him.

"I wish you were my date tonight." He admitted quietly. I looked back at him, nodded my head and then rushed downstairs without another word. I secretly wished the same thing, but I had to stop acting like such a little school girl. I had a boyfriend that was crazy about me. I had to block Bret out of my head or I would be caught in a downward spiral of betrayal and drama.

We arrived at Joey's house a little while later. I was a little confused as to why I didn't know about it sooner, but I pretended not to care. Joey had technically invited me that afternoon and I had blown him off. I didn't realize it was an all-day affair. I weaved in and out of the crowd, looking for my boyfriend. I was standing at the edge of the pool; when I heard someone call my name, then yell for Joey. I realized that Joey's friend, Garrett, was trying to protect his friend. I stared back in horror as I saw Joey making out with Makenzie Yarden in the pool.

"Shit!" I heard Joey exclaim, looking back at me

quickly. I spun around on my heel and tried to run away. "Brittany! Brittany, wait!"

I didn't know where I was going or why I was so upset. After all, I'd made out with Bret a few times while Joey and I were together and I didn't even know what feelings I had for Joey. Tears streamed down my face, I was shocked and humiliated by what I had just seen.

"Brittany, please wait!" Joey yelled after me. "Please? Can we just talk?"

"Leave me alone, please?" I said, as I raced to where my brother stood with his friends.

"Can you take me home?" I begged Drake. He looked back at me questioningly, realization dawning when he looked up to see Joey chasing me.

"Are you sure?" He asked. I nodded my head and tried to get away before Joey caught up with me, but I wasn't quick enough.

"Brittany please, just let me talk to you." He pleaded, trying to grab my hand.

"I don't want to talk Joey." I said, shaking my head vigorously. "Just go back to your new friend and have a good time."

"Brittany, it's not like that. I've been drinking all day and she just…she kissed me." He protested.

"That's not what it looked like."

"I can only imagine what it looked like baby, but that's what happened."

Drake and his friends had walked off, leaving Joey and I alone to work out our problems. I wanted to forgive him, mostly because I had no room to judge. Joey wrapped his arms around my waist and pulled me close to him. I felt his lips move to my ear lobes as he whispered an apology into them.

"I forgive you." I whispered tearfully. "But I need some time to clear my head."

"What do you mean?" He asked sadly.

"I think I'm going to hang out with my friends." I shrugged.

"Brittany I love you, I didn't mean to…"

"I just need time to think." I whispered, walking off before he could protest again. I didn't know where I was going or what I needed to think about. Everything in me told me to drop him right then and there, but I couldn't. Maybe it was out of guilt for what had happened between Bret and me, or maybe it was just the

fear of Bret rejecting me once he realized I was available. Part of me

believed Bret was just interested in the chase of an unavailable girl.

Most of me knew, however, that I was terrified of what Bret

McHalley could do to me if I fell for him completely.

Chapter 50

Two weeks later, I was dressed in a pair of shorts and a tank top, ready to hit the treadmill downstairs. I grabbed my mp3 player and bounded down the steps to our basement. I was going stir crazy being cooped up in the house constantly, I really wanted to go for a long run on my own, but no one would allow that. Chris was still out there somewhere and even though he hadn't shown himself since that night in my bedroom, my family wasn't taking any chances.

Joey had showed up on my doorstep the day after his party, carrying a bouquet of flowers and an extremely apologetic face. He told me he loved me and the kiss with Makenzie meant nothing, it was a horrible drunken mistake. He continued to tell me he understood if I couldn't trust him anymore, but that he wouldn't give up on our relationship. I forgave him and was touched by his surprise visit, it made me feel special, I guess. I may have accepted his apology but because of the circumstances with Chris and just because I was struggling with my own issues, Joey and I hadn't really hung out more than a few hours since the incident.

"Hey, where you headed?" Bret asked, running into

me on the basement steps.

"Treadmill." I said, faking enthusiasm and sticking out my tongue. Bret smiled back at me and motioned with his arm, allowing me to pass him.

"Hey, are you going to church camp with Marc and me?" Bret asked nervously. I shot him a weird look and shook my head. "I thought your mom or Marc had mentioned it."

"Nope."

"Well, do you want to go with us? It sounds dorky, but it's really a lot of fun."

"No, I think I'll pass." I shrugged with a laugh. "I'm not exactly the church camp type."

"What do you mean?"

"I'm not like you Bret; I'm not the church type, really. I'm not perfect like you are."

"No one ever said you had to be perfect." Bret laughed.

"Yeah, but *you* are. Besides, those people will take one look at me and all my secrets will persecute me."

"I am *far* from perfect, Brit."

"Whatever." I laughed. "Bret, you are super smart and super talented. You don't even have to study or try and you're phenomenal. You don't even have to attend study hall with the rest of us, because you don't need to study or do homework."

"Brittany, I get up at four o'clock every morning and go take care of the horses, whatever my dad needs me to do on the farm that day. I run inside to eat breakfast and shower, then run to school. I bust my ass in class every day and studying every night. I skip out of study hall because I'm either hitting the gym or running for the class period. I give one hundred and ten percent at every single practice or game, and afterwards, or on days off, I'm still practicing. I stay up all hours throwing the football, taking batting practice or shooting free throws and jump shots until my arms and legs feel like they're about to fall off. And then I get up in the morning and do it all over again. So, yeah I do have to try, I'm just extremely dedicated and disciplined. I'm passionate about everything I do."

"Well regardless, I'm not like you. Sure, I go to church but I know nothing about the bible or anything else. I sit in church with all the other people who are just trying to better their resume to get into Heaven and when I'm there, I feel like I'm being judged the entire time by the rest of the congregation. I don't really want to spend a week with a bunch of people who think they're better than me."

"*God* knows you're not perfect, he doesn't expect anyone to be. Who cares what the stuck up parishioners think anyway, everyone who knows you knows how wonderful of a person you are."

"Thanks, but I'm not going to change my mind."

"Fair enough, I just thought I'd try. I really just wanted to be able to spend alone time with you for the week, so I was just being selfish."

"Bret," I began, realizing he was holding my hand and moving closer to me.

"I don't get it Brittany, why are you still with Joey? He kissed another girl, you deserve better than that."

"Do I need to remind you that I've made out with you on at least *two* occasions? I mean, I can't exactly punish him for something I'm guilty of doing too."

"Yeah butI can guarantee that when Joey kissed

Makenzie, he didn't feel the same things we did when we kissed. I can guarantee he wouldn't have felt guilty, had you not caught him. He probably wouldn't have ever told you."

"And *I've* never told him about us."

"Us?"

"How can you judge Joey and Makenzie for what happened, when you're guilty of the same thing, Bret?"

"From the first minute I saw you Brittany, I knew you were the *one*. I should've acted on my feelings a lot sooner. I've had a ton of opportunities and I keep missing them, like an idiot, but fate keeps throwing them my way and I can't keep ignoring them. Brittany, I am in love with you and I know *we're* meant to be together." Bret rambled nervously. His lips were millimeters from mine and my heart was screaming to kiss him and accept everything he was saying. However, my conscience was telling me to run for the hills. There's no possible way he could be serious. We're fifteen years old and he's spouting about fate, *the one* and being in love with me? That's insane. Bret barely knew me, so how could he believe for a second that he was in love with me? All this time I've thought Chris had mental issues, but maybe Bret has us all fooled.

"You *love* me? You're crazy, you don't even know me." I gasped as I started to back down the stairs slowly. Panic was flitting through my stomach as terror gripped my heart. Terror or joy, I'm not sure what is going on, really.

"I know you better than anyone else does and you know it." He defended, obviously hurt and confused by my reaction. He took a step towards me and reached out.

"No, no." I murmured shaking my head quickly. "Get away from me, Bret. Get away from me, leave me alone and don't ever come near me again." I stammered nervously, backing away again and almost falling down the steps.

"Brittany I'm sorry, I didn't mean to scare…"

"No! Stop! Don't talk to me, just get away from me!" I warned as tears streamed down my face. I spun on my heel and tried to go back down the stairs, hoping I could escape from the basement. I couldn't believe what I was hearing, I had to get away to process his words. It was absolutely not possible for a guy like Bret McHalley to have any interest in someone like me. He was way out of my league, he could not truly have feelings for me unless there was more to this than what I was seeing.

"Wait, wait!" I yelled as I flipped back around and stomped towards him. Bret turned around and smiled excitedly at me, thinking his lies had worked.

"You are an asshole Bret McHalley! I can't believe I fell for your bullshit. You know about my relationship with Aaron, you heard all of Jeremy's lies about me and you know Joey and I are screwing. So let me guess, you thought if you laid it on thick, then I'd fuck you. Right?" Bret didn't respond, he stared at me blankly before he laughed. "Are you kidding me? I thought you were different, I thought you were this amazing guy and instead you're an asshole like the rest of them! I don't ever want to see you again in my life, Bret. Get the Hell out of my house!" I rambled angrily.

"No Brittany, no you have me all wrong. I said all those things because I mean them, because I want you to be my girlfriend." Bret defended himself. The look in his eyes even had me fooled; he looked so sad and hurt.

"I have a boyfriend and it will *never* be you." I stated icily, before I rushed past him and ran out of the house. I sprinted through the front yard and onto the road, I didn't know where I was going, but I knew I had to get as far away from that jerk as possible.

"Brittany stop! Please stop! It's not safe out here! I'll leave, just please come back!" Bret yelled as he chased after me. I dug deep and put more space between us, I knew if I could pull away from him that he wouldn't be able to keep up with me for long. I sprinted until I his voice sounded far away and then I kept going. I raced away until I felt like my legs and lungs were going to collapse. I stopped and bent down to catch my breath. Tears streamed down my face as Bret's words played on repeat. I wanted to believe him, but none of what he said could be true, it just couldn't be.

"Dang it." I spit as I tried to calm my breathing. I stood up and looked around, realizing I was in front of the cemetery where Aaron was buried. I looked around nervously, wondering how I had ended up here. It was over five miles from my house and I hadn't been here since the funeral, I couldn't bring myself to come back. It was almost as if I saw the headstone I would realize that he really wasn't coming back to me.

I began sobbing uncontrollably as I slowly walked through the wrought iron gates. I was so distraught on the day of the funeral that I couldn't quite remember where he had been laid to rest. Every horror movie I ever watched was spinning through my head as I

327

started getting an eerie sensation.

"Aaron, I'm freaking myself out here." I murmured to myself as I looked around at the headstones again. Something moved in the corner of my left eye, when I turned to look the sun was shining down on a large dark granite headstone.

I plopped down onto the ground and sat facing the grave marker, as if it were Aaron sitting in front of me. I buried my face in my hands and began to cry hysterically. This was why I hadn't been here since his funeral, I was avoiding the mental and emotional breakdown. Although, thirty minutes later I composed myself and realized I probably should've done this a lot sooner. I almost felt a little peace filling my heart.

"How could I have been so stupid?" I asked out loud. "How could you have been so wrong about Bret? He's so manipulative that he even had you fooled. Aaron, you've never been wrong about a person's character before, how could we both have fallen for it?" I sobbed.

"And people say *I'm* crazy? At least I don't talk to dead people." I heard Chris Kaplan say behind me. I began to cry harder, knowing without a doubt, that something bad was about to happen. How fitting was it that I would probably die right here at my best friend's grave?

No one knew where I was and if Bret explained we had a fight, they wouldn't begin to worry about me for another -hours. I contemplated running away, but I knew running would do me no good.

Chris wanted me and he would not stop until he got me. I felt my heart shatter for the things I didn't get to say or do. I braced myself for the blows; for however he was going to end my life right now.

Chapter 51

"It's time, Brittany. It's time for us to be together." Chris said, taking my hand as he squatted down beside me and whispered in my ear. "But first, you have to meet Heath."

"Chris, I need to get back home. I've been gone too long and the boys will be out looking for me. I was supposed to be at home for a phone call with Michael and if I miss that, they'll know something is wrong." I stammered.

"No they won't." He chuckled. "Joey called twenty minutes after you left and said you showed up on his doorstep, distraught because of an argument with Bret. He promised to have you home by curfew though and by then, we'll be long gone." He smiled proudly and I began to cry harder. "It's even better that Michael will be so pissed when he realizes you chose *Joey* over him." Chris just laughed wickedly as he stood up, grabbed my arm and yanked me off the ground.

"C'mon baby, Heath's been waiting so long to meet you. I'm so excited that I can throw you in his face. He's never believed that we're in love."

Chris grasped my hand tightly and led me to a mausoleum, a vault that was marked KAPLAN. Bret had been right, the brother that Chris always talked about was dead and I was about to be introduced to him. He looked around worriedly before he opened the door and led me inside. There were five spots total in the vault, two glass caskets rested against one side. The first casket looked as if it held a very small child dressed in blue clothing, but Chris didn't stop there and went to the decaying body of who I could only guess to be his brother, Heath. I closed my eyes, tears flowing freely as I prayed and prayed this nightmare would be over soon.

"Here she is Heath. This is Brittany, she's beautiful, isn't she?" He asked his dead brother. "I told you I wasn't making her up." Chris laughed as he pushed me forward. "Don't be a snob sweetie, say hi to Heath." I closed my eyes tighter, not wanting to look, ever. "Apparently she's shy." He chuckled as he shook his head in disbelief. He leaned down and kissed me on the cheek softly.

"Now Brittany, stay right here and bond with Heath. I need to go and get the car, okay?" He asked softly.

"Wait, I want to go with you. Please don't leave me here." I begged, my eyes focusing on Chris and nothing else. He shook his head and smiled proudly as his eyes darted to his brother smugly.

"I'll be right back." He grinned before he pushed me back gently and hurried to the door. I screamed after him and tried to follow, but he shoved me back so hard that I flew into the wall. Chris chuckled before he hurriedly slammed the door behind him.

"Oh my God, oh my God." I sobbed as I tried to get my bearings. The second I got to my knees the world started spinning and I puked. As soon as I was done, I focused on calming my breathing before I stood up the rest of the way. I went to the door and pulled, but it was sealed tight. I searched myself for my phone, but I knew I had left it in my room to charge. I had no way to call for help and I had no way to be tracked.

I kicked the door, I ran into it like an idiot, I pulled with everything I had but it wasn't budging no matter how hard I tried and prayed for it to move. I fell down into the floor and cowered in the corner of the crypt, sobbing and praying this was a horrific nightmare. No one would be looking for me anytime soon, no one would probably even care that I was at Joey's or that I was late for curfew. Chris could never come back and I would never be found, I would be left to starve to death in a crypt with two other dead people.

Chapter 52

Bret

"I screwed up Marc." I announced in exasperation as I fell down on his desk chair and buried my face in my hands. "I royally screwed up."

"What happened now?" He asked as he looked up from the book he was reading. He set the novel down on his bed and shook his head, already knowing it had to do with Brittany.

"I told her how I felt and, of course, she freaked out."

"What do you mean by *you told her how you felt*?" He asked with a raised eyebrow. I couldn't say it to my best friend out loud, he knew my feelings for his soon to be sister. Marc had known before we had even officially met Brittany, how I felt about her. "Oh shit." I nodded my head and scrubbed at my face.

"She told me I was crazy and sprinted out of the house. I chased after her, but I couldn't keep up."

"She'll be back." Marc said sympathetically. "Running clears her head, so I'm sure that she's already sorted her feelings out and is on her way back to talk to you."

"What was I thinking?"

"You did the right thing." Marc assured me with a roll of his shoulders. "I wish I had half your balls to tell a girl I liked her. Had you told her this a long time ago though, she would've never had to deal with Font and Kaplan's bs." I nodded my head, Marc already knew I was constantly beating myself up for those things. Had I come clean to Brittany the second she and Michael were apart, then she would've never went on a date with Chris Kaplan and she would never have had to endure the stalking, the fear and anxiety he's caused her.

"It doesn't feel like the right thing. I'm pretty sure I just ruined our friendship and any chance I may have *ever* had with her." Marc shook his head as he stood up.

"I don't know a lot about girls, but I'm pretty certain she has a thing for you." He nodded towards the door for me to follow. I pushed myself off the chair. "I'm starving. Let's get something to eat and she'll probably be back by then."

"I should leave. It's just going to be super awkward when she gets back."

"You're not leaving. No one is even home at your house." Marc chuckled as he shook his head and started down the stairs.

"What's up?" Drake asked as he nodded at Marc and me from the fridge.

"You seen Brittany?" Marc asked. Drake shook his head and rolled his shoulders as he pulled a meat loaf out and set it on the counter.

"No, isn't she in her room?" Marc shook his head. "You guys hungry? I'm starving and mom called to say they wouldn't be home until later so we're on our own for lunch."

"Why would we be in the kitchen if we weren't hungry?" Marc laughed as he pulled out a barstool and bellied up to the island. I followed suit and watched as Drake went to the oven and looked at it for a minute.

"How do I turn this thing on?" He asked as he looked back at us sideways. I laughed and Marc crossed over to the stove as he shook his head.

"It's not that hard. How can you not know how to use a stove?"

"Um, my mom or the girls always handle things in the kitchen." He said with a shrug. Marc put the oven on preheat.

"Go sit down, I can do this." Marc laughed. Drake nodded and crossed over to the refrigerator. As he opened the door, the house phone rang.

"Hello?" He asked into the receiver as he grabbed the cordless off the counter.

"Oh hey Joey, what's up?" Marc looked back at me with a questioning look and I shook my head, a knot forming in the pit of my stomach. "Brittany's there? She ran to your house? Okay, my parents aren't home so they'll call her if she needs to be home sooner." He listened intently and nodded his head. "I can't believe she forgot her phone, that thing is normally attached to her." He laughed. "Okay, see you later." Drake hung up and spun on his heel to look at me.

"What did you and Britty get in a fight about?" Drake asked accusingly. I shook my head and looked down at the countertop.

"He told her he liked her." Marc interjected. I looked up and shot my friend a dirty look, I was about to answer.

"Everyone already knows that." Drake chuckled. "What's the big deal?"

"It freaked her out." I said sadly. "I should've thought it out a little better. I know she's terrified of the word, because so many people that have said it to her, have left her."

"I've heard Joey say it to her." Marc said flatly.

"She doesn't love him though." I said quickly.

"Then why is she with him?"

"I don't know, because he's safe maybe? I'm still trying to figure that out." I said as I messed with a napkin on the counter. The oven beeped signaling it was ready to do some work. Marc jumped up and put the meatloaf inside.

"Why did Joey call on the house phone, doesn't he have your phone number?"

"Yeah, he does." Drake said as he rolled his shoulders. "He sounded weird too." He looked around thoughtfully before he jumped up to look at the phone's caller id. He pulled his cell phone out and scrolled through the contact info. "That's not his phone number."

"Maybe it's his parent's house phone?" Marc asked as

338

his eyes darted to mine.

"Do you have Kaplan's number in your address book?" I asked as I stood up. Drake nodded and looked for the number.

"Shit." He muttered as he realized the number matched. "I don't…" He called the number back and it went directly to voicemail.

"Does that mean she's with Kaplan?" Marc asked worriedly as we all stood around looking at the cordless phone as if it were an alien.

"He's not home, though." Drake said in disbelief. "He's supposed to be in Georgia."

"You should call your parents." I said slowly. My mind was racing as I thought of all the horrible ways this could end. Chris Kaplan had severe mental issues and there was no telling what he would do to Brittany. And it was all my fault.

Chapter 53

Brittany

It seemed like hours later when Chris finally returned with a grin plastered on his face.

"I hope you were nice to her Heath." Chris said as he shot a look at his brother. "She'll be meeting mom and dad soon, too. She's definitely a keeper." Chills ran down my spine as he crossed over to me and held a hand out. "I'll tell mom you'll be home in a bit, okay?" Chris asked his brother. He nodded his head as if there were a response. I have never been more terrified in my life by everything I was taking in, I could only continue to pray I would wake up soon.

Chris took me by the arm and led me outside to a black vehicle that sat in front of the tomb, the familiar license plates read; *HTHK*. The scenes from the car accident with Joey flashed through my head quickly.

"It *was* you." I gasped, realizing now that he had no problem taking my life.

"You're pretty sharp." He laughed as he tied my hands together with a thick nylon rope. No matter how hard I tried to fight him, his grip only tightened and made the rope bite into my flesh. "It's a good thing I never told Heath you were a genius, you would've just made me a liar." He popped the trunk, put a burlap bag over my head, threw me in the back and slammed the trunk shut with me in it. Seconds later, he started the car and I could feel us peel out of the cemetery.

Anxiety clawed to pull me under and I fought with all I could to stay sane, hoping in some way I could tell where we were going. The vehicle was fishtailing all over the road which meant he was flying, but I couldn't tell which direction we were going at all.

I couldn't see, I could barely breathe and I only wanted to cry and pray someone would save me. That was unlikely, however, and that reality was scarier than the situation. I will never see my family or friends again. Bret will always think this is his fault and that I think he's absolutely crazy and I will never be able to tell him any differently.

The more I thought about Bret, a memory popped into my head. We were watching a WWE movie a few weeks ago where a girl was abducted and thrown in the trunk. Apparently, there is a trunk release in all the newer vehicles for just this reason. I felt around in the dark and prayed that I would be so lucky. After what seemed like hours, I finally felt something and yanked, when I moved my legs I realized that I had indeed opened the trunk.

I sat up but Chris was swerving so bad that I continued to fall down. I was upright again when he slammed on the brakes and caused me to fly back against the trunk lid. I had never felt so much pain in my life.

"What the fuck are you doing Brittany?" He screamed frantically as he yanked me out of the trunk and threw me in the backseat of the car this time. "You could've gotten yourself killed."

"It would be better than this." I murmured. He was in the front seat and tearing down the road again before I could sit up and get my bearings.

More than once he cursed other drivers, swerving or slamming on the brakes making me think we almost crashed, but he didn't seem concerned. I kept my eyes closed most of the time, praying for the Lord to spare my life and to help my family find me before it was too late. We finally spun to a stop. Chris jumped out before I could move, threw the door open and yanked me out.

"Have you ever traveled the country Brittany?" He asked sweetly. I shook my head. "Well, today is your lucky day. We're about to do some traveling. I need you to behave though." He bent back into the car and pulled out a small bag, he unzipped it and pulled out a vial of clear liquid and a syringe.

"What is that?" I gasped.

"Just a little something to calm you down." He grinned. "Do you have any idea how easy it is to break into a veterinary hospital? You would think they'd keep these things locked up better. Of course, just wearing a set of scrubs into a hospital is a pretty simple way to get some good drugs too, but they didn't work on you last time." Chris laughed and shook his head as he filled the syringe with the liquid. He grabbed in between the rope and tugged me towards him, no matter how hard I fought, he was stronger. I screamed as I felt the needle go into my arm. "Sssshhhh." He hummed as things immediately got fuzzy. Within a few minutes, he was untying my arms, sliding me in the front seat and buckling me in. He put his head near mine and pulled out his phone. "I think it's time to tell the rest of the world that we're a couple, don't you?" He snapped a picture, looked back at it proudly before he pulled away, still messing with his phone. Finally, he started the car again and pulled out.

I couldn't focus on anything. I couldn't talk, my entire body was numb as the medicine did its job. I could only stare at the door handle, my hand wouldn't move towards it. Chris drove us out of town, obeying the speed limit signs now. I couldn't tell you how many signs I saw before we pulled into the city and he headed for the airport.

"Act right baby or they won't let us fly together." He said in a soothing voice. He pulled into the long term parking lot, pulled the car into a spot and turned the engine off. He got out, grabbed a few bags out of the backseat before he crossed to the passenger side of the car and helped me out. A bus pulled up beside us and Chris helped me board. People were barely looking at us, but it didn't matter because I couldn't even make a face to ask for help.

There were no questions as he took us through security, got our boarding passes and led me onto a plane. I thought security was supposed to be tight nowadays, but I wasn't seeing it. Seriously, no one thought it was strange that a nineteen year old was toting around a catatonic fifteen year old?

He gently shoved me into an aisle, putting me next to the window before he climbed in behind me. He sat down in the seat and grinned back at me.

"First class." He said proudly. "Only the best for my girl." We were the last of the passengers to board and the flight attendants were busy going through their spiel about safety and turning off cell phones. I watched as Chris quickly updated his Facebook and Twitter account statuses with *leaving on a jet plane.* He took another picture of the two of us, added it to the words and shut off his phone. The flight attendants started making their way down the aisles, asking if people needed anything. When the red head got to us, I could only pray she saw the weirdness of the situation.

"Do you kids need anything?" She asked with a sweet smile.

"Could we have some water and some pillows?" Chris replied, matching her smile. She nodded.

"Anything else?" She asked, her eyes darting to me worriedly. "Is your friend okay? She looks like she's intoxicated and…"

"She had to take some anti-anxiety meds." He answered sadly. "She lives with her mom here in Tennessee and just learned that her brother was murdered in Cali, where he lives with his father. She's pretty distraught, the doctors thought it was best to give her something for the grief. She has anxiety issues anyway, so they had to give her a pretty high dose."

"Where's the rest of her family?"

"They will be leaving later this afternoon." He said. "It's such a shame, really. They were very close." Chris slid his arm around my shoulders and pulled me close to him. The flight attendant nodded sympathetically and hurried away to get the things we had requested.

I closed my eyes as the plane took off and succumbed to the sleep that was desperately trying to tug me under. Maybe I'd wake up in a completely different situation.

Chapter 54

Bret

"Call Joey." I said quickly as panic started to rush throughout me. "Maybe she really is there." I took a deep breath and tried to ignore the heavy feeling in my heart and stomach. The house phone rang and Drake stared at it for a second before he answered it, immediately hitting the speakerphone button.

"Hello?" He said cautiously.

"Is Brittany okay?" Michael asked quickly on the other end.

"What do you mean? Have you heard something?"

"No, what do you mean by that?"

"Michael, tell us what you know." I instructed in a tight voice. "Please."

"I told her I'd call her at three, I've been calling for the last hour but she hasn't answered. She's ignoring my texts. Something has to be wrong for her to ignore me."

"She's with Joey." Drake said flatly, immediately flinching at his words.

"What?" Michael gasped. "She stood me up for Joey?"

"No. At least, I don't think so. Something is wrong, we'll call you back when we know something more." Marc explained quickly. "We have to keep the house phone open."

Drake hung up despite Michael's arguments and then stared back at it helplessly. "She wouldn't miss a call from Michael." He said to no one in particular.

"Where does she keep her phone?" Marc asked as he started up the stairs. "Maybe I'll find something on it."

"It's usually on her bedside table." Drake said. Marc hurried up the stairs and came back a minute later holding the phone up. Drake messed with the house phone for a few minutes before he put it to his ear.

"It just went to Kaplan's voicemail." He said flatly. "I called the number back and it went to Kaplan's voicemail.

"Look at this." Marc said in disbelief as he held up Brittany's phone. There was a selfie of her and Chris together.

"Those are the clothes she had on today." I said quickly.

"She had an alert on her phone saying Chris tagged her in a status update. It says they're in a relationship." Marc said in a soft voice.

"What?" I asked in disbelief as I stared back at the picture. I could only see terror in Brittany's normally bright blue eyes.

"Call your mom now." Marc said to Drake. I started pacing in the kitchen, scrubbing my face with my hands so I could clear my head and figure out what we needed to do next.

"I'm calling Joey first…we can't jump to conclusions." I looked back at Drake in shock as he picked up his cell phone and called Joey.

"Is Brittany with you?" He asked without greeting his friend. "Did you or did you not call the house about twenty minutes ago telling me that she showed up at your doorstep upset because she'd gotten into a fight with Bret?" Drake's face grew pale as he shook his head and swallowed hard. "That's all I needed to know." He hung up quickly, dialed another number. "Brittany is missing." He said quickly, before he went into everything that happened within the last half an hour. When he hung up, he looked back at Marc and me bleakly. "Mom's on her way. We're going to Kaplan's." He leaned over to the wall, grabbed his keys and strode out the door and to the driveway with us on his heels. He called Lindsay, told her to get home immediately just before we tore out of the driveway and down the road.

"What if she's not there?" Marc asked meekly from the front seat. Drake didn't answer, his jaw tightening as he pushed the accelerator a little harder. Five minutes later, he whipped into the Kaplan's driveway and barely put it in park before he jumped out of the car and raced to the door. He began pounding and yelling for someone to answer.

"They're not home son." An older man said as he came around the fence row. "They haven't been for a week."

"Do you know where they went?"

"No, I don't." He said with a raised eyebrow. "I'm assuming something happened with that boy, they tore out of here in the middle of the night. I heard fighting a few hours before, but that's not all that unusual." He explained slowly before he rolled his shoulders and turned back around. "You'd be smart if you stayed away from that boy, he's not all there."

"We think he kidnapped my sister." Drake said in a pain filled voice. "Have you seen a girl here?"

"No, but I'd start praying if that's true. He killed both his brothers."

"What?" I asked in disbelief.

"He only had one brother and he died in a car accident." Drake commented with a shake of his head. The man rolled his shoulders as he looked us each over very carefully, just as someone came out of the house.

"Hello Mr. Fletcher." Chris said in an overly polite voice. "Good to see you recovered from your fall so quickly." Chris laughed evilly as the old man turned around and hurried inside his house.

"Where in the Hell is Brittany?" Drake cried as he lunged at Chris and pinned him into a black car.

"At home?" He asked with a weird smile on his face.

"That's bull shit and you know it. You called

and pretended to be Joey and then you put that you're in a relationship on your social pages."

"We *are* in a relationship, we just made it official. Joey was pretty upset about it, maybe you should check in with him and stop wasting your time with me."

"Brittany wouldn't give you the time of day." I said icily.

"You're just jealous I won her over, even after you poured your heart out to her." He chuckled as he effortlessly pushed Drake off him. "Now, if you don't mind I have to meet my parents for dinner."

"You won't mind if we take a look through your house, right? I mean, if Brittany's not here than it won't be a problem, right?" Marc challenged. Chris's face turned dark as he glared at the three of us.

"Do not go near my house. I'll call and have you arrested for trespassing."

"Why don't I just call and have the police search your house, instead of us?"

"They'll laugh in your face and then probably

arrest you guys for the constant harassment you put me through."
Marc whipped out his phone and dialed. Chris shook his head. "I'm
out, I'm not dealing with your stupidity." I made a grab for him, but
he was in the car before I could. Drake got in front of the car, but
Chris just laughed as he floored it.

"Fuck!!" Drake screamed as he raced to get out
of the way, he got hit in the process.

"I need an ambulance and officers to 3813 Chestnut." Marc
advised calmly into the phone as I raced to Drake. "My brother was
just hit by a car in front of this house, the driver took off." Marc hung
up the phone and looked back at the scene before us. Drake's leg was
sitting at an awkward angle and he was screaming in agony.
Everyone was looking out of their curtains, but no one came out to
help us.

Chapter 55

Brittany

I don't know where I am, other than on a plane. I looked over at Chris, who was reading a magazine and smiling smugly. My neck wouldn't move, no part of my body would move. I was paralyzed from the drugs Chris was continuously shooting me up with.

We had changed planes seven different times. Never stopping too long, never allowing anyone to talk to us for more than a few minutes. I still don't know how Chris was getting away with tugging along someone who was obviously drugged, but none of the security guards were looking at us suspiciously.

"What did you think of Cali, baby? Maybe next time we'll be able to spend a little time at the beach. I would love to see you in an itty bitty bikini." He said, his eyes roving me lasciviously. I closed my eyes and pretended I was elsewhere. Chris kept talking.

"This jet lag is getting to me, four days of plane rides will wear anyone out." My eyes popped open. Four days? I'd been gone for four days?

"We'll be landing soon. I've got a hotel lined up for us. You'll love it, only the best for my girlfriend. I got us the honeymoon suite." Bile rose up in my throat and there was nothing I could do to stop it, but my body did before I made a mess and drew attention to us.

We landed sometime later, Chris helped me off the plane and out of the airport. He put us on another bus that took us to the rental cars, where he had one already reserved. Within twenty minutes, I was tucked away in a Dodge Charger and we were speeding through the city, as if Chris had been here a million times.

"Welcome to Arkansas." He grinned. "It's not spectacular, but no one will expect us to be here either." He turned the radio up to some pop station and sang along. It didn't take long before we pulled into a hotel. Chris left me in the car as he ran inside quickly. No matter how much I focused, I couldn't get any body parts to move so I could run. I sat there too drugged to save myself. All I could do was cry.

Chris jumped back in the car, drove to a parking spot and got out. He came over to help me out of the car and led me into a side

355

door, took me to the elevator and pushed a button for the third floor. The elevator began moving and Chris slid his arm back around my waist and pulled me tight into him.

"You're about to experience Heaven." He breathed in my ear. "Joey could never satisfy you, but I will." My body involuntarily shivered in fear, but Chris didn't notice. "The best part is, your dad is funding it." My eyes darted to him questioningly, just as the elevator door opened and he walked me out. He looked at the signs on the wall, then turned to the left. My body wasn't cooperating though, it continued to go limp and Chris was getting extremely irritated. He finally picked me up, carried me to the room, slid the card in the door and pushed through. He threw me on the bed as soon as he was close enough to it, he missed though and I landed with a thud in the floor.

"Jesus Brittany, can't you do anything right? No wonder your dad is paying me to take you off his hands." He picked me up off the floor and then dropped me back down. He pulled the comforter and sheets back and then stood me up and set me on the bed. He tugged my shirt over my head, removed my bra, pushed me back on the bed and pulled the rest of my clothing off. "I'll be back."

He mumbled as he grabbed the key card off the nightstand and stormed outside.

If I could just move enough to kick or hit the wall, I could annoy someone enough that they'd come to the room. If I could find my voice, open my mouth and scream, then someone would be at the door quickly. I tried with every inch of my being to do any of those things, but no part of me would move. Tears rolled down my cheeks, but I couldn't move anything.

When Chris returned a few minutes later with the luggage I was still lying in the same spot, staring up at the ceiling and praying for a freak accident that would cause my immediate death. I couldn't see him, but when I heard his pants unzip I knew I was in Hell and things were about to get worse.

Chapter 56

"Yes sir, yes sir, she's definitely enjoying herself." Chris said with a cocky laugh into the phone. "I appreciate everything you've done to get us together. I'll take great care of your daughter." He made a few more noises and then said goodbye. I felt like we'd been in this room forever, but it could've been because Chris was doing whatever he wanted to me, whenever he wanted to. Time was dragging on as I focused on everything but what was happening to me.

"Your dad says hi and you're welcome for bringing us together." Chris grinned as he looked back at me. "Our house is almost ready. I know, I was pretty shocked when he offered to buy us a house to live in, but he said he was tired of dealing with you. He's paying me very well to keep you occupied and out of his hair."

Chris stood up and went over to where his clothes were strewn everywhere. He started picking up his things, stuffing them in the duffel bags he had brought in with him. Once everything was picked up he looked around the room to see if he had missed something. His eyes landed on me, roved up and down my body before he grinned and crossed back over to the bed.

"We should really have one more for the road, it's a long drive back." He said in a soft, soothing voice as he grabbed my hair and pulled me to the edge of the bed. He put his hand on his hard cock, opened my mouth with it and stuck it inside. I lay there gagging and drooling as he continued to move my head up and down until he came all over my face. He chuckled as he cleaned me up, kissed me and then flipped me over on my stomach. He entered me again and as much as it hurt, I couldn't even scream out loud.

When he finished, he picked me up and dropped me into the ceramic bathtub and turned on the ice cold water. He grabbed a washcloth, some soap and scrubbed me roughly before he washed my hair. He finished, grabbed a towel and dried me off. He pulled a comb through my hair, yanking and tugging through the many tangles that had formed. My head was pounding by the time he carried me back into the bedroom and dropped me on the bed again.

He dressed me, grabbed a baseball cap and tucked my hair under it. He left me on the bed as he grabbed all the luggage and left the room. He hadn't drugged me all day, but I was still drowsy and lethargic from the remnants of the medicine. I pitched myself off the end of the bed before rolling to the door. Chris had left it cracked and somehow I was able to open it and crawl out the door. I heard the elevator open and prayed it was someone who could help me.

"What the Hell are you doing?" Chris growled as he raced towards me. He grabbed me up by my hair and drug me back into the bedroom. He picked me up and punched me in the stomach, then in the face before he threw me back on the bed. "What is wrong with you Brittany? Someone could have seen you." He fell down onto the foot of the bed and buried his face in his hands. "Don't you understand Brittany? Can't you see? I'm protecting you, I'm saving your life. Your dad wants you gone. Your family wants you dead. They're tired of the bitch you've become, they paid me to dispose of you. I couldn't do it though, I love you too much to lose you forever so I offered to leave the state, to take you with me. We're going to make our home together baby, you'll be safe. That's all I want, is you safe with me baby." Chris rambled in a broken voice. He continued to mumble about my father paying him off and Mr. Curren helping with the escape plan.

He picked me up and carried me out of the room. No one passed us, no one else was in the elevator and there was no hope for me to be able to grab someone in a last desperate attempt for help.

He put me in the front seat as soon as we got to the car, buckled me up and then closed the door behind him. I could feel blood trickling down my face from where he'd hit me earlier, but he didn't seem bothered by it. He grabbed the medical bag from under the front seat, filled another syringe and inserted it into my vein expertly.

"I don't like drugging you Brittany, but if you won't behave I have no other choice." He sighed as he reached over and kissed my cheek sweetly. The medicine pulled me back under and I slumped down, just as Chris pulled out of the hotel parking lot.

Chapter 57

"Home sweet home." Chris said happily, as he tugged me awake. I squinted, as my eyes tried to adjust to the glare of the sun. "This is so exciting Brittany, our first place together, it's going to be like we're married. Which we will be soon, it won't be long before your dad signs the papers and we can find a preacher to marry us. We'll be together forever." He gave me a quick hug and put me in a tight arm lock as he drug me up the steps and through the front door of an old wood cabin, effectively keeping me from looking around at my surroundings. Once we were inside a horrible stench smacked me in my face.

"Brittany, these are my parents Phyllis and Charles Kaplan. Mom, dad, this is Brittany, the girl I've been telling you about." He announced proudly to the two bodies that sat on the couch, slowly rotting. Vomit shot up and out of me before I could stop it. "Gross. There's no reason to be so nervous, they already love you." He said as he looked down at me sincerely. "I'll get you something to clean this up. Hey mom, Heath said he'll be home in a bit, he had some things to do in town." I stared in horror at the bodies on the couch, at the multiple holes in their chests. I looked around the room desperately trying to find a quick exit. There were guns littered throughout the cabin; rifles, shotguns, handguns…I didn't know what their technical names were, I just knew I was dead.

"Here you go honey." He said cheerfully as he handed me a mop and bucket of water. "Hurry and clean up, we've got to get you settled in before dinner. Mom's making her famous Chicken Tetrazzini tonight." I was surprised to feel myself move, it felt like I was moving through thick sand though. Chris stood over me, looking around the room cheerfully and chattering away with his parents, who weren't responding.

I finished mopping up my own vomit and fought the urge to just keep puking. Chris took the cleaning supplies from me, put them against the wall, grabbed my hand and tugged me into a nearby bedroom.

"I don't care what you say mom!" Chris yelled over his shoulder. "I told you she'll be sleeping in my room with me and that's final!" A shiver ran down my spine at the amount of venom in his voice.

The inside of the cabin was surprisingly clean and decorated as though someone had been living there. Immediately, I realized this is where Chris had been hiding. That's why his parents didn't believe he was home, technically he wasn't. I'm guessing when they found out, it sealed their fates. Chris beamed back at me as he proudly produced a single red rose.

"I thought of everything for you Brittany. That's why you fell in love with me, isn't it?" He asked.

"I don't love you, Chris." I announced sharply, my voice rough and gravelly from not being used for so many days. He looked back at me angrily.

"You know that's not true. There's no reason to pretend here, it's just us."

"I don't love you. You need help, you are seriously diluted. Your brother is dead and you think he's still alive, that's not right. Your parents are dead. You killed them." I rambled angrily.

"Why would you say that? He's not dead, you met him and you talked to him. My parents are right in the living room, alive and well. Seriously Brittany, maybe you're the one who needs help." He shot coldly, before he walked out of the room quickly, slamming the door behind him.

I seized the opportunity, I opened the door, sprinted out of the house, and made a beeline for the car. I flung open the door and dove inside. I locked both of the doors behind me and then began to frantically search for the keys, knowing I had watched him drop them in the floorboard. Chris tapped on the window, chuckling as he dangled the keys in the air. I buried my head in the steering wheel and cried.

"Now why would you do that Brittany?" Chris asked, yanking me out of the car. I raised my leg and nailed him in the balls as hard as I could. He dropped to his knees with a yell and I sprinted into the woods as fast as my legs would carry me.

"Brittany!!" He screamed shrilly after me. I wouldn't stop, I wasn't turning around and I sure as heck wasn't slowing down either. I have no clue where I'm at or where I'm going but anything is better than the fate before me. "Brittany!" He continued to yell. "Don't make me do this!" I heard a loud boom and dropped to the ground, knowing he was shooting at me.

"Oh my God." I sobbed. "Brittany, get your shit together." I scolded myself as I turned my head to see where he was. He'd shot in the air because he couldn't see me. I had screamed, though and alerted him to my general whereabouts. So I crawled

behind a huge tree, caught my breath and stood up to run again. I was

making an excellent getaway when my foot hit a root, my ankle gave

way and I fell flat on my face. I screamed again out of stupid habit

and I could hear Chris chuckle somewhere behind me.

Chapter 58

Searing pain shot through my body and I almost passed out when I forced myself off the ground. I looked down and saw bone protruding.

"Brittany!" Chris yelled again. I glanced over my shoulder knowing the pain in my leg was nothing compared to what I would face if I didn't get away from Chris Kaplan. I gritted my teeth and took a step; my body wilted, but I started moving with strength I didn't know I had. He screamed my name again and this time I fell to the ground as I heard two bullets whip by my head.

"What is wrong with you?" Chris growled as he found me face down in the mud and debris. He yanked me off the ground and looked into my face angrily. "I don't know why you think I'm not good enough for you. Honestly, if you would just get off your high horse and realize we're meant to be together, things will be a lot easier for you. But now, now you have to be punished, Brittany." He grabbed me by the hair again and dragged me behind him. When I passed out from the pain, he didn't even notice or care.

Chris jerked me up by my shirt and pulled me up the wooden

steps to the cabin and then throughout the house until we were at his bedroom. He pulled up a piece of the wooden flooring in the corner and started down a set of steps, still dragging me behind him.

"This used to be part of the Underground Railroad, it was one of the places they hid the slaves. A lot of people say this place is haunted, I guess you'll find out first hand, won't you?" He laughed wickedly.

"Chris please, I won't run away again. I promise, I'll be good. I'm sorry. My leg, I think it's broke." I lied quickly, pleading for him not to lock me away in the dungeon.

"Knock it off!" He screamed, slapping me away from him. I flew against the wall and watched as he came back at me. Chris grabbed me off the ground, ripped off all my clothes and kissed me roughly. "Nobody else wants you anymore Brittany, you're tainted and you always will be. I'm just trying to make your life better. Why can't you see that?" He asked sadly as he kissed me again. "I love you and I will always love you. Joey Hawkins just used you for sex and *you* are too stupid to see that." He shook his head disgustedly as he pushed me away again, grabbed my clothes off the door and bound up the steps out of the room, slamming the door down on me.

What in the heck was I supposed to do now?

I wallowed in self-pity and desperation for a while. I tried to focus on anything but the searing pain in my leg and the constant nausea wafting through me. As my eyes adjusted to the darkness I looked around the tiny room, familiarizing myself with everything in it. There were no windows, no means of escape other than the hidden doorway. I crawled up the steps and tried to bang my way through the old, rotting wood.

"You dumb bitch!" I heard Chris laugh from the other side, "There's no way you're getting out of there on your own. The sooner you learn that, the better off we'll both be!"

I fell back onto the stairs, completely defeated. I was naked and extremely vulnerable, but most of all, I was devastated. Ironically, my life was going to end in the cellar that had originally been built to help slaves start a new, free life.

Panic was welling up inside me and, out of habit, I felt my neck, grasping for the friendship necklace Aaron had given me before he died. Anytime I felt helpless and lost I reached for the pendant, hoping to get some sort of serenity. It was gone, I searched

369

frantically for the silver necklace but it was nowhere to be found. I finally let the panic take over as I buried my face in my arms and sobbed. I would die down here, Chris would probably never realize I was dead either.

Chapter 59

"Hey babe?" A voice called down the hole. I was in and out of consciousness. "It's dinner time." I moaned groggily as Chris came down the steps. He picked me up, carried me up the stairs and threw me on to his bed. "You are filthy; you can't go to dinner with my parents like this." He clucked his tongue and looked around the room carefully. "We can skip dinner though. I would be crazy to choose dinner over a naked girl in my bed." I closed my eyes and fought the urge to vomit again; I rolled over and tried to get up. "Don't get up baby. I'll come to you."

"I need…I need to go to the bathroom." I said breathlessly as I stood up and clamped down on my lip in an effort to redirect the pain.

"You're not leaving this room." He said flatly.

"I have to…"

"I don't care. You're not leaving this room, you'll try to run again."

"No, I won't." I stammered. Chris looked around the room, then he hurried out of it and came back with the mop bucket I had used earlier.

"Here you go."

"I...I can't."

"It's this or nothing, Brittany." He said angrily as he rolled his eyes.

I fell in the bucket three times before I was able to get my business done. Chris cleaned me roughly before he threw me back on the bed. He started undoing his belt, took off all of his clothes and climbed onto the bed as he grinned down at me. He used his belt to tie my hands to the bedframe, just as he bent down to kiss me roughly.

"No, no."I hissed through my gritted teeth as he laughed and climbed on top of me.

"I know you're not a virgin, I'll just pretend you are." He said nonchalantly as he grabbed my thighs before I could kick him and slid his knee in between my legs. I was begging and pleading, screaming for help as he climbed on top of me, put himself inside me and raped me again.

After that, Chris would come downstairs from time to time

with food and water, sometimes he would violate me and others he would try and get me to tell him that I loved him. If he was able to rape me, then he would reward me but otherwise my punishment was starvation, a physical beating or he'd flip me over and take me from behind, being rougher than usual.

I don't know how many days I've been here. I don't know how many times he'd come down and pulled me out of the cellar, only to put me back down there again just as quickly. I was weak and delusional, my broken ankle was infected. I wasn't a genius, but I knew that without a doubt.

I contemplated lying and giving in to him, but I feared it would only endanger me more. It's possible he would believe me and let me go, or at least allow me to see the sun. I couldn't take that chance though, if he caught me in a lie I feared his anger would outweigh any conscience I could ever imagine he would have for me.

"I'm going to die here." I sobbed softly. "I don't want to die like this." I felt a coolness to the air and peace filled me quickly. I closed my eyes and inhaled. "Please, please get me out of here." There wasn't a response, I knew there wouldn't be. "Aaron, if you're here looking out for me like you promised you would…it's okay to leave me. It's okay to leave me, because I can't bear for you to watch this. Please, please go get help. I don't know how you're going to do it, just please get me help." I cried even harder when the feeling of peace left me alone in the darkness.

Chapter 60

Bret

"How in the Hell could you let this happen?" Mason's accusations were on repeat in my head and had been for the last few months. As soon as the Rhodes' family learned Brittany was missing, they returned to Stitlin. They were staying at a hotel, no matter how often Mrs. Hoffman told them it wasn't necessary. "I thought you would protect her, I'm never wrong. How in the Hell could you let Chris Kaplan anywhere near her?"

"McHalley!!" Coach Seffenson screamed at me from the sidelines. "Get your head on the field." Football two a days had started, but I was a robot. I couldn't focus, I was just going through the motions and begging God to give me a do over for that day.

For the first two weeks after Brittany had disappeared, Chris had been posting status updates, selfies with Brittany and check ins at various spots throughout the country. Mr. Hoffman had gotten a notification that various credit cards were being used randomly throughout different states as well, he cancelled them all and it was

375

the last time we knew Brittany's exact whereabouts. The police had thought when Chris tried to use one of the cards again they would catch him, it hadn't happened yet.

"Bret." Justin said as he came up behind me. "It feels good to pretend the guy coming at you is Kaplan. Just saying." I shook my head and tried to focus. Justin's words didn't help and I was grateful when practice was finally over.

"You guys headed out to look again?" Jeremy Font asked as he hurried after Marc and me. I nodded my head.

"Haven't you been all over the county?"

"Yeah, so?" I asked angrily as I spun on my heel and got in his face. Jeremy immediately took a step back and put his hands up in surrender.

"I'm just asking." Marc put his hand on my shoulder and shook his head.

"They've had people searching in the four surrounding counties because Chris's car has been seen in those places."

"Chris's parents had a cabin somewhere…did they check there?" Jeremy asked thoughtfully. My eyes grew wide.

"Where?"

"I don't know. I've been there a few times but we were drinking." He said as he rolled his shoulders and shook his head. "I figured the police already knew about it since his dad is Sherriff."

"You need to call it in to the tip line." I demanded quickly as I searched for my phone. "Now." Everyone was looking at me oddly. "Now." I repeated a second time through gritted teeth. Jeremy searched for his phone, found it and dialed the number I recited to him.

"Look at that shit." Justin growled as he came up beside us, nodding to where Joey was talking to Mackenzie Yarden. The girl was all over him, flirting with him and Joey was eating it up. "I'd like to deck both of them."

"Apparently, he's forgotten about his girlfriend going through Hell right now." I hissed. I wanted to flatten Joey right there, but it wouldn't get Brittany back to us. Although, it would feel incredibly amazing to take my frustrations out on him. How could he be flirting with another girl when his girlfriend was missing? He hadn't helped with searches, hadn't put up flyers or even seemed concerned that she was gone. I half thought maybe he was relieved by her disappearance or maybe he and Chris Kaplan had been working together all along.

"They're bringing out the cadaver dogs." Mitchell said as he came down into Marc's basement where we all waited for our next instructions.

"Why?" I asked innocently. Michael shook his head, tears filling his eyes.

"Because they think she's dead."

"But Chris just posted a picture of them together two days ago."

"Doesn't mean it was recent." Matt said drily as he shook his head and stood up quickly.

"She's not dead." I growled.

"I'm not saying she is, they are." Matt spit as he pointed upstairs. "I will never give up hope she is alive somewhere. Sometimes I wonder though, if he's as crazy as we all think, maybe she's better off dead." I lunged at him, but Mason grabbed the back of my shirt and yanked me back.

"Get the fuck out of here Matt."

"I didn't." He started before he shook his head and

bounded up the stairs to the first floor of the house.

The room was absolutely silent and filled with tension. The television was on the local news channel, waiting to hear what their latest update on Brittany was. I had developed a website for people to offer support, prayers and give any tips if they'd seen Chris recently or not. The page had blown up and had reached a national level, we'd gotten some good things from it, but we were no closer to finding Brittany.

Chris's parents were missing as well. Police had searched his house after Chris had ran over Drake. Inside they'd found signs of a struggle and blood, but there weren't any bodies. Chris was nineteen years old, he was bound to screw up somewhere, right? That's what the police were counting on but now that the Kaplan's were missing, people were coming out of the woodwork to talk about how disturbed their only living son was.

Originally, there were three boys in the household. When Chris was four, his mother had another child named Kory. The baby had a series of unfortunate events growing up, so many that the Kaplan's were being watched closely by child protective services. The parents were throwing a huge birthday party for him when he turned two, complete with a magician, bouncy house and pony rides. Five minutes before the cake was to be cut the child fell out of a second story window, chasing a balloon, and died. Only a few people saw Chris in that window, but nothing ever came of it.

Three years ago, Heath Kaplan was a senior at Stitlin High School and blowing up the football field. He'd already been offered a full scholarship to University of Alabama. Heath got into an argument in the high school parking lot with his parents after a football game one night, because Heath wanted to go out with his friends and they wanted him to take Chris with them. He yelled that he didn't want to take his weird little brother anywhere with him…well he did and ended up dying in a car accident that night, while Chris walked away without a scratch. The police believe Heath somehow just lost control of the vehicle.

Neighbors had come forward about run ins with Chris spanning the last sixteen years, the stories all ended with dead animals or pets being left on their porches. Gruesome things being done to the animals. There were threatening messages left in their mailboxes, but no one ever saw anything. No one had ever come forward before.

If all these things were true, it meant Chris was a sociopath. He had killed before and would kill again, the chances of Brittany being alive were slim to none. The odds of her surviving and coming back as the girl we all knew and loved, were nonexistent.

"We should've never left." Mason mumbled quietly as he shook his head sadly. "I wouldn't have let Kaplan near her." Guilt ripped through me. Mason blamed me for Brittany's predicament, it was bad enough I knew it was my fault but the backlash from others was starting to wear on me.

"We would've still been together, so it wouldn't have been an issue." Michael interjected.

"You should've never broken up with her in the first place!" Mason yelled as he shot off the couch, Michael did the same and the two brothers squared off to each other. "You supposedly love her and you dump her? Who the fuck does that?"

Michael was speechless but he didn't back down. Everyone just stood back and watched, knowing this had been escalating since the Rhodes returned to Stitlin.

"You two idiots aren't helping us find her, at all. This isn't about you, it's about her and getting her to safety as soon as we possibly can."

"You think I don't know that? I'm going absolutely crazy thinking of what that bastard is doing to her!" Michael exploded as he turned on me.

"Then shut up, stop bickering and get your ass out there and do something about it!" I spit back at him. Michael's jaw clamped tight as he glared.

"So we'll be going to a new church next Sunday." Lindsay announced drily as she trotted down the stairs. She stopped at the last step and rolled her eyes as she saw Michael and me at each other's throats. "Pastor Fred apparently told mom she needed to accept that Brittany is dead. Tom and Mr. McHalley just escorted him to his car." She laughed wryly as she shook her head and plopped down on the couch. "Idiot."

"They're getting ready to drag the pond at the park." Alex said sadly from the top of the stairs. "We should go."

"She's not there." I hissed in a low, dangerous voice. No one responded, we all just filed to the door and to the cars in the driveway. The police weren't giving up, but they had exhausted their manpower in an attempt to cover up the fact that they'd been notified of the situation and brushed it off because of who Chris's father was. They were fairly certain that if they found Brittany, they would know where their missing Sheriff was as well. It was probably the only reason they were still searching.

We left the park hours later, Brittany wasn't there. I knew she wouldn't be and I was grateful I was right. I was going stir crazy, not knowing was driving me insane. Thoughts of what he could be doing to her, if she was even still alive, kept me up every night.

Chapter 61

"I think I'm going to walk home." I said to my father a few weeks later, as we stood in the driveway of Brittany's house, loading into our car. "I'm going to take the trails."

"I don't think…"My mother started, but quickly stopped when my father held up his hand.

"Do you have your cell phone on you?" Dad asked. I nodded my head. He reached into the car, dug in the side pocket of the door and threw a flashlight at me. "Please be careful." I nodded again. I'd had many conversations with my parents about my feelings for Brittany, about how I got her in this predicament and how I wouldn't rest until she was found. My father knew I needed to clear my head since they'd officially called off the search today. Chris hadn't posted recently and no new leads had come in for over two weeks, they'd done all they could. School started tomorrow and I was supposed to go like nothing had changed, like Brittany wasn't out there going through Hell.

I didn't need the flashlight but it felt nice in my hand, it was there in case I needed a way to protect myself or scare something off.

I looked down at the ground, focusing on the thoughts running through my head rather than the path I was taking. I'd walked, ran, rode these trails so much over the last two years that I could take them blindfolded. Marc and I rode four wheelers through these woods before he ever moved into that house; it was just a bonus that we were practically neighbors now.

"How can everyone just give up on her?" I asked out loud. "She can't be dead, I would know if she were, right?" I shook my head at the horrific thought. I loved Brittany Hoffman more than life itself, she was my soul mate and if she were dead, I would know. I would've felt the world shift, *I know it.*

I tripped on a root, caught myself and looked up. Apparently, I couldn't take these trails blindfolded because I didn't recognize where I was. I grabbed my phone and prayed for reception…the GPS on this thing had to be good for something. As the navigator loaded on my phone I looked around to get my bearings, nothing looked familiar.

"What is that?" I said to the wind as something was glowing near a large tree. I turned on the flashlight and walked towards whatever was shining under the leaves littering the floor of the woods. I pushed everything out of the way and picked up a silver iPod, the song "Time is Running Out" By Muse was displayed on the screen. I flipped it over in my hand and shone the flashlight at it.

Brittany Marie Had been inscribed in the back of the mp3 player, a gift from her father when she graduated grade school.

"How?" I started, wondering how it was possible that the thing still had a charge to it or that it hadn't been found before now. I know they'd searched these woods, hadn't they? The song ended and "Supernatural Forces" by Sebadoh appeared. "Aaron." I murmured with a smile. "Thanks." The wind picked up and then eerily quit, and I was all alone in the woods again. I grabbed my phone and called my dad.

Chapter 62

Brittany

"Aaron, will they ever find me?" I asked into the small space. There was no answer, no matter how hard I wished there was one. "Actually, that doesn't even matter anymore. I wish I were dead."

I could hear Chris moving around upstairs and I prayed he wouldn't come down to get me out of the cellar today. I didn't have the energy to fight him anymore, I didn't have the energy to cry about my situation anymore either.

I have been in the dark for so long, hidden from reality for an unknown amount of days that I've had a lot of time to think. I reflected on everything in my life. It had been days since I had told any of my family or friends that I loved them, when Aaron passed I had promised myself that it was something I'd never forget. I lied.

I was always so hateful to Mr. Curren and he deserved better. Most of all, I was extremely sorry for the horrible things I had said to Bret. The more I thought about his words, his sweet blue eyes that day, I knew he had spoken from his heart. He was too good to be as horrible as I had imagined him to be.

Regardless, I had never felt those emotions from a kiss before and that had to mean something. Something that terrified me to the core. Bret had somehow developed a very important part in my life, without me really noticing it. I couldn't handle not having Bret in my life and that's no doubt what would happen if we acted on our feelings. Besides Aaron, Bret was the person who I thought about the most while I was in this captivity. I would think of his smile or his laugh and I would instantly feel at ease. I'm sure that isn't normal, but my life isn't exactly normal compared to other people's at this point.

Joey's faced popped into my head and I instantly felt guilty for the fact that it was the first time I had even thought about my supposed boyfriend. I never told him about kissing Bret and I should have. I regretted sleeping with Joey so soon, I wasn't ready. I honestly think my rash decision had hurt our relationship, because I knew after our first time that I didn't see him in the same way. I knew I didn't love Joey.

I missed Bret, but after my psychotic blow up, he was

probably happy to see me gone. At least, that's what Chris continued to tell me. I prayed I could at least salvage our friendship if I ever made it out of this torture chamber alive.

I heard the familiar scraping of furniture moving above me and knew Chris would be with me in a few seconds. Sometimes he would pretend that he left, knowing I couldn't see him in the darkness. He would lie at the top of the steps, breathing heavily. I ignored him and would sing "Amazing Grace" or the few words I knew to "The Old Rugged Cross". Depending on the day, he would either attack me or get so frustrated that he'd leave in a huff and not come back for a while.

"Brittany?" He called with a lilt in his voice. "Come here baby." I stayed where I was, I refused to move for him any longer. I could hear Chris chuckle as he came down the steps and sat behind me. His legs moved to either side of me, and then his arms did the same. "What's the matter baby?" He breathed in my ear, kissing me softly on my neck. Tears rolled down my cheeks as I fought every urge I had to cringe, scream and run. I learned the hard way that Chris didn't react well to those things.

"I'm hungry." I murmured as I inhaled slowly.

389

"I love you too." He remarked with a smile as he continued to kiss my neck while his hands ran gently up and down my arms, before they began to explore wherever they wanted.

"That's not what I said." I mumbled as I closed my eyes and tried to focus on my breathing. If I focused on that or the pain in my ankle, I wouldn't realize Chris was kissing and touching me.

"When will you learn not to defy me?" He murmured as his hands went to my breasts. "You wouldn't be down here in this tiny hole; shitting and pissing where you sleep, trapped in the darkness, if you would just admit that you love me."

"I won't." I said hoarsely. Chris's hands clamped down on my breasts, I squeezed my eyes shut to block out the pain. I wouldn't scream, it was fuel to his fire and I wouldn't give him any more than I already have.

"You will." He hissed as one hand went to my hair and he yanked until my neck was at an awkward angle so I was facing him. "You do love me and you will eventually see things my way." I could hear the venom pouring out of his voice as he went to my neck and bit down as if he were a vampire. I remained still, fighting every urge I had to move and seek shelter away from him. "I have risked so much for you, why can't you see that?" In one movement, I was underneath Chris and he was violating me before I could even react.

Pushing, shoving and begging him to stop only made things last longer, so I just laid there praying for it to be over soon. He pulled out and ejaculated all over me, laughing as he did, before he pulled me up the steps by my hair and threw me onto the bed.

He walked over to the dresser and fingered his father's gun belt as it hung off one of the wooden knobs. I whimpered in fear, certain of what my future held and knowing there was nothing I could do about it. Chris chuckled to himself before he grabbed me, handcuffed my arms to the bedrail and used a rope to tie my legs spread eagle.

"I'll be back in a minute baby." He drawled lasciviously as he walked out of the room. I struggled to get loose, to break the old spindles on the bed frame, but I couldn't do it. Chris only gave me food or water in spurts and it was never enough to sustain my hunger. I was weak from dehydration, starvation and the infections coursing through my body from my broken ankle and the numerous gashes from the belt he liked to use on me when he was raping me.

The door flew open and Chris carried his deceased brother under the armpits and dropped him on top of me. I screamed and flailed, the smell of rotting flesh surrounding me as I vomited everywhere.

"Kiss him." Chris said coldly. "I know you love my brother more than you love me. That's what always happens. I find a girl, fall in love with her and fucking Heath steals her from me. Kiss him. Fuck him. Get it out of your system." Chris stormed out of the room as if he'd just caught me sleeping with his brother and slammed the door behind him.

"CHRIS!!!!!!" I screamed, with a voice I didn't know I had anymore. "Please. Please, I'll do anything you want me to." I cried after him, but the door didn't open again. I was left alone with Heath Kaplan's dead body on top of me and I could do nothing about it.

Chapter 63

I stared out the window across from the bed, focusing on anything but the dead body that lay on top of me. The sun had rose, set and rose again before Chris finally came back in the room.

"Are you done fucking my girlfriend Heath?" He spit as he grabbed his brother by the shirt and threw him in the floor. "You're not even going to deny it?" He kicked the body, before he turned and glared at me. "Is it out of your system now? Is there anyone else you would like to fuck before you decide to settle for me?" Chris walked over to the dresser and grabbed the pepper spray can out of the gun belt.

"Answer me!" He screamed as he aimed the can at my vagina and sprayed when I didn't answer. The second the chemical hit the most sensitive flesh on my body I screamed and writhed in agony, but I didn't respond as he screamed for me to answer him so he sprayed my face and anywhere he could. I couldn't see, I couldn't breathe, I couldn't scream anymore and I passed out from the searing pain.

"Wake up!" Chris hissed as an electric shock went

throughout my body. "How could you fuck my brother?" He screamed in a broken voice as he put the Taser gun to my leg again.

"Please God take me now. Kill me. Please." I begged in my head as I latched on to anything to keep me sane from this excruciating torture. "Please kill me." I begged Chris this time. He shot me again with the Taser gun before he roared out of the room in disgust.

Chris upped his torture methods to an all new level. At one point, he threw his naked father on top of me and then his naked brother again. He forced me to kiss them, to touch them in ways that would disgust the most perverse psychopath. He finally took them out of the room and came back to me alone.

I was drifting into unconsciousness when he returned with a handful of cattails that he had yanked out of the ground outside. The second my eyes fluttered closed; he would run the plant along my already hypersensitive skin slowly, lightly. It was a new kind of torture.

When he climbed on top of me and placed himself inside of me, I was actually grateful to be raped and not subjected to the other methods of Hell.

Chapter 64

Michael

"Joey has started dating someone else." Mason said disgustedly as he plopped down on the couch in the Hoffman's basement. Everyone else was at actual school, my mom had given my brothers and me a break from our home school courses for the next hour.

"How do you know that?"

"Drake." He replied plainly, as if it were the obvious answer. "I'd love to beat the Hell out of him for that. Sometimes, I wish we never would've moved. I could've watched out for her better."

"Me too." I murmured softly as I went to Brittany's social media pages and prayed for an update. There was, of course, nothing good so I went through her pictures and stared at her gorgeous, smiling face. "I asked mom if we can take our house off the market."

"I know. I did too." He mumbled. "I'm not leaving

until they find her."

"Me neither."

"What if…" Matt began as he came inside the basement door. "What if they never find her? Kaplan is nineteen years old, he should *not* be able to outsmart the police and everyone else. He should be making stupid mistakes and he's not. He obviously planned this out and…"

"We're going to find her." I said through clenched teeth.

"And if she's still alive Mikey, have you thought about the emotional and mental damages he's probably inflicted on her?" Matt questioned in a broken voice. "Bret said he was threatening her, stalking her and that he had gotten physical with her. His parents are missing. There are rumors that he killed them, his older brother and his TWO YEAR OLD brother. He is crazy and…"

"I think about those things until I make myself sick Matt. I know she's not going to be the same girl, I know that." I snapped. Tears filled my eyes and I shook my head disgustedly. I couldn't sleep at night for all those thoughts flying through my head on repeat.

"I heard someone say that the Kaplan's family vault had been broken into." Matt announced quietly as he looked down at the carpeted floor. "They found some of Brittany's hair in there. But…but they also found that the two bodies that should've been in the coffins, were gone."

"No." I growled. Matt nodded his head but wouldn't look up at me. Mason rushed out of the back door and all I could do was stare after him. "How could no one see him take bodies out of the cemetery?" Matt shrugged his shoulders and stood up.

"Can you tell mom I went for a run? I'll be back in an hour, I just need to clear my head. I cannot sit here and wait, it's driving me insane." I nodded my head, understanding the feeling well.

Matt hurried out the back door too and I was left in the basement to stare at the television. Brittany's kidnapping was old news; they rarely talked about her or the ongoing search anymore. The story had gone viral though with the help of Marc and Bret, more people than we could have ever imagined were offering some sort of help in aiding in the search. They would've ended all the efforts a long time ago if it weren't for the funding coming in from all over the world.

My phone rang and I didn't even have to look at the screen to know it was Ashley. She called at the same time every day.

"Any news?" She asked in a tiny voice.

"No." I mumbled.

"Each day I pick up the phone and pray you'll answer differently before I call. I hope that someday soon, God answers that prayer." She admitted softly. "I wish I were there with you guys. I feel like, if..."

"I know. I'm constantly thinking if only I'd..., what if we didn't move, what if I never broke up with her." I said as I exhaled a breath. "None of it is doing any good though, because we're not helping her by blaming ourselves."

"I know. I just wish there was something I could do."

"I know." I replied. "I'll call you if I hear anything."

"Thanks." She sighed before she ended the call. My heart hurt because I could only imagine how insane Ashley was going being in California while her childhood best friend was lost in Tennessee.

I couldn't be alone anymore so I went upstairs to see what

Mrs. Hoffman, Mrs. McHalley, Mrs. Harper and my mother were doing on the home front. They would find some busywork for me to do so I could help in the search for my girlfriend and keep myself focused on something else.

Chapter 65

Matt

I jogged down the Hoffman's paved driveway and took a left, heading away from the subdivision. I just needed to get away from people. Brittany Hoffman had been in my life for as long as I could remember, she was the sister we never had, in a way. Michael was supposedly in love with her, but it was more of a crush that he didn't know what else to do with. They had been a couple for two years but did that even really count in grade school?

I'd always thought that Stitlin, Tennessee was a boring little town with nothing exciting ever happening. Unfortunately, I was wrong, we all were. You never think something like this could happen in your hometown and you sure as Hell never think something like this would happen to someone you know, to someone in your family.

I never thought I'd know someone who died from childhood cancer either though. It was almost like once I hit high school, shit got real. I'd much rather go back to my stupid naivety, it hurt a Hell of a lot less.

It was an adjustment to get used to not seeing Aaron at our house constantly. It took a lot of getting used to when I'd pick up a basketball and he wouldn't join in the game. Now, I would turn the corner all over town, throughout her house, and expect to see her beautiful smile greet me. But it hasn't yet and I feared that it wouldn't ever again.

If Brittany didn't survive this, if she is already dead somewhere, it would change the course of a lot of lives. It would tear my brothers and me apart, for sure. Mason would blame Michael, Michael would blame himself and I would blame them both. I never wanted to pursue our music career, yeah I love to sing but I was content to live in Stitlin and be a football God here. That's all I needed for now. I just wanted to have a normal teenage life, there was so much future ahead of us to pursue our music dreams. We had a lot of maturing to do and the world didn't need to see us do it.

Drake and Lynsey would never survive the loss of their sister and Mrs. Hoffman would probably never get over the grief. Mrs. Dalkman shattered into tiny pieces on the day Aaron passed away, Mrs. Hoffman would follow suit. Justin and Alex would go down a dirty path, there was no hiding the fact that they relied on Brittany just as much as the rest of us did.

Who would think that a little blonde haired, blue eyed fifteen year old girl would hold the fate of so many people in her fragile hands? It sounds crazy, but it's so true. My heart hurt to think of someone being cruel to such a sweet, innocent girl.

I ran past the cemetery where Aaron was buried, noticing police were all over the place. That confirmed the rumor about the missing bodies. My stomach clenched at the thought of why someone would steal bodies from their resting place. It was just wrong on so many levels.

I kept running until I was well past Bret McHalley's house and stopped to stretch my cramping legs. I should probably turn around before I was too tired to run back, especially since I'd left my phone behind. I went into a runner's lunge and tried to stretch out so I could walk tomorrow. I stood up, grabbed my right leg and stretched my thighs just as I heard a car coming down the road. I moved off into the grass, knowing that out here they probably weren't expecting anyone to be in the road so they wouldn't be paying attention.

The black car plowed down the road, swerving all over the place. I just shook my head. "Drinking a little early dude." I said to myself as I put my head down and continued stretching. I looked up once the car passed and my heart stopped. The license plates read HTHK. I started running again and cursed myself for not having my phone. I would know that car anywhere since it had been all over the media since the day Brittany went missing. However, I also remember seeing Heath Kaplan driving it around all the time before he died.

Chapter 66

Mason

I'd been walking for too long and honestly had no clue where I was at. I'd gone straight out of the Hoffman's basement, past the stables and into the woods behind the house. I'd known from growing up in Stitlin that this was a part of the Savannah Estates charm, the subdivision Brittany lived in was built with the woods in the middle. There were rumors of the woods being haunted, that the Underground Railroad had supposedly travelled through here but it was unlikely.

We'd been through these trees a lot on four wheelers growing up, since the Dalkman's used to live just down the road from here. However, I never remembered seeing so much as an outline of a shack being out here. There were spots where the trees got extremely thick, sucking the light out of the day and then there were spots where the birds sang and the light was bright.

There has to be something I'm missing about Chris Kaplan, something that we all haven't seen in his posts or pictures. Matt was right, Kaplan is nineteen years old and he should have screwed up already. He could not be an evil genius, I'd known the guy for a while and he really wasn't all that smart.

The fact that he was posting randomly, flaunting that he and Brittany were together and that no one had found them yet, made me think he was cocky enough to be close by. He thought he was smarter, better than everyone else and I would be willing to bet that he thought he was untouchable because his father was the Sheriff. Even the mightiest will fall.

Brittany's old house was abandoned, waiting for a buyer and so was our house. Do the realtors check them on a regular basis? He's conceited enough to take her to either place and laugh at the fact that it was so obvious. My fists clenched at the thought and I would definitely be looking into it when I found my way out of here.

Brittany was like my little sister, no she is my little sister. I vowed a long time ago to protect her from all the assholes of the world, but I had failed miserably. I should've called to check up on her, asked who she was dating and so on. I should have told her to steer clear of Chris Kaplan, Jeremy Font and Joey Hawkins. Of course, I was not expecting my stupid brother to flat out dump her, I thought those two would be together forever.

However, I really thought Bret McHalley had taken my place. It was obvious he had an unspoken thing for her. When we were playing football at our going away party just before the school year started, Bret came out of nowhere and tackled Brittany, but he did something so extraordinary that I still can't believe what I saw. Instead of tackling her to the ground, he somehow spun so he was on the bottom and cushioned her fall. I'd never seen anything like it and, at the time, I couldn't help but think he would protect her no matter what. I guess I was wrong.

I heard a car, which meant I was near the road. That was good, I could probably get cell reception once I got to the road and possibly get my GPS to work and tell me where the heck I was. It would be a cold day in Hell before I called to tell someone I was lost.

I hurried towards the sound, there wasn't a road but my heart immediately stopped when I saw the black car skid to a stop. There was nothing around it. I moved closer, taking cover in the trees as I prayed Kaplan couldn't see me out in the woods. He looked around, looked behind him a few times before he started away from the car.

I saw the house then. Well, it wasn't really a house but it was some type of structure. I could see the cement outline of a house

jutting out from the grass, there was more than one of them making

me think that at one time there was more than one house in this spot.

Chris walked away from me and then disappeared, almost as if he'd

fallen off a cliff.

I hurried forward staying as covered as I could, just in case

Chris popped up out of nowhere again. I got to his car, peeked inside

and then ducked down by the tire.

"Brittany, are you in there?" I asked hopefully, praying

she would answer and I could get us both out of here quickly. No

such luck.

I looked around and tried to figure out my next move. I

closed my eyes and focused on my surroundings. I grabbed my

phone and texted my mother that I had found Chris Kaplan, but I had

no clue where I was. I silenced my phone immediately and then

looked underneath the car to see if Chris was coming. I sprinted to

the nearest tree and realized Chris had just dropped down to another

plane. It was about a ten foot drop, but there was a house. It was

basically built in to the side of the hill and absolute perfect

camouflage. Even if they had searched this way, it would've been easy to miss.

Chris had apparently just dropped onto the top of the house, then taken a ladder down. I couldn't do that because the noise would alert Chris to a visitor. If Brittany were still alive I wouldn't risk him flipping out and doing something irreversible.

I scoped out the area and saw a way down about 800 yards away, so I took the long way down and inched closer to the house trying to take in as much of the surroundings as I could. Chris was laughing from inside the house and then I heard Brittany screaming. I closed my eyes, grateful to hear her scream but I also had to force myself not to run in guns blazing. Chris's dad was a cop, there were more than likely guns inside this house and I wouldn't be able to take out a gun. I would have to have surprise on my side.

I found a window and peeked inside. Chris had his back to me but Brittany was staring out the window, she didn't even acknowledge me. She was handcuffed to the bed, her body was emaciated and an array of sickening colors. Her normally bright eyes were dull and lifeless; if I hadn't heard her scream, I would've thought she was dead. I tried to get her attention but she was staring right through me. I crouched down the second Chris started to turn around.

She was alive but she was by no means okay. I needed to act fast, but I sure as Hell didn't know what I was supposed to do to save her.

Chapter 67

Matt

I had lost the car. I can't believe I lost the fucking car. I cursed myself as I continued to run in the direction I'd last seen Chris going. I should probably turn around and go back to the McHalley's house for help, wherever that was. I could at least have the police search this area again, surely it would turn up something, or Chris would mess up and they'd catch him driving down the road.

My gut was telling me to turn around and get help, but my heart was saying that Brittany was close and I had to find her. I could be the only thing between her death and her life.

I kept going until I found a dirt road that had been traveled recently. I turned down it, the dust finally settling from Chris's trip down it. God was smiling down at me now. He is leading me to Brittany, I know it.

Chapter 68

Brittany

Blinding, searing pain had taken over my entire body as the chemicals from the pepper spray reignited at their will, intertwining with the open wounds on my body. I couldn't scream any longer, I had no voice left. Chris took pleasure in the screams though, it was obvious because of the bulge in his pants. The more pain I was in, the more excited he got and, ever since he had pepper sprayed my private spots, the quicker he was to flip me over and enter me anally. I had never known so much pain or shame in my life and I begged God to have mercy on me and take me quickly.

Once Chris had finished his latest attack, he went over to the dresser and began putting his tools away for the time being. I stared out the window, trying to mentally escape from the Hell I was in. The pain was roaring in my ears as tears raced down my cheeks. The agony was so intense that I had finally started hallucinating I was seeing people in the window. I certainly didn't think I'd ever imagine that Mason Rhodes would be my rescuer, I thought for sure my fantasies would star Bret McHalley as my white knight.

"I'll be right back baby, mom has dinner on the table."
I didn't respond, just laid there lifelessly and prayed that my delirium
meant I would be dead soon. He inserted a syringe in my vein again
and I welcomed the paralyzing medicine. It was the nicest thing
Chris could and would do for me, the drugs took away the pain and it
was the only time I felt a hint of ease. He leaned down to kiss me
before he hurried out of the room.

Ten seconds later, there was scratching at the window.
"Please be a bear." I thought to myself. Anything is better than this.
I closed my eyes and inhaled deeply, praying it would calm the
painful sensations that were all over my body, that it would make the
medicine take hold faster.

"Brittany." I heard a harsh whisper in the room.

"Aaron? Please tell me you've come to take me." I
begged tearfully, my words slurring as the medicine seeped in.
"Please."

"It's Mason sis." He answered in a broken voice. My
eyes flew open as I saw that he was looking at me through an open
window. "Where is Chris?"

"Kitchen, eating dinner with his dead family." I said flatly. Mason's head tilted trying to comprehend my sentence.

"I'm getting you out of here." He said as he started into the window.

"No. I can't walk. I can't move. He drugged me." I said in a broken whisper. "I can't. He'll find me." Mason's face contorted with anger, disgust and disbelief as he looked me over.

"What in the Hell has he done to you?" He hissed. "C'mon, I'll carry you." He searched for the keys to the handcuffs, but I had watched Chris put them in his pocket.

"He has them." I mumbled as I forced myself to focus on Mason. The medicine was in my blood stream, the nausea took hold as did the sleep. No part of my body would move now, it was taking everything I had to keep my eyes open.

Mason hurried to the bed and hovered over my head, looking for a way to get me out of the handcuffs. He reached down to feel the spindles.

"No!" I gasped. "Don't...don't touch me."

"Britty, I'm not going to hurt you." Mason said sadly. "It's me sis." He didn't stop his movements and I screamed silently.

413

Mason's face dropped as he looked back at me helplessly. He exhaled loudly as he bent down so he was eye level with me. "I'm going to get you out of here, okay? I have to go for help though. I can't...I can't get you out of here on my own. I'm so sorry Britty. I'm so sorry that I can't take you out of here now."

"I can't leave." I mumbled, shaking my head. "I can't leave. He'll find me."

"I will kill the son of a bitch before that ever happens." He spit. He closed his eyes and forced himself off the floor, to the window and out of it without looking back.

"I love you Mason." I whispered after him as he closed the window silently. I knew I would never see him again. It was just a matter of time before I was dead. At least, I prayed it was only a matter of time.

Chapter 69

Matt

I jogged another three miles down the road before I saw Chris's black car in the distance. I sprinted, knowing Brittany was close by. Chris came out of nowhere and I saw red, the angry roar in my ears was telling me not to stop. I charged and tackled him to the ground before he even knew what hit him.

"Where in the Hell is Brittany?"

"Who?" He chuckled, evil flashing in his eyes. "How did you find me?"

"I knew you'd fuck up sooner or later." I hissed as I dug my knee into his stomach while I pinned him to the ground. "Where is she?"

"You'll never find out." He laughed sardonically. "No one will ever know." My hands went to his throat and I squeezed.

"You crazy son of a bitch, tell me where she is right now or I will kill you with my bare hands and not think twice about it." Chris roared and before I knew it, he had overtaken me. He stood up, pulled a gun from his pocket and took aim. He didn't hesitate

when he pulled the trigger. Everything went black.

Chapter 70

Mason

I dropped to the ground when I heard gunshots; I instinctively looked around for the shooter. When my breathing slowed, I realized they had come from quite a distance. I wasn't the target. My heartbeat quickened with the fear that Chris had figured out I'd been there somehow and had killed Brittany because of it. I warred with myself to go back and make sure she was okay, but I couldn't help her that way, I already knew that. I sprinted through the woods. I had no idea where I was going or where I had even been, I just knew I had to find someone to help Brittany. I had to get her help now.

I finally came up on the back of a house, I pounded on the doors and yelled for help but no one was home. I caught my breath for a second as I looked around, trying to decide what to do. I pulled out my cell phone. I finally had towers, so I called 9-1-1.

"I found Chris Kaplan. I found Brittany Hoffman, she's alive. Chris has her tied up in this hidden house. I just…I don't know where it is, I found it by accident and she needs help. She needs an ambulance, I couldn't get her out of there on my own." I rambled hysterically.

"Slow down sir." The operator said drily. "You found Brittany Hoffman?"

"Yes."

"Where?"

"I don't know exactly where. I went for a walk in the woods, got lost and came up on Chris's, Heath's car. The house is built into the side of a hill and…"

"You found her, but you don't know where you found her?"

"No, I don't. Listen, I know it sounds crazy but I saw her, I talked to her and I tried to get her out of there but she has burns and gashes all over her. She has broken bones and couldn't…I couldn't touch her without hurting her. She said his family was all dead. I need your help."

"Can you give me a location?"

"No, I just told you that I couldn't. I can tell you where I'm at right now, send the police to me and I will take them to where I was."

"Sir, the officers are extremely busy and cannot go on wild goose chases." The operator said dismissively. "It is not funny to call in false tips and hinder the search for this poor girl."

"I'm not…I'm not calling in false tips. I'm telling you the truth. She is like my little sister and I want her home more than anyone. She wouldn't be in this situation if you assholes would have listened to her in the first place. You blew off her accusations like they were nothing and this is what happened."

"What's your location?" She asked. I looked at the front of the house, then to the mailbox and read off the address. At the same time, I noticed a boat in the driveway. I hurried to it, ripped up a seat and pulled the emergency kit out from under it. I grabbed the four flares inside and started back into the woods.

"Tell the officers to come to this address and look for flares. When I get to the house where she is, I will shoot off flares. She needs me, I can't wait on you guys to get here." I rambled quickly as I hung up the phone and immediately called Drake.

"Listen to me very carefully." I instructed in a flat voice. "I found Brittany and it's not good. She's alive but she is hurt,

419

bad. I walked out of your house, past the stables and into the woods and I got lost. I don't know where the Hell I'm at, other than I just left this house at 438956 Gable Road and I'm headed back to where I found her. I have flares. When I get there, I will shoot one off, then another one an hour later if you haven't found me yet. I have my phone, but I can't get reception out there."

"You found her?" Drake gasped.

"Did you hear everything else I said?"

"Yes. I'll get everyone together and we'll go out into the woods and watch for the flare." I stopped immediately and looked around the house for a weapon of some sort and a lighter, I would need a lighter for the flares. I found a grill in back with lighter fluid and a lighter resting on it so I grabbed the lighter and then went into the broken garage. I found an ax and a screw driver, at least it was something.

"She is not good Drake. Just, make sure there is an ambulance on standby."

"How…how bad is it?"

"I will murder that bastard for what he's done to her." I growled before I hung up the phone, put it in my pocket and started back in the general direction of where I'd come from.

When I finally found Chris's car again night had fallen, which was perfect because it would be so much easier to see the flare. I braced myself for the backlash if Chris heard anything go off, I would be ready and waiting for him when he pounced.

Chapter 71

Brittany

Mason was dead. Chris must've found him and shot him. He was dead and it was all my fault. How was I going to look Mrs. Rhodes in the face, if I ever got out of here, and tell her that I killed her child? "I'm so sorry Mason." I said to the empty room. "I wish it were me, instead of you."

Chris barreled into the room, shaking and covered in blood, a disgusting sneer on his face. He paced the floor, rubbing his hands across his cheeks and back of his head as if he were incredibly agitated.

"How the fuck did he find me? How did he know where we were?" He repeated in a panicked voice. "We have to leave. We have to go. They'll be here soon." He was wringing his hands in front of him, pacing frantically. He left the room just as quickly as he entered, and I heard shouting from outside.

Sometime later, he was dragging a bloodied body behind him.

"Matty." I gasped in agony. "No." I sobbed as I took

in the massive amount of blood covering his pant leg. He was unconscious, completely lifeless as Chris threw him in the floor.

"Why is he here Brittany?" He asked in accusing tone. "Why is Matt Rhodes here?"

"I don't know." I croaked as I struggled to get to my friend.

"You want him to fuck you too?" He spit.

"NO!" I screamed in shock. "Please let me help him. Please." Chris looked back at me with absolute hatred as he shook his head and kicked at my friend. He grabbed a chair from the corner of the room, put Matt in it and tied his slumped body to it. He slapped his face repeatedly, screaming at him to wake up, but Matt was barely coherent.

"Fuck you." Matt growled quietly. "I. Will. Kill. You."

"You want to fuck Brittany? Is that it? You want to fuck the little slut too?" He roared as he got up in Matt's face. "Is that why you're here?" He punched him in the stomach and Matt only moved from the force of the blow.

"NO!" I screamed. Chris looked over at me hungrily,

ripping his pants down and dropping them to the floor in front of Matt.

"Why don't you watch while *I* fuck her?" He hissed. I was screaming, flailing and frantically begging for Chris to leave me alone. It was bad enough that if this ever ended everyone would know what he did to me, I couldn't stand for Matt to have to watch any of it. Chris didn't care though, it only turned him on more to hear my screams and protests as he uncuffed my legs and wrists, flipped me over on my belly and rammed himself inside of my tightest spot. "Don't you wish this was you?" He spit, he was spouting rude remarks the entire time before he finished and ejaculated all over my back and hair.

"You want her now?" Chris growled as he untied Matt and threw him on top of me. "You can have her." He tore out of the room.

"Matty." I sobbed. "Matty, please answer me." I begged as I tried to push him off me. His dead weight was too much for my already weakened state, but after a long time of trying, I was finally able to get him beside me. In his angered state, Chris had forgotten to tie me back up so I was able to tend to Matt's wounds. I should've paid better attention to the first aid classes we were given in health class and I relied on my foggy memory to staunch the gunshot wound in his thigh. It was the only massive wound I found and for now the disgusting pillow case from the bed would have to work in slowing the blood.

"I'm so sorry Matt." I murmured as I hobbled to the corner of the room and went for the window. "I'll find help." I started out the bedroom window, but Chris was right outside and tackled me before my good foot hit the ground.

He started punching and kicking me, screaming at me that I was a pregnant whore. He kicked my already broken ankle and I could feel the blood starting to pour out of the wound again, it didn't take long for me to pass out.

When I awoke sometime later, I was naked and laying on top of Matt on the stairs to the tiny cellar. He was unconscious, his breathing shallow and growing labored. My whole body screamed in agony at the feel of Matt under me, at the pain from the blows and everything else. I shuddered as I pushed myself off and moved to the bottom of the steps.

I could hardly breathe and when I inhaled there was a sharp shooting pain. He had broken my ribs and, if I was lucky, the bruising on my stomach meant I would die of internal injuries before the day was over.

"Aaron, don't worry about me. Please, just save Matty." I sobbed. "Please save him."

Chapter 72

Mason

This was it. I had just watched Chris leave in a hurry. I could get her out and get her help before he came back.

As I hurried towards the drop, there was a dark spot on the ground. I bent down and felt the wet, sticky liquid on the patches of dirt and grass. Blood and a lot of it. Was it Brittany's? Please, don't let it be Brittany's blood. My stomach dropped when I realized the blood pool was right next to where Chris's car had been sitting. I grabbed the lighter, a flare and lit the end and held it up towards the sky. I prayed help would be here soon as I dropped the empty case and hurried down to the drop off. This time, I went straight onto the roof and let myself down the ladder. I went in the front door and vomited the second I walked in and was hit with the smell of death.

The entire Kaplan family, minus Chris, sat on the bare couches, watching a television that been drawn on the wall. Two were just skeletons, but the other two, his parents possibly, were rotting and resembled any zombie you'd ever seen in movies.

"Brittany!" I called as I sprinted through the house and into the three other rooms. She was no longer in the bedroom. I puked again when I looked at the bed and saw the amount of blood covering the filthy mattress. The room reeked of sex and blood. An empty gun belt rested on a nearby dresser and the handcuffs hung from the bedframe. I screamed her name, but she didn't answer. They were gone and I had royally screwed up by leaving her here.

Chapter 73

Brittany

Things had been quiet, mostly because I was in and out of consciousness so much from the infection coming back into my leg. Matt was unconscious at the top of the stairs, but he was still breathing and that's all I cared about at this point. I had heard Chris come back into the house at some point. Then he had gotten into a fight with his parents and brother earlier...there was lots of screaming and yelling from him, anyway. I heard the front door slam, the car start and Chris tore away from the cabin. I had gotten the door open and almost escaped so many times that he had finally put something so heavy over the opening that there was no way I was getting out. He had been expertly administering the drugs so I was addicted, he would stop them cold turkey so I was weak with withdrawal before he would pour them into me again. He had also been starving me so I couldn't fight him off, I was weak and infected, I couldn't fight my way out of a sheet. It had been at least a day since my last dose of medication, since Mason Rhodes had been murdered because of me.

I trembled from the need of the medication.

I was half awake when I heard voices outside of the cabin. I heard people hollering and I screamed back, but my voice was so weak, I'm certain they didn't hear me at all. The voices got closer, I could hear them right above me. I screamed until I thought my throat would bleed. I pulled myself up the steps and banged on the wooden door, but there wasn't a reply.

"It's all in your head, Brittany." I murmured as I fought back the tears. "It won't be long now before you die of starvation. No one's looking for you, you've been too hateful and horrible to everyone who has ever been nice to you. Hallucinations are the first sign you're about to go." My voice was raw from screaming and it had honestly taken everything out of me, so I closed my eyes and let the infection pull me back under.

Chapter 74

Bret

"They matched Brittany's blood type to the blood found in the woods." Marc announced sadly as he walked into my bedroom.

"What does that mean?"

"That she was there." He shrugged, two weeks after I'd found her iPod in the woods. They'd sanctioned off those trails and went through them with a fine tooth comb and found blood, skin, hair and a piece of cloth, but nothing that pointed in her direction.

Chris's social media statuses or pictures were few and far between, but they were unable to be traced because he would post them in obvious spots, tagging himself at various locations just to tease people with how close he was. He would make light of the fact that no one had caught him yet. It would only be a matter of time before he messed up.

To make matters worse, Matt and Mason had both gone out for runs four days ago and neither one of them had returned. Mason had contacted the police and Drake, saying he'd found Brittany, but he didn't know where he was. The police thought it was a hoax until Mason went missing as well. We could only pray that the three of them were together and safe, surely they would be able to overtake Chris.

The last picture he had posted with Brittany, she was unrecognizable as she was so thin that she looked almost like a skeleton next to him. He had said he'd gotten into a fight with his brother and parents but that his relationship with Brittany wasn't changing and that kept him going. I was starting to fear Brittany was dead, too and Chris just hadn't realized it yet.

"We already knew that." I muttered as I turned back to my trigonometry homework and tried to focus on it. "She's got to be close by."

"They've looked everywhere, numerous times and nothing is coming up."

"Tell me you're not giving up."

"Never." Marc said, forcing a smile. "I just…I just wish we'd catch a break." I nodded my head as I abandoned my homework to check our website again. There was nothing new, unfortunately, but the email account I had made specifically for the website had two new messages.

"Hey Marc, this person sending this email said they just saw Chris's car in town at the grocery store." I informed him slowly.

"What time?"

"The message was sent one minute ago." Marc picked up the phone and immediately called the tip line, while I responded to the message. There was an instantaneous reply on the other end stating they were looking at the car as he typed. They took a picture, uploaded it and sent it to me to verify. I was up and out of the chair before Marc could finish his conversation.

"MOM!" I yelled as I rushed out of my room, grabbed my car keys off the kitchen table and almost ran my mother over. "We just got a message saying that Chris is at Taylor's Grocery, that his car is there."

"Bret, you can't go. Did you call the police?" Marc hung up the phone and looked back at my mother.

"They're on their way."

"I'm going mom, I can't risk them losing him. Maybe

he'll talk to one of us."

"Bret it's too dangerous!" She hollered after me as I slid by her with Marc at my heels.

"I don't care. The longer Brittany is out there, the more danger she is in. There's no telling what that…"

"I know buddy, but you can't…"

"I'm going mom." I said in a flat voice as Marc and I sprinted out of the house and to my restored Mustang convertible. My father chased after us, I technically didn't have my license yet, but that wasn't going to stop me. I tore out of the driveway, sped down the dirt road into town and to the grocery store where Heath Kaplan's car sat shining brighter than a new penny.

"What if it's a decoy?"

"Too much work." I said with a shake of my head. "He most likely doesn't have help. It would be too much work for him to use more than one vehicle at a time and it would risk his identity."

"Good point." There wasn't a spot near the car, so I pulled up across from it as Marc and I raced to see if anyone was inside.

434

"Boys, hold off." My dad growled as he grabbed his cell phone and called the police. He handed me his phone and went to investigate the car. I could not sit back and watch, I handed the phone off to Marc and he started talking without hesitation. I followed my father, watching the soldier come to the forefront. "Bret, stay back. I cannot risk you getting hurt."

"I cannot watch. I have to...maybe he'll talk to me."

"Or maybe he'll kill you." He hissed. "You have to think of the bigger picture, son."

One look inside the car showed there was no one inside, my father tried the doors and they were unlocked. He leaned in, found the trunk button and I heard it click open. I rushed to the back, praying she'd be there smiling back at me.

She was not.

Mason Rhodes was there in her place. He was limp, gagged and bound, slowly spilling blood everywhere. My father went back to the car, yanked a shirt out of the front seat and came back to the trunk where he searched Mason's body for the source of the bleeding.

"Call an ambulance and stay out here and wait for the police." I instructed Marc as I hurried into the grocery store. I could

435

hear my father scream after me, but he knew if he didn't stop the bleeding, Mason probably wouldn't make it much longer. I could handle myself and I hoped he knew that. Brittany was my only concern, they could get help to get Mason out or he'd do it on his own. I didn't care, I was only concerned with Chris and getting Brittany back.

There were about ten other smaller businesses in the little strip mall, but an employee would be able to remember Chris's face too easily. He hadn't been in hiding this long by being stupid, he knew what he was doing and wouldn't risk a little business.

I hurried through the store, scoping out every aisle for someone who resembled Kaplan, knowing he would at least try to hide his identity. There he was. A young guy dressed in camouflage pants and hat, a yellow tee shirt and muddy boots. He was wearing black ray ban sunglasses and he was flirting with the cashier as if he weren't a psycho. I started to approach when I felt someone bump into me and then shove me into a display of fruits and vegetables.

Chris glared down at me, standing over me as if he wanted to murder me.

"She loves me, not you." He hissed.

"Where is she?" I growled, trying to get up. He kicked me back down. "Is she still alive?"

"Not to you, she isn't." He chuckled. "I'm protecting her from you assholes, why can't anyone see that?"

"I will…"

"Do nothing, because you'll never find her if I go to jail." He grinned smugly before he walked out of the store as if nothing had happened. Every time I tried to get up, I fell back down on some slippery mess.

"Someone stop him!" I screamed, but no one listened. They were too busy laughing at the people who were falling in the mess all around me. "That's Chris Kaplan!" Finally, the entire store stopped what they were doing and looked back at the entrance and Chris was nowhere in sight. I could only pray that my father was waiting for him in the parking lot.

When I was finally able to get out of the grocery store, Marc was on the ground and the police were tearing out of the parking lot after the black car that Chris was speeding away in.

"What happened?"

"We were getting Mason out of the trunk. Chris attacked me from behind, just as two squad cars pulled in. He hopped in the car and took off."

"Where's my dad?"

"Um, he threw himself in the car."

"What?"

"Yeah, he sprinted to the passenger side and hopped in. I don't imagine they'll make it far before your dad has him apprehended." I laughed and shook my head, I couldn't believe what Marc was saying but knew it was something my father would do. He was a soldier, he had no fear and would do whatever he could to keep us safe.

"What took them so long?" Marc shrugged his shoulders as I held my hand out to him. "You all right?"

"Yeah. You?"

"I've been better." I said with a disgusted shake of my head. If Chris Kaplan got away, I would hold every member of that police department personally responsible. One squad car pulled into the parking lot while three others sped in the direction of the police chase. A small female officer climbed out of her car and motioned for us to come over. I didn't have time to answer questions, I needed

to get to Chris and find out where Brittany was. I could only pray my

dad kept him alive long enough to get that much out of him.

Chapter 75

Brittany

Chris had been gone for too long. I needed out of this cellar. My fever was raging and so was Matt's. If Chris didn't come back soon, the two of us would die and be buried in this cellar forever.

I just wanted to go to sleep and never wake up, but I couldn't do that to Matt. He hadn't woken up since Chris had thrown us down here so I was the only way he was getting out alive. I couldn't let him die, because of me.

I crawled past him and tried with everything I had in me to get the cellar door open, but it wasn't budging. I collapsed on to the cool cement and closed my eyes.

"I'm sorry Matt." I breathed before everything went black.

Finally, Aaron was there smiling back at me with his arms were open wide and I ran to him. Matt appeared out of the corner of my eye, grinning peacefully and waiting patiently for his hug too.

"Nooooooo!!!" I screamed.

The end

About the author

Melissa Logan is a work from home mother of five; three boys and two angel babies. She is a Veteran of the U.S. Coast Guard and an online fitness coach. In her spare time she loves to workout, read, write, photography and spending time with her family. Melissa was raised in a small southern Illinois town and currently resides there today.

Other books by this author

Callatin Academy #1 New Beginnings
Callatin Academy #2 Trust Me
Callatin Academy #3 Crazy Girl

The Brittany Files: Crossroads

Available in print at Amazon.com

Connect with this author

You can friend her on Facebook at the following:

www.facebook.com/melissa.logansanders

www.facebook.com/authormelissalogan

www.facebook.com/melissasandersfitness

You can find her on Twitter @melissalogan79

Amazon author page at http://www.amazon.com/-/e/B00HFHBI02

Or at www.smashwords.com/profile/view/lissalu7997

Made in the USA
Columbia, SC
05 November 2022